# PRAISE FOR *WOMAN OF INTEREST*

"A funny, effervescent addition to the memoir-as-detective-story genre." —Nicole Chung, *Esquire*

"A fascinating and immersive look at identity, dedication and unanswered questions." —Tobias Carroll, *InsideHook*

"In cool, noir-tinted prose shot through with wit and compassion, O'Neill presents her inquiry as a sort of metaphysical detective story. Readers will be riveted." —*Publishers Weekly* (starred review)

"Resembles what experimental jazz would be like if it were a written narrative. Funny, shocking, and emotionally charged, the memoir takes readers on [O'Neill's] journey of self-discovery and finding what family means." —*Library Journal*

"O'Neill's prose brims with intelligence, energy, and humor." —*New York*

"[An] urgent, atmospheric memoir meets noir about family shadows, writing, and the pursuit of searching for answers we know we might never find." —*Oprah Daily*

"This is a work that is funny, moving, mean—an exceptional book from an extraordinary writer." —Kevin Nguyen, *Literary Hub*

"[A] genre-expanding noir memoir-detective story, full of drama, intrigue, bizarre characters, even more bizarre behavior, and unexpected twists." —*New York Journal of Books*

"Dark, deeply funny . . . Framing her narrative as a detective story, [O'Neill] writes in a comedic voice that's at once old-fashioned and contemporary—Dashiell Hammett meets *Fleabag*." —*The New Yorker*

T0356712

"There are some new summer books that have nothing to do with fiction, but read like a mystery novel. This is one of them."

—Brit + Co

"Her memoir at times reads like a thriller and does so right at the beginning. . . . O'Neill captures in her writing the complexities of family and the pain caused by separation and by keeping secrets."

—*Asian Review of Books*

"*Woman of Interest* is a brilliantly constructed Russian doll of a memoir—a profound meditation on language and desire within an insightful family mythology within a propulsive detective story. How does Tracy O'Neill hold it all together? With a rare combination of exquisite prose, good humor, and intellectual rigor."

—Nadia Owusu, author of *Aftershocks*

"Know this: Tracy O'Neill has a novelist's sense of narrative, the eye and ear of a poet, and the luminous mind of a young philosopher—gifts woven into an innovative, propulsive, and trenchant memoir about the search for self and one's roots as well as the evolution of family myths. This book, as is Tracy, is an exemplar of literary brilliance."

—Mitchell S. Jackson, author of *Survival Math*

"With *Woman of Interest*, Tracy O'Neill solidifies her status as one of our greatest living prose stylists. With a singular wit and brilliance, O'Neill expands the horizons of the memoir, pushing the boundaries of the genre into the realm of detective noir and thrilling quest narrative. O'Neill's formal innovations and bracing prose create a new and invigorating lens through which readers can view a universal theme: the desire to search for the self and one's source." —Chloé Cooper Jones, author of *Easy Beauty*

# WOMAN OF INTEREST

## A MEMOIR

## TRACY O'NEILL

**HARPERONE**

*An Imprint of* HarperCollins*Publishers*

WOMAN OF INTEREST. Copyright © 2024 by Tracy O'Neill. All rights reserved. Printed in the United States of America. No part of this book may be used or reproduced in any manner whatsoever without written permission except in the case of brief quotations embodied in critical articles and reviews. For information, address HarperCollins Publishers, 195 Broadway, New York, NY 10007.

HarperCollins books may be purchased for educational, business, or sales promotional use. For information, please email the Special Markets Department at SPsales@harpercollins.com.

FIRST HARPERONE PAPERBACK EDITION PUBLISHED IN 2025

Designed by Yvonne Chan

Library of Congress Cataloging-in-Publication Data is available upon request.

ISBN 978-0-06-330987-6

25 26 27 28 29  LBC  5 4 3 2 1

*For Ali*

Young women not in desperate need, not saddled with children and old enough to say *Hell no* and *Get out of my face* evaded capture.

—SAIDIYA HARTMAN

What woman, in the solitary confinement of a life at home enclosed with young children, or in the struggle to mother them while providing for them single-handedly, or in the conflict of weighing her own personhood against the dogma that says she is a mother, first, last, and always—what woman has not dreamed of "going over the edge," of simply letting go?

—ADRIENNE RICH

# CONTENTS

CHAPTER ONE

# MOTHER OF RECKONING

Brooklyn to Poughkeepsie, 2020

A few years back, despite a lifelong renunciation of the urge, I surrendered to obsession with a woman. So I was beside myself. I was myself. It was no time to basket-case through life. I did. I wanted her, wanted everything, and all of her was missing.

Circa that revelatory, sad-sack time, I left S, the man everyone thought I'd get around to marrying. I skipped out on my beloved Brooklyn for a job in Poughkeepsie, the lesson of which was that gas station stench had reach. I did not see friends. I saw a peaked white wedding tent on the campus lawn, where I taught writing classes; then, once COVID-19 spiked, I saw for nearly every waking hour the one-bedroom apartment of drop-ceiling tiles where I taught over Zoom. Time itself felt "dark with something more than night," as Ray Chandler might have written, or maybe I just overidentified with the theorist Lauren Berlant's sentence: "The crisis is of what to do when one's long habit of doing the work of being oneself no longer works." In fact, myself was no longer recognizable, or I was a dunce, or else I contained multitudes—was, in other words, both a dunce *and* someone unrecognizable to herself.

But suppose I had an interest in getting my story straight. I could level with myself. On paper, I was thirty-three, adopted, Korean-born, New England–bred. Profession: writer. And because no one made a living writing anymore, profession: professor. My net worth was, roughly, dog. I had not evaded taxes, but I *had* evaded children. There were consolations in my back pocket, most notably that prior to this period in 2020, during which much of what I did resembled impotent riot, I had been many selves besides a person who wanted this missing woman.

I had been a wannabe Olympian and a minor child actor. I had been a zealot for friendship, hedonist for ideas, and bartender to men baroque in their disappointments who, ordering Tecate, would say dumb things like "Take me to Tijuana, baby." I had been a kid in a household where bras were referred to as "over-the-shoulder boulder-holders" and the doctoral candidate whose dissertation was originally to postulate an emergent nineteenth-century chronotope. I had been associated with a man, alias S, for ten years, to whom I would not apologize for remaining at my writing desk for days and then staying out all night. I had written a couple of books. I had been someone who detained herself theorizing about the meaning of this missing woman to her own life before making any sudden moves, which meant I had also become someone who agonized over tardy recognitions, forgot to eat, and paced.

Therefore! my own raving mind thought.

TRACY
O'NEILL

In conclusion!

Why should I not also be a person who found a woman named Cho Kee Yeon?

I am saying I was sick of reason. Rather: the belief I needed good reason to justify the search. I did not know how to "process," as psychotherapeutic professionals say, but I did know my own loitering mental process was to blame for rude timing; now I had to locate my woman in a pandemic that had miniaturized life by way of lockdowns and social distancing protocols. I did not want to endlessly rationalize, dispute, rationalize on different terms, poke holes, poke back, call into question the person suspected of misjudgment on the count of Cho Kee Yeon—who happened to be me. I wanted to run on pure feeling, be a body that *did*. I had a body and its gut was, reputedly, gifted with instinct. My gut had spoken—if only metaphorically—and I would listen! I found myself thinking like the nutjob I was, perhaps, becoming.

What, then, was next: I filed missing person paperwork. Shot emails to agencies that tracked down the sort of errant woman I was after. COVID did not generate prime conditions to find missing persons. Such-and-such department was temporarily closed—unless it was going to remain closed forever. So-and-so who might have further information was out of office for the foreseeable future—unless the future remained as unforeseeable as it had been in the run-up to the contemporary moment when it was abruptly postulated that your best friend's breath could kill you. I'd ransack the paper for better news, though the prevailing global sentiment now resembled the scene in *Touch of Evil* in which Orson Welles's dirty cop asks Marlene Dietrich's madam to tell his fortune. "You haven't got any," she says. "Your future is all used up."

During the time in question, detectives I consulted enjoyed precisely enough courage to name a sum without warranty, grandstand on realism, then augur failure in a tone implying me foolish. I, too, could see I looked foolish, but I was less concerned with foolishness than with sensible waits that never ended.

So in November 2020—having lost my deference to procedures, to the thankless patience and appropriate pauses between emails—from my little Poughkeepsie apartment of drop-ceiling tiles, penned in by fried-chicken boxes and books, I did what I estimated anyone in my position would do. I left a message for a PI who claimed he'd paid for his Corvette with the proceeds of training Contras.

His name was Joe Adams. He'd once infiltrated a white supremacist doomsday cult. A .25-caliber pistol was, to him, an offensive little-shit firearm. Reputedly, he did not kill people out of anger, save that one time. He'd once caught someone on the FBI's Most Wanted list. We shared an aesthetic in sports cars.

That Corvette money had been funneled through the maneuvers of Oliver North. The CIA sent Joe Adams to Honduras and to Nicaragua, and because when Joe Adams shot, the bullet hit its aim, the rebel paramilitary Adolfo Calero had called Joe "Tirador," his marksman. This PI was a good shot. Maybe my best.

According to my notes, after all, Joe Adams had operated in several countries, including South Korea. And according to my own misguided ardor for the idea that you did not know what was impossible unless you tried everything, I had to do something.

Had to, though I'd few facts on my missing person, save that at thirty-eight she had a bad eye for love. All I knew was she fell for a man so far, she lent the shirt off her back to keep them skin to skin. When she managed a café, he was a regular—if not one to count on. I mean he was married, and not to her. Anyone could see how easy it would be to go missing in that kind of love.

This is where I confess that when I began my investigation, the case had been cold over thirty years. And you can live with a cold case. You do. The coldness of a case is how it is. Solving is the aberration, and I'd copped no novel leads. But I had a clincher for Joe Adams. I did. Namely: my life depended on this missing person. I mean she had been one of my mothers.

"You know," Joe Adams said when he returned my call on the first of December, "I almost went to jail once for what I did, trying to find someone."

"If I'm hearing you correctly," I said, "sounds like you're my guy."

———

In the months leading up to my first call to Joe Adams, the line I fed myself was that I was fine. When I remembered to, I hammed up my own impression of "fine." To friends, I declared I was only late to the party—as usual—on my own rotten mommy issues. Privately, I held on to the wisdom of a friend who, as he told it, recovered from his quickly enough when a therapist shrieked, "If I hear *one more word* about that woman!"

As it happened, no one would have exercised that particular form of therapeutic disgust on me because, prior to 2020, I had uttered few words about "that woman" who didn't raise me at all. I had for many years suspected that my life paradoxically was conditional on and had little to do with her, but I could not summon what the logical stakes of apprehending her were. My stance was that when I determined the name for the feeling I had about Cho Kee Yeon—if ever I did—then I'd know how to act, and I would. The operant fiction I told myself was that if I chose to find her, it would be a garden-variety matter of execution.

It was only in the spring of 2020 when I, preposterously, ransacked the paper for better news than the city's storage of surfeit corpses in freezer trucks that I'd read a *South China Morning Post* article. It reported that a sixty-three-year-old man had died of COVID in a locked Korean ward with no known friends or family—no one to be contacted about the matter of his ashes. The paper referred to his death as "lonely," and it was observed, not without poetry, that the dead man, weighing ninety pounds, "barely took up any space in this world."

That last phrase did it. That phrase got it through my own thick skull that my woman could be dead or dying alone, no one to contact about the matter of her ashes. And though I could not define what it meant to die well, let alone how she hoped to, I was afraid that she was afraid. It did not stretch the imagination that someone might wish to die alone, then in the grand eventual rue it.

As it turned out, I could not stomach the image of an orphaned old woman. My regret moved forward and backward, inside out, and in the dizzy reckoning with a phantasmal urn of Jane Doe, I couldn't see where anything started or ended, so that pretty soon my own thinking resembled a regrettable little obverse poem:

Were I not someone who had lived without her
I would have known why it mattered not knowing her.
Immaculate of doubt,
I would have found her.
Roland Barthes said, "Only a mother can regret."
Imagine believing that.

Imagine believing that
Roland Barthes said, "Only a mother can regret."
I would have found her.
Immaculate of doubt,
I would have known why it mattered not knowing her
Were I not someone who had lived without her.

I'm saying the new nausea tripped a wire organizing my life. I'd come up with a particular O'Neill ethos in which family was formed not by nature but by the fact that you wanted enough to be family at all. That ethos had allowed me to be—despite material evidence to the contrary—"Irish American"; for my mother to say we both had olive complexions that looked like puke in yellow; and for me to recklessly hang on to the narrowing effect of *wanting enough to* as the primary feature of my identity.

And I loved wanting enough to. Or, if I got aboveboard, wanting too much. In obsession, I didn't give a shit about the fat slice of life. If asked, I had my answer. I was already giving all my shit to the one thing. My shit had been spoken for. I'm writing. I'm writing. I'm writing. I adored the William James idea, "My experience is what I agree to attend to," the thought that I could narrow my perception to white peony, big dogs, dance, whiskey, poetry—and if I succeeded, that would be my experience. This was how writing worked: what I agreed to attend to was my story. Until 2020, my story was that I had been too busy wanting to write a novel, write another, write a dissertation or article about marginal sports to resolve my ambivalence about secondary subjects such as marriage, children, and Cho Kee Yeon, who had something to do with my birth but not my life.

Perhaps this historical tendency is why, when in 2020 I mentioned the burgeoning fixation on Cho Kee Yeon, my friend Maggie said, "But I thought you didn't care about finding her."

"I didn't," I said.

Maggie was in a position to know that, of course. She was the first friend I'd made when I'd moved to Brooklyn thirteen years before. When we were neighbors in an infested Bushwick dump, she'd witnessed our landlord call out to me as I'd pet a stray, "Hey, Tracy! How come you don't take care of me like that? I want to be that cat! Meow! Meow! Meow!" When she was twenty, I'd snuck her into filthy aquarium-looking bars where we drank Jack and Cokes. I loved her because she was sharp, exacting in her intelligence, and when her father was dying, she flew to Iowa to mow his lawn.

"I'm not angry," Maggie said on the phone. "I just don't know where this mother thing is coming from."

"It's coming," I said, "from me."

"I don't understand."

"Which part?"

"You always said you didn't want to!"

"I didn't," I said.

"So what happened?" and I could hear the sense of betrayal in her voice, as though I'd taken her on a ride.

I understood. Sometimes, we'd share each other's stories to explain how we saw the world. She liked to tell people who referred to sexual abuse allegations as witch hunts that her friend Tracy said the metaphor was imprecise since it wasn't as though there had been actual witches running around Salem, whereas there *were* real live abusers cruising for a bruising. And I liked to say that if you wanted an idea of what decisive looked like, Maggie once quit a job by carving a clementine skin to resemble a jack-o'-lantern, then attaching a paper speech-bubble resignation. Never had our repertoire included a near-idiopathic impulse to find a stranger who might be an apologist for her own unchained life or in hiding, a sad figure in an alley or, sadder still, dead.

"You know what? Never mind," Maggie added. "Just don't become one of those assholes who leaves the city 'for the children.'"

"Girl," I said. "You do realize I'm in Poughkeepsie."

I missed her. I missed an unlocked-down life, where it wasn't so easy to forget we no longer lived in the same city. In those days, most everyone I knew missed each other, whether or not any of us had gone anywhere.

And all fall, men who claimed my case was hopeless disappointed me. I sat tight, sprawled stupid, waiting on developments—until in fevers I contacted more disappointing men. There were so very many! I did consider the words they offered, but I also considered how in that lousy shut-down world, language had been debased in pandemic articles, directives, directives contradicting previous directives, statements on the virus, statements on bleach, statements on not drinking bleach. Writing had long been my modus operandi, and while I did sometimes think that maybe I ought to just write a noir novel about a woman whose committed crime was a birth, I'd lost sight of the ascendance prose offered when there absolutely was no "there there"; there was quarantine.

Which is to say: I forgot that I was quote, unquote fine. Then, I decided I was again. An old, blackballed suspicion that life turned on chance's autocracy returned. Apropos of zip, you could wake up in another world, country, house. Without S in the mix anymore, my conversations largely entailed complimenting the big, beautiful dog who, on first sight years before, had been nothing but a scared, clumsy blur of black fur with one and a half ears who came to me as soon as I inexplicably called him Cowboy.

During dark hours, I would startle from sleep, as though a fool had flipped on a lamp, believing that light would reveal the forgotten thing. The thing I'd forgotten was what was real and mine, here and now, but also what might come: a sense of stakes to my freedom or a soft edge of home, a direction for love or a place to put it away, a confirmation I was a woman still able to write a new narrative into her life. Now, it was incumbent on me to track one down I could live with. Here, I told myself, is a story: time passes, but it means something. That's all I needed.

Where does a woman go on her own? I wondered. What's her story?

———

Therefore, ergo, next, I was in a hurry to catch up to the past when I first got Joe Adams on the phone.

To do: Set down yesterday's cold coffee. Unlock cabinet. From a green folder came a collection of documents, its skinny prose cataloging the details I had and implying those I did not.

I did not have dates of birth, I told Joe. I did not have resident ID numbers, the Korean equivalent of Social Security numbers. I did have an indefinitely delayed search request with an agency in Seoul.

And yet.

I could say papers in my possession indicated that on September 18, 1986, Cho Kee Yeon lived in Chollabuk-do, that she was a divorcée with a high school diploma. I could say, too, that my secondary person of interest was named Kim In Kee. Bona fides: he was, or had been, a farmer.

For most of my life, what I knew of my birth mother was

TRACY
O'NEILL

what my parents had said: my birth mother was five foot seven, and I was born in Seoul.

In fact, I was not born in Seoul. I was born at the Song Obstetric Clinic in Daejeon, according to records held by the Eastern Child Welfare Society. My birth mother was 160 centimeters tall, approximately five foot three.

These discrepancies might be chalked up to many factors, but I think it's not unfair to say that my family had accepted a mode of vagueness in which my given name, Seon Ah, could become my middle name in America, one my mother said was "basically" Shauna, an Irish name—so obviously, I was Irish.

To an outsider, our vagueness could be seen as a condition of love. But the interested parties would deny it. My mother would recall that once when a taxicab driver began harassing her, I, a child at the time, stamped my foot down hard against the floorboard, shouted, "Don't talk to my mother that way," and the driver stopped the car. There is this, too: when I was an adolescent and we disagreed, she would say, "I'm the mother" and "You got it so bad? Save it up and tell it to Oprah. Tell her what a rotten mother you had."

It wasn't until college that I found the slim, green folder holding seven documents, including my Korean passport and a letter from the Immigration and Naturalization Service of the United States Department of Justice, plus papers stating that Seon Ah was, at two months, "a cute and mild-tempered Korean baby girl" who'd nonetheless "push herself upward when crying bitterly . . . in a loud voice." This cache of documents was how I knew that Cho Kee Yeon was 160 centimeters tall and that I was not born in Seoul. It provided my first bit of biography: Seon Ah "tries to hold up her head but feels uneasy."

It was also, I'd learned, the metric of my case's viability to private investigators.

"I'm gonna stop you right there," Joe said.

At some point, I'd sat down. Now, I thought to stand up, as though then Joe Adams wouldn't walk off the job before it had even begun. Cowboy slapped a paw down on my thigh, supplicant.

"I want you to have my full attention," Joe Adams said, "but I'm currently in the attic of my home, recovering Christmas tree decorations."

There had been no picture in my mind for the voice on the other end of the line. Now came a vision: Here was a man in a navy work shirt, resting a cardboard box of artificial branches and sleigh bells against a banister, a doorway framing him by a half-moon picture window. The box would sit on his hip. The phone would be at his ear. He would say—

"So what we do is can you call me back this afternoon?"

"We can do that," I said.

"Anything comes up, you text me to reschedule because you got a lot of information, kid."

"I won't need to reschedule," I told him.

I knew now, after all, that whether patience was a virtue depended on your timing. More than three decades after my last sighting of Cho Kee Yeon had blown past standard-issue virtuous waiting.

"By the way," I said, "she would be seventy-two or seventy-three."

"Better hurry up."

No explanation was required. Find that mother, I knew Joe Adams meant, before she gets dead.

# CHAPTER TWO

# THE SECOND CALL

On the Line, December 2020

What I told Joe: A man from an organization known to find my brand of wayward woman had suggested that at her last known location, my woman of interest had left (1) some hospital paperwork and (2) a fake name.

This man—last name: Ripp—had a take, and it was that assuming a false name was a frequent sham. A woman might do this if she was wanted or if there were debts to skirt. With minor hoaxing nomenclature, she could hide in the open.

That explanation I understood. But, in September, I had asked how he'd concluded that she had left a false name.

"The database returned the message 'This is not a person,'" he said.

"This is not a person?"

"This is not a person."

"My mother is not a person," I said.

His voice tipped out of the laptop speakers, halting and cheerful, hands flapping around his face. "According to the database, no!"

*This is not a person* signified a mismatch between the name and resident ID number. The information didn't match, so this was not a person who could be linked to an address. That Cho Kee Yeon did not want to be found could not be discounted, but neither could a dumber story. A clerical error. Clumsy fingers typing. If the story was, indeed, a dumber one, the correct resident ID could yield an address.

On that day in September, I was told there was nothing more that man Ripp could do for me. I looked at his soft features and neat, red mouth. When, on Zoom, my face stiffened then vibrated—but did not fall—then stiffened again, he looked away, a courtesy. Head down, wire-rimmed gaze averted, he mumbled about the kismet of personnel changes. Sometimes you asked the right person at the right time at the right agency or police station to try an alternate spelling of the name.

It violated procedure, so you couldn't ask this kind of thing over the phone. It was just that sometimes if you waited two years or eight, you could strike that right person's right mood if you went into the office, and bam, you found your missing person. I asked if he was advising that I fly to Seoul every so often on the off chance whoever was working the desk that day had taken their meds.

"A search only ends," he said, "when you want it to end."

I didn't want it to end.

———

And so, what I also told Joe: Though I was short on facts, there was more information about Cho Kee Yeon in Korea. I even knew who had it. During an extended email exchange that I'd imagined back in 2019 to be a passing whim, the Eastern Social Welfare Society revealed a potential trail: "Documents about your parents in the States, Post Placement Reports, Counselling notes are not released."

Until that email, it had not occurred to me that a counselor had taken notes on Cho Kee Yeon. Knowledge taught me more to want. And more, according to Ripp, likely did exist. Eastern tended to keep a binder on birth parents, withholding all but a few facts.

"That's where I got this idea," I told Joe, "that people acquire binders with bribes."

"That's not crazy," he said. "You read my mind, kiddo. We're on the same page."

I picked up a legal pad, flipped to fresh blue lines. A whole unmarked sheet for this, our second call. "You saying that's the way to go?"

"No, no, no, sweetheart," he said. "You'll pay for positive results. Not bullshit. You do that and how do you know you aren't paying for bullshit?"

"I wouldn't."

"What do you do, anyway?"

"Well, some would say because I can't do, I teach."

"Teach what?"

"English," I said.

"I always liked English," Joe said. "But you're not rich. If you were, you'd have figured this out already."

I was sitting in my white chair with the little sheepskin blanket. From my seat in the living room, I looked into the abbreviated kitchen, where the counter space permitted a microwave but not a toaster. The toaster was through the kitchen on the bedroom floor, where it fit. I stared at the Cuisinart, as on occasion in my early days in Brooklyn I'd gazed at my garments to determine which could be sold at the used clothing store when rent was due. This was after, say, I'd had a bad run of bar tips because I had done things like, when a customer specified that their twenty-five cents in change was not a tip, toss a roll of quarters back, saying, "For you, a drink on the house."

I thought, too, of when I'd wanted terribly to study at a university in Rome and could not get hired at Market Basket or Shaw's, CVS or Barnes & Noble or Chili's. There was no work for me anywhere other than a strip club and billiards hall called Mark's Showplace in Bedford, New Hampshire, owned by a couple who'd opened and closed a topless donut shop in Maine.

I'd taken that job, then one night, my parents had shown up as I was making gin and tonics, had sobbed and screamed and pulled my arm, and in the moment I knew I could leave with them or I could continue to stand behind the bar—and, consequently, step foot beyond America for the first time since birth. I watched them escorted out with a sick stomach, as a woman who didn't care for me at all looked out with pity from beneath potato chip–dry bangs to ask if I was okay. In the cigar smoke and the cast of blue bulbs, I said I was fine, sliced a lime. I worked all summer, then turned twenty aside golden ruins, spit bones off my first fish served whole, and walked the city corridors of gold light drunk, guilty, free, and elated.

Several years later, when I was broke and wanted to be a writer, when I had a few hundred dollars and didn't want to drop out of my MFA program, I'd once more briefly resorted to a job at a strip club. For twelve hours at a time, I walked on spiked shoes in vinyl shorts, miserably soliciting tips. I'd think I'd not gotten very far, then think if I was to be a writer that wasn't the thought to think. I got back out on the floor.

"You know, you never know what you're going to find," Joe said finally. "You sure you want to do this?"

Before me were a cold coffee cup and a warm water glass. I concentrated on them. Drained them down. It was possible that I had convinced myself I did not want to find Cho Kee Yeon when I was younger because such desire was too expensive. Even a few years ago, I'd been denied a Bloomingdale's charge card. I'd made my living on ill-advised, ill-remunerated, and altogether dicey adjunct teaching work for eight and a half years, and I could not have afforded a plane ticket and an extended stay in Korea until I began the job at Vassar College in the fall of 2020. Did reasons matter anymore? No.

"I'm aware they might be dead."

"That's not what I'm talking about," Joe said.

"So what *are* you talking about?"

"There's something wrong here to begin with," he said, "in your whole conception, and you're going to go right back in, and it could be hurtful."

"Yeah, well," I said to Joe, throwing my campy voice through the phone. "I been hurt before."

But Joe did not laugh. Joe kept to his track. He said, "If the literature is right"—and I suppose he was referring to a few

suggestive sentences in the paperwork I had in my possession—
"Your father could be in jail."

This, I supposed aloud, would mean he'd be easier to find—
and so would Cho Kee Yeon. It could be perversely useful.

Joe Adams paused.

Joe Adams cleared his throat.

"Okay," he said. "So here's your homework."

CHAPTER THREE

# LEAVE NO WITNESS

To Mahopac and Back Again, December 2020

For a long stretch of the pandemic, the official directive had been *Everyone, sit pretty*, and I'd done the pedestrian thing. After an SUV crashed into my car in October, I had said to the EMT stumping for an emergency room visit, "The car is totaled, but I am not," then never replaced the Subaru. But Joe Adams said I'd need a vehicle to do my "homework."

Maybe it was odd for a PI to request that a client do homework; I was more struck that Joe Adams's process seemed workable at all. And I liked workable, other than when I loved the impossible. I detested bromides, except for when swallowing them whole got me through a day. There might have been more to ask Joe Adams, but at the time, my mind was on Wittgenstein: "Why do I not satisfy myself that I have two feet when I want to get up from a chair? There is no why. I simply don't. This is how

I act." It was time to quit counting feet and catch a rideshare to the dealership.

The night I got on my homework, the driver and I were women in fur-lined parkas. Her hair and jacket were gold in the front seat, and my hair and jacket were dark in the back. It was five or so. We were masked and hooped, buckled. There was an elaborate decorative crust on her nails, gem-bright on the steering wheel. We took the way out of town past flashing houses and blow-up nativity scenes. CHILLING WITH THE SNOWMIES, an inflated sign read. The white of snow looked blue.

"Where are we?" the driver said after a while, a little lost on the road.

As though it addressed the question, I said, "The dealer's in Mahopac."

"You say it *May-o-pac*, FYI," the driver said.

"So long *A*, silent *H*. Like *today*?"

"Like the stuff you put on sandwiches." She laughed, said, "I'm sorry. I'm corny."

I tucked my phone away. The sky, color-wise, was in flux. "But your pronunciation is perfect. Here I was going to say it corn-*ay*."

We merged onto the Taconic State Parkway, took curves fast. I looked into her curls, distinct with gel, as we talked about monthly payments and how you could get got on trims. There were, we discussed, a vehicle's advertised MPGs, and then there were real-world contingencies. We were women who had ideas about crossover SUVs and all-wheel drive, salesmen who took us for fools, and maybe it was some residue of the mawkish car commercial aura, the sense that on wheels you got somewhere, but I was happy.

TRACY
O'NEILL

"I did good on this car, you feel me? Because a lot of my friends went to name-brand places, and what did they get?"

"The blabber of unabashed crooks," I guessed.

"I like that," she said. "What did you say again?"

"Unabashed crooks, middlemen high on huffing margins, corporate toadies in Eddie Bauer vests and half-zip sweaters."

"Motherfuckers."

"*Definite* motherfuckers," I said.

Pretty soon we were streaming down a ribbon of Route 6 cramped with auto body shops. We cut around water. Even through a KN95 mask, the air in the car was high on Garnier Fructis and hot rubber. Even through masks, it was apparent that what we were up to was laughing back and forth in the mirror, and the whole time in the back of my mind was Joe Adams's strategy. Namely, according to Joe, chasing clues first in Korea equated to "jumping to square seven," whereas around square one—the United States—we spoke the language, knew the rules and agencies, and could chase leads face-to-*I will-catch-your-lies-so-don't*-face once I had my own car.

And the latter, in fact, was my homework. And I, if nothing else, had been endlessly a good student. And the driver said, "Look, it doesn't work out today, you go to MAG Auto tomorrow. *M-A-G.* MAG. Tell them Kiara sent you."

"MAG," I said.

"Kiara," Kiara said.

"Got it."

"I got you," she said. "You tell them. Tell them Kiara sent you."

My neck nodded in the rearview reflection. She got me—and not in the rascally way where someone had to lose.

What I'd remember later was that we rode toward the horizon as Megan Thee Stallion rapped on the radio that she did not cook or clean. I pondered how to torture a sticker price down. I pondered my missing woman. Out the window, shambly wood buildings had been done up in strand lights like delinquents in pearls, and for whatever reason I took them as premonitions of luck.

———

This left me at procurement of Outback: check. Procurement of backup: pending. Pending because though Joe and I had already spent hours on the phone that first week in December, there was a certain wander to our conversations. We were going to need reinforcements in Korea—or we should exercise caution on that count, since people posing as PIs there were selling clients' information on the black market. I had a lot of information, kid—yet I needed to do my homework on further facts to run with. He was soliciting me, or I was soliciting him, and as whoever whatevered, we kept tripping on circling riffs.

"I'm an old-school detective. I would want to be on-site, go through the US Embassy," Joe said.

"South Korea's going to be a tough one. But it's not impossible," Joe said.

"The question is, How do we find a private investigator in Korea who won't rob you?" Joe said. "If you had an investigator worth a shit here in the United States who could oversee the project and know when someone's bullshitting and when they're not, that would be beneficial."

It seemed to me the investigator worth a shit Joe was referring to was himself. It also seemed to me that though South Korea had legalized private investigators only four months before, Joe's plan required not one investigator worth a shit, but two.

Still, it was worth following Joe's lead.

Because I was someone who, seeking insight into detective work, would read the psychoanalyst Jacques Lacan's writing on a Poe mystery—itself an interpretation of Freudian repetition compulsion—then ludicrously think it a clue to my own story. But Joe had picked up ways to probe I'd missed while sitting in libraries. He'd hunt down someone's whereabouts by sales receipt, and he was practiced in hopping a jet. He knew what to tell a jet pilot to do should he not make it back from an investigation. Better, he knew how, in the end, to make it back with a missing person.

"The spooks at the embassy have their guys they trust. Locals," Joe continued.

"Are you suggesting that I hop a plane and show up at the embassy to ask who's their favored Daejeon operative?" I asked.

"Can I speak honestly?"

"Speak honestly." From a chipped china cup, I fed Cowboy chicken so that he'd not bark over our conversation.

"You walk into that embassy, to them you're a dumb girl. You're not a PI. You're not retired military personnel."

The chicken worked. No beg. No bark. No noise at all. I twisted at the smoked quartz beads gifted from Maggie, who'd claimed they'd save my neck—spiritually anyway.

"The problem's going to be getting someone over there to pay attention," Joe said. "In the spook world, that's usually because there's something they want to trade. And they're not talking about money."

"So what *are* we talking about? Government secrets?" I thought I said ironically. "Because I don't have any of those."

"Like once I traded over 4,100 rifles in a cargo shipment that went over to Pinochet in Chile for a favor. But we don't have 4,100 rifles to trade off as a favor to the intelligence community."

"I don't even have one."

"It's going to be easier to find someone who's not dead because the paper trail continues," Joe said, almost to himself.

"Right," I said. "Dead people don't swipe credit cards."

I put that thought aside, and others. *It's going to be easier to find someone*—I kept that part, and the notion that a promise connects two points in time, two people in time.

———

Joe's consolation: his Rolodex included a "lazy, fat bum in Tampa" who might just know which Korean detectives the US Embassy considered trustworthy. Absent the bum's referral, I hunched over my desk, hot on the air of a lead. Joe had heard from an FBI friend that there'd been some funny business involving Korean child imports around the time I'd been adopted.

Anyone could tell that Joe liked the warp and weft of that detail, but as far as I was concerned, there was little evidence to suspect that I, like other children whose export from Korea had been orchestrated by the Eastern Social Welfare Society from the 1960s through 1980s, had been kidnapped, abused, enslaved, or all of the above by one of Eastern's affiliate sources, Brothers Home, then shipped off. That funny business at "The Child Farm"—Joe's shorthand for the pipeline—was terrible and somewhat beside the point to finding Cho Kee Yeon. At least, so I decided.

Rather, one-half of myself decided that. The other conveniently believed his hunch enough to take down the names of individuals who appeared in news articles and public records, since any of these names might possess facts pivoting to Cho Kee Yeon.

Except, I found, they couldn't.

Most of the people on my list were in possession of zero facts—that is, deceased.

That I was no closer to Cho Kee Yeon might have gotten me off drafting theories on who'd know her whereabouts, but I did not shake the game. Staking out possibilities was, after all, a writer's long racket. I'd run the numbers on several scenarios for myself: live a life like art, love a love like art, get wasted on free ideas. Go to town, go to school, come what may—but not really. Dance with people who weren't a spouse, have a baby, have no one, be someone. Find her. It went on, it could interminably go on, that rolling the dice, and it was a bad habit, if not my worst.

Not the worst because staying in the game turned up one alive-and-well name from newspaper coverage of a trial later depicted in the movie *A Change of Heart*. The name from that article was Margaret Cardona. Margaret "Marty" Cardona, who had taken the witness stand in that trial. She had been a social worker at the now-defunct Pennsylvania adoption agency Love the Children, which brokered my passage to the United States from Eastern.

I wrote down a phone number. I checked my watch. It was rather late to call. I called.

"I'm looking for Marty Cardona," I said. "Is she in?"

Through the window to my right was a contracted vista

running the length of a faculty housing parking lot, anonymous legs behind sheer drawn curtains. Dampened sounds stirred. I watched the black whip of dog tail turning, turning at table height, radiator heat hot on my back, and still my fingertips were cold.

"Who?" the switchboard operator said.

"Marty Cardona, Margaret. Margaret Cardona."

A sigh coming through the switchboard. "I don't know who that is."

———

And maybe this was preferable, until I got up to speed on certain skills. By Joe's estimation, if I were to establish certain facts about Cho Kee Yeon, I needed to interrogate as though I were not interrogating. The job was to get answers, not frighten strangers with intensity. My charge: appear to want information only casually, but—

"You know how people say someone's heart is on their sleeve? My heart's all over my face," I told him. Even as a girl, my mother often told me to get a look off my face, and I couldn't. No matter what she threatened to do if I didn't, my heart was right where I'd left it. That, Joe observed with a laugh, was an inconvenient quality.

"So here's what you do," Joe Adams advised. "Dustin Hoffman."

"Dustin Hoffman?" I asked.

"In the movie."

"Which movie?"

"With Dustin Hoffman and what's his name? I turned down his autograph once. It was embarrassing."

Joe Adams did not sound embarrassed at all.

"Robert Redford?" I asked.

"Robert Redford and Dustin Hoffman."

"As Woodward and Bernstein. *All the King's Horses*—no, *All the President's Men.*"

"Right," Joe continued, as I turned a new page in my notebook to write *December 3rd*. "Scene I'm talking about, they've got to get information off a secretary. Watch how Hoffman maneuvers. That's classic PI work."

In fact, those procedures were not PI work. They were journalism. It occurred to me then that Joe and I did not know each other, really. He did not even know I was a writer. He was advising that life imitate art—by mimicking Dustin Hoffman.

But there were worse things to try. I'd tried the conventional wisdom on searches, and all that got me was the inducement of organizations, agencies, and other PIs to call my case dead on arrival. With Joe, the case lived.

"You turned down Robert Redford's autograph?" I asked.

———

Who I most wanted to tell that I'd found my guy in Joe Adams was Ali. Ali in Berlin, who called me his sister. It wasn't that we looked like each other or any bosh like that. Brother and sister was just what we felt like to each other. I was his sister in that we were people who preferred dogs over nearly anyone. We found ideas emotional, and not only the ones about God. People presumed we were dark, and we could be, but I think we were also just optimists with penchants for cigarettes.

No matter. We didn't care much what other people thought. In college, we sang Patti Smith songs about claiming your own sins and gloried in the inimitable scent of a photography darkroom.

When he said he planned on moving to New York after college, I picked up a ticket from a cut-rate line known to run buses that occasionally burst into flames, then rolled my suitcase and pocket full of six hundred dollars to Brooklyn, because I trusted him when he confided that in that city you could live fast, lit, and best, free. He was right, and we thrashed through the Lower East Side together for a few years, and when he moved back to Europe, he was still right.

Now, I aimed to share that I'd found my guy in Joe Adams, not least of all because of a conversation we'd had three months before. It had started like this: Because he wanted me to laugh, Ali had declared *Poughkeepsie* was his safe word with his wife. He had never been there, but he loved the sound of it—not what the experience of the city sounded like, just the phonetics of the word itself.

"Poughkeepsie," he whispered. "I don't know, I always liked it. Listen. Poughkeepsie. Poughkeepsie! Poughkeepsie, Poughkeepsie, Poughkeepsie!"

"I love you," I said. "And you're deranged."

"What's wrong?" Ali asked. "Are you sad?"

"Of course," I said.

"So then cry."

I knew what he meant. He meant because it happened to be my first birthday without S in a decade. "Okay."

"Are you crying yet?" he asked.

"No."

"Maybe you want to talk about it."

"You've already heard it. You've been hearing me moan about it for ten years."

"So go ahead and cry," Ali said. "Cry. Here, help yourself to some crying, Tracy."

"Oh, I couldn't," I said. "I'm watching my weight."

"No, you aren't," he said.

"No, I'm not," I said.

"Why won't you cry?" Ali said.

"I don't know," I said. "Just clogged up. Call the plumber."

I did not call the plumber, euphemistically or otherwise. I took quack nostrums, drank blue moon booze. When the nostrums proved quack, I doubled down on calling detectives.

Now, three months later, with hours of Joe Adams's counsel under my belt, I wanted Ali to know that I'd recovered something fast, lit, and free. Events had turned. I had. It wasn't my second wind that I'd caught, but I'd caught air.

"This PI's in Korea?" Ali asked.

"No," I said. "He's in St. Louis, Missouri."

———

It was four hours, by my math, when I realized that Joe had disappeared. Since we'd first corresponded the month before, he'd been prompt in communications. But when I texted him on December 21, 2020: nothing.

Give it a day was reasonable. Give it until the next night was bargaining. I knew what would follow.

Days passed. No word from Joe.

When I did receive calls, they principally involved topics like the progress a friend was making on their glutes. My massage therapist friend had resorted to a stint as my essential oils online salesperson friend. Nearly everyone else I knew was horizontal and immoveable as distressed couches, yawning pledges of self-improvement and complaint. On good days, we were going to stop missing our old lives next year. On bad days, we were going to stop missing them the year after. Or never—this pandemic might never end. No matter how grandiose the public discourse about heroes, we'd the sense that no one was coming to save us. No one knew how.

We enumerated consumed food, how busy we were with sludgy time, sludgy dishes, sludgy minds. One friend hundreds of miles away said, "Apparently I'm the last asshole who still believed the anarcho-communitarian ideals everyone pledged allegiance to in our twenties, and now the pods are organizing down the breeder-childless divide." Maggie hit her stride on diatribes about desk job jerks who didn't tip on takeout. One aspired to remember humor.

**Ali:** I can't believe Jesus was a Capricorn
**Me:** That the worst sign?
**Ali:** There's also Sagittarius
**Me:** What's wrong with that one?
**Ali:** Stalin was Sagittarius.

Hours pulled by grading papers and asking Cowboy, "Are you a puppy or a flower? Are you my baba ghanoush?" And I, a glum bum in track pants, recalled that it was S who'd started calling Cowboy "baba ghanoush." He'd carried Cowboy in his arms like a baby on the trip back from the shelter.

This was a year or so after he began picking me up for coffee on a BMX bike that he pedaled through Manhattan traffic as I balanced my feet on the back tire pegs, holding his stomach. We worked the other nine-to-five then, professionals only in night-life. At six or seven in the morning, when we were very tired after our shifts at a filthy downtown club, he built cocktail straw tee-pees to float on my whiskey. If ambitious, we walked to Sullivan Street Bakery for first morning bread. He lost a shoe in a concert mosh pit from which we later hopped home, me licking from the wrapper a candy hippo crushed in his pocket.

All the same, because I was a dumb kid with a dumb mouth, I said, "I'm not sure why people commit to relationships." I didn't understand how to settle down without giving up some unad-ministered, inventing edge.

Then, one afternoon on a cab ride downtown from a mu-seum, I made my admission: I liked how he said words beginning with a consonant and an *R*, like *fruit*, from right behind his lips. As I slipped out of the taxi, he said, "I love you." Later, coming off the daze, I had to call, say, "I didn't say it, but you know."

In this way, we got to be idiots to each other but also for each other, and I decided that what mattered was that he was my id-iot. Maybe all that meant was we mythologized ourselves and in turn believed.

Maybe that was all I ever did. Make up stories. Believe them. I'd refused or failed to notice when I'd lost control of the story of my life—and more than once. I needed to notice my life as I was living it, before more of it careened off permanently. Joe, for instance, and Cho Kee Yeon.

Instead, the retrospective glance: when we'd needed an expres-sion that upped the ante on love, what S and I said to each other was, "You're my family."

But, too: "Why are you testing me?" I shouted once as he sped us through Brooklyn on an ailing motorcycle and I incorrectly predicted we would die young together, in leather jackets. That question I asked when, complaining of nausea from a round of Plan B, he said, "So next time, don't take it."

Now, in comparison, I said, "Is my Cowboy barking at his own farts?" Said to my black mutt, "Just say it in plain English."

I said, to Joe's voicemail, "Call me when you can. Call any time at all."

———

For many years, I'd had a good routine that involved doing things too much or not at all. I read books and wrote. I put in hours thinking myself into oblivion, and when I couldn't think more would call my friend and neighbor Jelly to go get in a bit of minor liberal arts–style trouble at the bar down the street. If I complained of writing drivel, he'd tell me, "You know why you'll finish this book, pup? Because you have a chip on your shoulder in all the right ways." Then it was back to the desk, and back to the desk, and at the desk, I wrote in one novel, "To orchestrate terror was to tell young men what to do with tomorrow, an ir-resistible charm." Now, it was time to do something else with tomorrow.

Sometimes, I'd catch myself checking my phone for Joe's name. I resolved and unresolved not to poke it, thinking of Joe's exhortation to hurry up. One night, I sat down to write. Write what I'd tried, write what was still possible, was the thinking. This was process of elimination, or maybe some people would call such a record of efforts autobiography, and since altogether I'd gotten the distinct impression I either was losing track or had lost it, it was the only way I knew to sharpen the outlines of what I'd gotten myself into. I did this, then recalled to my own chagrin the psychoanalyst Marie Langer once writing, "I was studying my umbilical cord while the world was blowing up around me."

And so for perspective, I went out the door. There, I could count on the incession of a ponytailed troll on Rollerblades who gargled milk from a gallon jug, skated gravel noise down the block, then liked to shout that I was going to die.

"What, can't talk?" he called out.

"Glide on, Ponytail," I suggested.

The thing to do was get past the troll. Take a left off the rotary. I'd go down Raymond Avenue past the two-for-one church that offered double the denominations of God under a single roof on alternating days. In fact, I never went and had no idea how to find Jesus, only that if you headed that way, you'd take a turn and get to Popeye's.

I went to Popeye's. I walked through the drive-thru. Children hung off women's wrists.

"Please," they cried, and I felt that.

I was one man down, zero ideas who to call when the missing person was the missing persons detective.

———

Which is why when Ali called, I told him I was beginning to wonder whether, when it came to Joe Adams, anything had even happened at all. If the investigation had been real. My life was newly witnessless. I was. I wasn't myself. I was crazy now, maybe. Crazier. It was easy to be crazier when witnessless. But I had known things before, I was sure of it.

Because whatever you could say about S, I told Ali, at times I learned to know what was true by what he did not. S had refused to admit that a clove and a bulb of garlic differed. On moving in, he had arranged our bed with the head pushed to the back of a closet, which I loudly noticed meant we woke as though in the middle of a car wash made of garments smothering our faces.

"You're always right," S said, accusatory.

I said, "Well, babcek"—the nonsense term of endearment I'd invented for him—"How about join me?"

And he did join me, in a way. This, at least, was the promise that we made to each other: to keep joining each other, keep coming home. We did. In the years S and I lived together in Brooklyn, our living room was taken up in large part by a picnic table, his idea of discipline was dancing with the dog, and though we had no fireplace, we had a hot pink mantelpiece.

Lately, I told Ali, I had the distinct impression that I wanted to go home, and I didn't know where that was anymore.

And on the phone, for whatever elusive reasons, I kept scratching at history. That S made declarations that we would one day live in a sailboat parked in a cement lot in Brooklyn. That he was always losing the rent money because his savings account was whatever misplaced book. That when S allowed me to use his phone, I programmed Google Calendar to remind him, at 2:00 p.m. each day, that he was loved.

"Don't worry," Ali said. "If you still feel bad next year, we'll get you another one. There's plenty more where that came from."

"Oh yeah, where?"

"Come to Berlin, darling. We've got loads of mediocre men."

I told my friend that it was correct to leave when I did. I knew that—however twinging I might sound now—because S and I were always arguing about what words meant. He believed love meant not making someone feel bad. I believed love meant that when S had been out of work and I had been in grad school, I had taken a third job, then extra one-off gigs to settle our tab with the landlord. In December 2020, I was repeating myself on the phone, and I knew it was pointless repetition. Still my mouth had legs. I kept going, as though then something of me would resolve.

For months—or was it years?—at a time S would not find a job, but I *would* find baggies hidden under the sink. I complained of squalor, even as I remained bored by an imaginal self who, presented with an exciting invitation, imperiously declared, "Maybe if I were younger, but *I* have a mortgage!" Sometimes, following the exhaustion of stacked shifts, I felt a grip around my neck until a wild hand splashed in my chest, and I'd have to leave the house. For the fourteenth time, the fiftieth, I don't know, I told Ali that I shouldn't have scolded S for longing for children for whom we were not equipped to care.

Because, in fact, even once I'd gotten the tenure-track offer that meant we could finally afford a child, it stretched the imagination that the person doing motherhood would be the same one I was in the habit of thinking of as myself: the one who read and wrote several hours a day, caroused when I couldn't write much more, and got lost on walks negotiating storylines, theories of social reproduction, or polemics regarding whether climate change meant that the moral calculus landed against procreation. In tempers, I'd quote Arlie Hochschild on "the second shift" of chores women cohabitating with men worked at home after their "real jobs." To S, I cited research that found men benefited more from marriage than women. I recapitulated the claims of a self-indulgent writer who compared motherhood to imprisonment and noted that I, too, was self-indulgent. I was afraid I would regret a biologically irrevocable decision, and I was afraid I would regret the other biologically irrevocable decision. And anyway, I kept making yet another biologically irrevocable decision, which was smoking cigarettes.

I asked S to leave, then let him stay. After I let him stay, I asked him to leave. We argued about the ceiling for the household MDMA budget, de facto his budget. I made pronouncements that I would not proxy his mother, then wondered how I could walk away from this person who, as a boy in socialist Poland, had flung paint on a statue of Feliks Dzierżyński, this symbol of the Red Terror. S brought home to his mother a hunk of the landmark destroyed in the revolt, and that story had taught me how to love S before we'd even met, but the relationship had devolved into one where you nag someone for turning you into a nag. The primary nag was stop riding the edge of crises, a nag that could persist between ten and sixty years, depending on how devoted either of us were to crises. In other words, I'd lost a grip on our life, and I couldn't remember when I'd ceased to belong to it.

By that December in Poughkeepsie, I could no longer remember how many times these cycles had cycled. I could only, it seemed, live in the virtual reality of books. For instance, Barthes: "Someone tells me: this kind of love is not viable. But how can you *evaluate* viability? Why is the viable a Good Thing?"

After I asked S to go, I found myself accidentally saying to grocers handing me receipts, "I love you."

So, the admission: indeed, in December 2020, I did want to cry as Ali had suggested months before. Did, especially, thinking this: because once S had pushed his way through a wall of police to find me when a school where I taught went on active shooter lockdown, I knew that he'd die for me, but for some reason, it had become untenable to *live* with this person.

"Thing is," I said. "You die once, but every day I live."

"You're very good at it," Ali said. "Keep doing that."

"Believe me, I didn't mean I was thinking about the other thing."

"I know," Ali said. "That's why you did what you had to do. You always do."

"Eventually," I said.

But what did I have to do now that Joe was gone, too? I couldn't get a handle on next week, on a few hours out. I didn't know what I needed to find Cho Kee Yeon. I didn't know how to know. And if I sounded like someone smack-dab in the middle of psychological transference from one absent love object to another, which I could only half refute, it was worth remarking that identify the psychic machination or not, I felt, irritatingly enough, still. I felt!

The gestures that followed the call will be familiar. I got my hair going in something like a balloon animal on the top of my head. It fell as I snapped an elastic. The Platonic ideal for a microwave burrito is seventy-three seconds. The Platonic ideal for a cigarette is no seconds. I reread the Borges story that got me every time. The detective Lönnrot quibbled at the inelegant design of his murderer's plot then, still a hopeful fool, asked his killer, Scharlach, to promise that in the next universe, his death would be more beautifully controlled, that there would be more art to it, that in the next universe Scharlach would murder him on a labyrinth unspooling in an endless line, unverifiable to the human eye.

———

Try again. Notice.

In the days after Joe went silent, in the absence of fact, I cultivated theories. Theories about Joe, theories about me. Theories having to do with Lacan's exquisite renderings of what he called a "dead chain of desire," or what those outside psychoanalytic circles understand as something like you can't get what you want—your all-fulfilling mom—but you take what you can get, and you still want more. I could develop a new theory while buying apples or batteries, looking at the cashier in the dollar store behind his taped-up Saran Wrap curtain. I had a theory for every day of the week, in multiple.

None of them mattered, though.

The facts are that December 3 was the date of our third call, according to my call log. Review of my notebook showed that on December 3, Joe had not yet phoned "that lazy, fat bum in Tampa." But he *had* been told by an FBI friend that investigating Eastern was "a bag of worms."

A momentum had accreted behind Joe's self-descriptions—"a freak," "a master"—when it came to inspiring people to share information. He lamented that such an art was nothing he could teach me, until he was, in fact, playing coach. PI work, I recalled he had said, relied on connection, even if a lot of people thought technology had outpaced hitting the streets. A man who'd once not had the time to talk to Joe about a case had abruptly found plenty of time to talk to Joe about horseback riding, for example, once Joe noticed a framed photograph of a girl in the saddle and said that horseback riding was a terrific sport.

My case was going to come down to finding the horse in the hearts of those people once employed by that adoption agency in Doylestown, Pennsylvania, he declared.

But my sharpest recollections were of other things Joe said.

One was "I'm gonna get an embassy contact and make sure you don't end up dead someplace."

Another, regarding Korean investigators, was "If they say give me fifty thousand up front, then they're liars. They're thieves. Then that's where I might have to come in."

"Are you saying you want to take this case?" I asked.

"No," he paused. "Well."

I waited. I hung on *well*. For a moment, I hoped like an innocent, and maybe I was.

By this point, I had investigated the investigator. I'd learned that Joe had pleaded guilty to bribing a public servant in 1997. Reportedly, another time, Joe plea-bargained his way out of weapons smuggling and conspiracy charges, then spent his entire probation knocking back liquor with Dade County cops. There may or may not have been some incident at a courthouse involving the waving of a weapon. And I trusted him.

Or else, I trusted going the whole nine yards, and that was what Joe's mythology was.

"Listen," Joe said quietly. "My wife's already going, 'I know what you're doing. You're getting involved in this thing.' I go, 'No, the girl's got a problem. She's got a right to find her parents, at least find out who they were.' My wife said, 'I saw your notebook. I see what you're doing.'"

On December 3, Joe and I had sat on the phone a while longer. We were two people who had never seen each other's faces, strangers on the phone line, strangers looking for strangers in the prickling mood of cahoots.

"You know what my call sign was when I was in the military?" Joe had finally said that afternoon of December 3. "It was Lone Ranger, because that's the way I operated, by myself. That's who you are. That's who you're going to be there. The Lone Ranger."

"Maybe in a couple months, when I've found stronger leads, the pandemic is over. And then we go over together, do things on the street your way," I had said.

"Yeah, all right," he had said. "Maybe."

A theory is not a fact, but that *maybe* is.

That he said "maybe" is a fact.

So is this: One day later in December I called Triple A. Another day my front shocks gave. On an afternoon glowing gray-blue with snow, from an auto body shop in the grayest part of town, I kept on in the revolving logic of snow, little almost-nothings building brightly underfoot. The two miles resisted contraction as I thought how all year a phrase had returned to me, gotten to the point of near-prayer in its senseless sense of meaning through repetition—if an interrogative reached the benchmark of faith required of prayer at all.

A young writer in class had asked me, "How do you know when a story is over?" *Will the end knock too softly, or will I quit my story before the end has begun?* she seemed to wonder.

I said what I wanted to be true: you just do. The end, I told her, appears in your consciousness as though it's always been a fact. I said the end is an unimpeachable feeling. I, who questioned as though to question is to answer, said something clicks. Certainty lands. The sentence goes dry. Punctuation. The end.

From the Poughkeepsie auto body shop, I walked those two miles, and it took so long, I felt as though the apartment on College Ave. was being sucked away as I stepped. A friend had told me the city figured in the Charles Bradley song "Why Is It So Hard." I thought of that, and I remembered that only one person didn't know who Marty Cardona was. Another person might.

I did the thing that aphoristically defines insanity: I tried and tried again. I didn't know how else to go about a day. That's all it was. One morning, when I was dumb with desire as ever, when I rued that I wanted a paradox ineffable as clean slate love I'd always had or else a paradox ineffable as a path through shapeless freedom, I dialed a number again.

Then, Marty Cardona asked how she could help.

# CHAPTER FOUR

# WHAT WE WERE REALLY DOING

New England, 1987–Poughkeepsie, 2020

In December 2020, I mostly hadn't a clue. But for whole years we knew what we were really doing. We were O'Neills. We were relentless. We believed in *wanting enough to*. Because just think: wanting enough to got two Korean orphans home and made us all Americans, all O'Neills. To know that was to know we could make anything mean something else.

In those days, when we spent, we were really building credit. When we were tough, it was really love. Rain on a wedding day: luck. We had our ways of slinking around facts—had, in our minds, getaway cars and side doors. I knew where to point when someone said, "No, I mean where's your real mother?" She was the one who wanted us to have jimmies on our ice cream, try shrimp cocktail. Said, "You need me to get you some pads and plugs for your period, or are you just in a real foul mood?" When proud her children lived better than she had as a kid, she said we made out like bandits. We got away with murder.

To celebrate that, out came blue plastic plates on the February anniversary of us turning family. Noodles neon with curry. On the wall hung framed pictures of animals carrying babies home. Truth be told, I had no idea who had carried me or my brother to the United States. I knew that if you had ambition enough in the late 1980s and early 1990s, you could hit the airport and get yourself a baby.

Only years later would I learn ambition was not itself sufficient—which is to say, I cost $5,300.

The blue plastic plates were sectioned like pie. My father always misidentified the noodles as "chow my," but we still caught the drift. The correct name was a detail of diminished interest in our homes in New Hampshire and Massachusetts, where my father added "chow my" to the Chinese order, where it was common knowledge that cinnamon sugar pita chips were Korean food, that Chinese was essentially Korean, and that some of my mother's relations called it all gook food anyway. We stuffed our faces, deciding February foods were tradition from the get.

And why not? To the four of us, it was clear one way to get away with murder was decisive approximation. We decided fruit-flavored ice cream was fruit, then ate it for breakfast. We decided we were sick to play hooky every third day and that making a deal was never negotiating.

The plan: work hard, play hard. In fact, never did learn to play without playing too hard at all. Then when working and wanting hard didn't work, there was being hard. We said, were told: cut the shit. If shit wasn't cut and you were still allowed around, you were family. *We* was *I* was *we*. My mother bought her sister Pall Mall cigarettes when her sister wasn't turning on her.

On Thanksgivings, an uncle by marriage, a black-haired *eye-talian*, proclaimed that I was his "little guinea," and he would tell everyone get a load of this, my hair—this was little guinea hair, and to be called a little guinea was really to be told you belonged.

———

In retrospect, the best times involved collusion on the homemade script. My mother recited her line about my brother stinking up the place like high tide at Revere Beach, long after we were anywhere close to Revere or Southie or Lynn. My father said, "Oh, God," and that he was exasperated was a bit, too. If he was really angry, he said, "Jesus H. Christ." Someone cruising for a bruising could ask what the *H* stood for.

Afternoons, we went to Marshalls and HomeGoods, went to T.J. Maxx. My mother would dog a clerk until a return went through on a twice-worn shirt missing tags. There was always another store. Return one thing for the other. In those manias, we would put anything we wanted in the cart, run high on the wealth of discount garments that, in the moment, we practically owned. In the gathering phase, we behaved as though money was no object. Money was an object. And so, there was also the phase in which my mother threw things on racks where they didn't belong, since you and whose army gonna stop us. Trashing stores, we understood the love in taking the wrong side and the dignity of asking for it so long as you went down swinging.

But on the whole, we weren't people who asked. We didn't knock on doors. Summer nights we slept on my parents' bedroom floor, where the strong fan blew. We stayed on top of each other, even in other rooms. Our voices were always in other rooms. Did we ever once mosey over to ask a question? No, we kept each other's names in our loud mouths.

You see, we were loud to be heard. We did not take lip. We mouthed off. "I'm the mother," my mother said. "Me." We couldn't say why we were so angry when we asked why a door was closed, never did learn to notify each other we were wanted politely. Only later was it apparent that the raging confrontations when our answers didn't come came of fear.

It came down to some of us had seen things, and that meant we lived life with an ever-creeping sense of stakes. We could, as the poet Elizabeth Bishop said, lose something every day, but we never took it wryly. What didn't kill us did not make us stronger. It made my mother hide food. She couldn't help herself, the poverty still in her bones, the years of dime-store peanut butter–cracker dinners a gaping memory in the stomach. We ate "like we were in a tent in Damascus." Of course, we'd never been to Damascus. We'd never been anywhere, really. We'd been to Roslindale High and Lynn. We'd been to aunties' and nanas', Southie to New Hampshire by way of Marshfield, Mass. In these places, someone was always on painkillers, and still, we felt on the outer rims, orating spectacular pronouncements.

"I'm the mother," my mother said. And "I would walk through fire for you."

In this way, we knew what it was to be made legend by love. We had, roughly, everything when we knew this, had knowledge in our guts that should we not get away with murder, then we were loved enough for someone to play the race card on our behalf, and we knew there was a race card because we needed that imaginary card to imaginarily win. When I began to write, no one said, "Hold your horses." My father asked, "So you're going to write the Great American Novel?"—just as, when we spent money we didn't have on skating lessons, I would win the Olympics. That ardor, we shared it, for the idea that go-getters got.

Consequently, that expression about the forest and the trees never made much sense to us. What did was that when my blue-eyed mother insisted she, too, had been called "Chinese Eyes" by neighborhood morons, she wanted it to be true, and my father wanted it to be true when he claimed she wasn't making it up. There was a scientific explanation correlating my mother's eye shape with that of a Pacific Islander, honest to God! For spells, we forgot where we came from. To draw a laugh, we did our best Fabio impression: "I can't believe it's not butter."

————

A writing teacher once told me experimental writing is seeing what you can get away with, and when I think of that now, it's clear what we were doing. We O'Neills were making up history as we went along and seeing with which metaphors we'd beat the rap. Who we could be was who we were. For years, this was my entire idea of freedom.

Or else there was freedom in continuing to ask questions. To those who did not see a family resemblance, my mother asked, "Says who?" For my entire life, I'd return to that question, senti-mental for the long con of language. That long con got us far. It also sometimes got us so deep in our alibis that we forgot what, in pursuit of a story, we missed.

I don't know exactly when I became confused about what par-ticular metaphors meant, how fruit-flavored differed from fruit, and what that had to do with the containers we chose for our lives. Only years later did it occur to me that we O'Neills had constructed an avant-garde story, like a book in which a designated letter never appears. In the experimental narrative of our family, what was not explicitly spoken of was, of course, her, the mother who did not keep me. In this way, we got away with something like murder.

But the mother who did not keep me was, as well, seeing what she could get away with. She was seeing whether, without family and marriage, she could make out like a bandit. Without a word of evidence, I believed she went after the experimental life like a crime spree. In December 2020, I did not know what I was really doing. But perhaps a woman of interest never did.

CHAPTER FIVE

# THIS IS NOT A ROAD TRIP

The Road to Victor, December 2020

December 29. Since Theresa W.—as I first heard her called—was dead, I got in the car. I passed gray sky and got more of it. Radio personalities said, "Go forth and find the lost sheep of the house." Then later, "South Koreans have not received the vaccine yet." I listened to the map, heard "9 West to 299," "299 to I-87," so on, so forth. I did these things as instructed, then as WAMC shrugged off fuzz, pushed eighty in open-road mesmerism.

On the highway, with its long stretches without exit or pause, it was easy enough to see the matter at hand as unfinished business. The sky was not broken, after all. Black cracks ahead were trees simplified of foliage. Though I'd learned no cause of death for Theresa W., I had picked up a last name: Weisberger.

*"She leaves no immediate survivors,"* the obituary had said.

It had been news to me, the *Boston Globe* clip, though it had been published in May 1990.

As a result, I was making the haul from Poughkeepsie to Victor, New York, in pursuit of more old news on Theresa Weisberger, now thirty years in the grave, and her relationship to thirteen crucial digits. These thirteen digits, if I understood correctly— and this, indeed, was an enormous hypothetical—might have once been written down by Theresa Weisberger.

*Find the number* I'd written in my own notes. *Find her.*

Her, of course, was not the dead woman, not *that* dead woman, anyway. I'd meant: find the number; find a mother.

————

*Find the number; find her—*

This had been written not as fortune or maxim but as procedure, a procedure that, it struck me, still remained in a protracted process of elimination. Police databases held the name, date of birth, resident ID number, and address of every known entity in South Korea. With two of the first three items—a modest fraction, I supposed—a person's location could be found. The shortcut was the resident ID number, since its first six digits already represented the citizen's date of birth.

*Find the number; find her.*

A poet would notice the sublime technique: the anaphoric repetition, the rhyme. The scientist could apprehend an elegant logic. And anyone could see how neat a trick it was, how like a place for everything, and everything in its place.

Everything had not, of course, been in its place. I needed that number. But then, December 23, the break came. On the phone,

Marty Cardona said she'd held on to her "own" notes on Love the Children clients.

In fact, I had not been one of them.

My mind paused. My mind barreled. If the deal was to go long on logic, what remained possible was picking the resident ID off notes kept by someone named Theresa W., who Marty said had been my social worker. There was a chance that this Theresa W. had written that number down and that Marty Cardona had a location on the dead woman's effects. I had a penchant for chances—compared, especially, to none.

*A plot,* I thought. *Suppose memory is dispassionate. Suppose a number remembers.*

"I promised I'd always do anything for the children," Marty Cardona said on the phone.

"Am I one of the children?"

"You're one of the children."

"So name a place," I said.

She said, "Do you know the way to Victor?"

---

I got there, of course—to Victor. Marty Cardona sat at a table by the door with an empty Panera Bread soup carton and a spoon set in a damp napkin. Hunched over refuse, she wore a gray shirt and a dark down vest. She was smaller than I'd predicted, softer. Off a tan, I could see that until recently she'd hung around outdoors. Something hurt in her eyes reminded me of my mother.

"Marty?" I said.

"Are you Tracy?" she said.

"That and late," I said. She was messing with a napkin.

"Do you want to order food?" Marty Cardona asked.

"I'm all right," I said.

"Coffee, water?"

"I'll just sit," I said and sat. "I'll be fine."

I had not come to be fed. The article in which I'd first picked up her name stated, "Agency social worker Margaret S. Cardona of Rochester testified." So she might now spill, too. We breathed into our face coverings.

"The first thing you need to know," she said finally, "is you might not like what you find out."

"I don't need to like it," I said. "I just need to find out."

"A lot of people think that," she said.

"But then," I said.

"But then," she said.

"But there's always a then, isn't there?"

"No," she said. "There isn't."

Nearby, teenagers assaulted each other and ran in jerks of new love. ("You stink." "No, *you* stink!" "Did you *really* just say I stink, stinkass?" [He did.] *Kiss*.) I considered how to assuage Marty Cardona's fears. What I had for her was this: The night before, I'd written a letter. I'd decided it was worthwhile to begin thinking of what I would say to Cho Kee Yeon, given the chance. By the time—if the time came—that I had an address on her, I would be prepared.

"Dear Cho Kee Yeon," it began.

*My name is Tracy O'Neill, and the reason for my letter is that you gave birth to me. I am referring to the labor that occurred on September 18, 1986, at 11:45 a.m.*

*I am flying to South Korea expressly because I wish to meet you, so I will be forward: Would you like to meet me?*

*Please do reply, even if your answer is* no. *Your explicit rejection will be helpful, in that I will not then fall into magical thinking. You can imagine how easy it would be to, in Kubler-Ross's terms, bargain. I could decide that this letter never arrived and look all my life.*

*I will hope for your answer.*

*Tracy O'Neill*

Only in rereading the letter had it occurred to me that I had not used the conditional tense regarding my mother's rejection. I had written "will": "Your explicit rejection *will* be helpful."

"So you see," I told Marty Cardona, "I cannot be disappointed. That's evident in the tense."

And yet, I suppose she noticed, the tense had not stopped me from driving five hours to meet her.

The analyst D. W. Winnicott figured mothers hated their babies before babies hated their mothers. Of his eighteen reasons why, one was "The baby is an interference with her private life, a challenge to preoccupation." The more famous kicker: a mother couldn't eat her kid. I could see how hunger could be demoralizing.

———

Marty Cardona had stopped messing with her napkin and was talking about the Thruway. She was well acquainted with the Thruway, it having once been her frequent route for work. She was sure I must have taken the straight shot of the Thruway to get to her. Its recommending attribute was how you could just stay on it. She said, "So."

"So," I said.

"Tell me about yourself."

I knew what my father would say—rather, what he had. "Who am I?" he had written in the personal statement accompanying the adoption application. "First off I am not a writer as, undoubtedly, I am now proving."

In a well-worn autobiographical tradition, the beginning was his biological family. Six O'Neill brats, two parents. Home was Lynn, Lynn, the city of sin, as the neighborhood rhyme went. His mother taught her children numbers by playing poker. She said, "Trust everyone, but always count the cards." Though my grandparents hadn't gone to college, my father realized he wasn't a great big dummy after high school and never forgot it:

> *Despite academic success, I graduated with honors, I was not accepted to any medical school. I was, however, offered a full grant to stay on at the university as a research assistant to pursue a master's degree in Genitics [sic]. . . . When the research grant money was not renewed I decided reluctantly to leave school.*

When interviewed by the agency, he'd have presented friendly. He dropped his *R*s more than my mother, and his hands moved abruptly. He tended to begin sentences, "Honest to God," though he'd always told me I should be less honest and learn to brownnose a little, and I'd never been good at it. He'd said that, with my personality, I was best suited to a career as a forensic pathologist. I guess some people were people persons and some people were dead-people persons. My father liked the idea of being a dead-people person, liked the idea of competition, but never cultivated the heart of a competitor. I remembered that when he asked my GRE score, I didn't want to tell him but did, and he laughed a laugh that was a little shocked with hurt and also proud, said I'd beat him, made excuses for his inferior score, and when I professed I didn't care about anyone's score, even my own, was perhaps more hurt. He'd always thought I was the cold calculator of the family. I wasn't. I think it must have been terrible for him to see he didn't know his daughter much at all.

"Me?" I asked Marty Cardona.

"You," she said.

"Whaddya wanna know, and who's asking?" my mother used to say, pretending to pretend to be a tough guy, when she didn't know an answer.

"I'm thirty-three years old, went to college once and can still speak English if there's any demand for it. There isn't much," the private eye Marlowe said in *The Big Sleep*.

But—*find the number; find her*, I thought.

"What do you want to know?" I asked.

"I don't know. Are you married? Do you have children?"

"No, I have two books, a mutt, and a PhD," I said.

"So you graduated?" Marty Cardona said. "Good for you. A lot of the children don't graduate."

I had better start asking questions. My attention had latched on to Theresa Weisberger, because her name resembled Therese, the paternal grandmother after whom I'd been named, or else because she was another woman on her own. Theresa Weisberger—something in me caught on her. This woman who died in Cambridge, not far from my relatives. I thought about her enough to vanish distance. Enough, anyway, to drive five hours and three hundred miles to a Panera Bread. Marty Cardona gave a little start in her jaw, as though she was about to say something, then thought better of it.

TRACY
O'NEILL

"What do you write?" she asked finally.

"Literary fiction."

"So," she said, "what is that about, literary fiction?"

"Chiefly," I said, "it's about failure."

―――――――

It was time to ask Marty Cardona about what I had come for, so I said, "What can you tell me about Theresa Weisberger?"

"She was a hard person to know."

"Who isn't?" I said.

"Sure," Marty Cardona said. Then, sighing, "Well, you can imagine how her clients felt."

Actually, I could not. We were strangers in a Panera Bread, sitting under the voice of Kelly Clarkson, winter light already spent down and salt on our boots. I didn't know her middle name.

"Given the timing," she continued carefully.

"The timing," I repeated.

"It was awful," she said.

Awful, meaning: Theresa Weisberger had been ambitious. Marty's territory was Rochester, Theresa's Boston, but they'd see each other on occasion for business. What Marty remembered was Theresa had always wanted to work at Harvard, to be an intellectual, have weight to her thoughts. Under that desire, Theresa had worked as though it was the only thing worth much. Marty knew that but little else, because Theresa was hard to know, and because there'd been no one really around to know her. That is, Theresa had never married or had kids. And then, of course, there was the fact that Theresa Weisberger had killed herself.

"With a kit," Marty Cardona said.

"A kit?"

"From the Hemlock Society," she said.

"The euthanasia people."

"That's right. You'd mail out for a suicide kit, and they'd send you a bag."

"For the body?" I said, stupidly.

"To asphyxiate yourself."

Theresa Weisberger would have had to address an envelope to receive her kit. It would have arrived in the mail, like any other package. There must have been instructions. There also would have been several chances to decide to live, but where there's a will, as the saying went, there was someone prepared to die.

Down my lower abdomen, hot and cold took their turns, and I was off topic; I pressed one thumb into the other palm.

"Look," I said. "I asked you to come here because I wanted to inquire whether you knew what happened to Theresa's notes. You said you took notes. Maybe she did, too."

"I wouldn't know about that."

"Do you know who would? Who was Theresa Weisberger close to?"

"I don't know if she was close to anyone," Marty said.

"Sure, okay." I leaned over my own elbows, crossed forearms. "But just for my information, would you have had access to a mother's resident ID number? You're making phone calls. You're liaising. On the phone with Eastern, does a moment come where, I don't know, your associate in Korea dictates the resident ID number for your records? Would Theresa Weisberger have had that number?"

"Oh no, nothing like that," Marty Cardona said.

"Your associate in Korea," I began again, and I didn't know why I kept saying "associate," "they tell you things. The resident ID isn't fundamental?"

"I wouldn't need that kind of information," Marty Cardona said. "The birth mother is not my client."

"Home studies, interviews; those kinds of things you handled. But nothing with a resident ID number."

"That's right," she said. "Now, you could try Eastern."

"I tried Eastern," I said. Then, "I also read about the Eastern revelations. Maybe you know something about what happened there."

"Oh, yes, I think I heard something about that."

"What did you hear?"

In one article on the trial in which she'd testified, it had been reported that she'd wept on the witness stand. She had broken down during testimony. It was possible, if she was lying, that she would break down now, too, but I could not see what her mouth did beneath her mask, and even in the moment I could see the lunacy of my preference. I preferred a lie about lurid plots over no information to give.

"I just remember there were articles last year, the year before maybe."

"You don't think Theresa Weisberger's suicide had something to do with it?" I said.

"What do you mean?"

"Was it guilt about what happened at Eastern? The kidnapping. The abuse."

"Nothing like that," she said. "We didn't know anything about it."

The trial in which Marty Cardona testified had concerned a child she'd placed with a couple who were, by regulation, ineligible for parenthood. The woman had been dying of cancer, then dead of cancer. As a result, the child had been taken away. Then the father, later played by Andrew McCarthy in *A Change of Heart*, sued for her return, and Marty Cardona wept on the stand. Marty Cardona had made a careless mistake that meant the child lost two mothers, or else she had taken pity on this couple. Seeing her soft face, that hurt behind her eyes reminiscent of my mother, I thought it had probably been pity.

"What do your parents think about this, anyway?" Marty Cardona said. "Your adoptive parents."

"They don't," I said.

"I see," Marty Cardona said. "So they don't know."

"They don't know."

"They don't want you to do this."

"Maybe."

"But you suspect."

"I could theorize." I didn't, out loud anyway.

Because, when my mother asked me as a child, "You don't want to find your birth mother, do you?" I'd said I did not. I wanted to stand by my words. I wanted language to mean absolutely, as it had in the declaration that we were family.

"Sometimes with adoptive parents," Marty Cardona said, carefully, "the search isn't easy for them. They feel like they did everything."

I hooked her eyes on mine. "They did," I said.

*After about eight months of being married, John and I decided we would like to start a family,* my mother had written in her personal statement. It continued:

TRACY
O'NEILL

*We tried for a year on our own then went for professional help. I had several tests that were negative until the laparoscopy that showed extensive stage IV endometriosis. I was referred to a fertility expert specializing in microsurgery and on January 29, 1985, I had extensive reconstructive surgery, had hormone therapy, and continued with the painful task of awakening each morning to taking and charting my temperature. In addition, John has had fertility problems of his own. We don't know if we'll ever be able to conceive a child, but do know we really want to have a child. My sense is that doctors are somewhat reluctant to tell a couple that there is no hope, there always seems to be one more procedure around the corner. . . .*

*Very early on in this process we decided that we would go as far as we could and that if either of us couldn't take any more, we would stop. I think we have reached the point that we feel we have done everything we could, short of very costly experimental procedures. There is some disappointment in arriving at this stage but there is also great relief. . . . The prospect of our being eligible to adopt is getting more exciting by the moment for us.*

So, why then, did I want more? This was a reasonable question. There was something terribly juvenile in the will to remember the mother who refused to mother, when I had parents who'd done everything. Or else they'd wanted enough, and there I was: wanting not enough but more.

And more for what? In the rogues' gallery of self-inflicted armchair analysis, I could conceive stakes to the search for Cho Kee Yeon. To see her could be to encounter my future. To see her could be to find that cradle-to-grave offered rewards outside those of the nuclear family or that the clincher was that love came back around. It could be to witness every day in the good life was amateur night, and though time passed through screwups, it still meant something. It could have something to do with controlling destiny, controlling story, dulling down my own historical sense of life's arbitrariness and contradictions of character. Get down to the brass tacks of belonging. These stakes appeared to me, but as though through a stranger's window, plausible and deniable as fiction. I couldn't explain, even to myself, why I so wanted to find her.

And in fact, there had been places to go other than Victor. A month prior, my friend Crystal had called to tell me that as friends we were soulmates. In the long term, this meant she wanted our children to grow up together. In the short, she'd like me to join her COVID pod with other Connecticut families. I was happy to imagine my friend in her home, and I was happy to imagine myself with her generally, but I was not happy to imagine myself with her in her home, her life. I couldn't say why.

"You all right?" Marty Cardona said.

"I'm all right," I said.

"I appreciate you coming here anyway," I said. "Talking."

"I promised I'd do anything for the children," Marty Cardona said.

"It's just Theresa," I said.

"Yes?"

"Why then?" I asked. "Why do you think she did it then? I saw in her obituary she'd gotten the job at Harvard."

"She *did* get the job," Marty Cardona said, nodding, "and it wasn't enough."

TRACY
O'NEILL

"So what you meant about the timing," I said to Marty.

"She did it on Mother's Day," she said. "I had to call her clients. They wanted to be parents, and the person who was supposed to help them become parents killed herself on Mother's Day."

I had come for one thing, and that was Cho Kee Yeon's resident ID number. It was not here in this pastry franchise with all its tricked-out variations on coffee. I had come to be dispassionate, to—without Joe Adams—operate as though I were my own detective; yet I was getting hung up on the details, one in particular about Theresa Weisberger that later I would learn was not quite correct. Theresa Weisberger did not commit suicide on Mother's Day, but it had been close enough to, in memory's make-do inventory, check the box on dramatic irony.

"You said she was a hard person to know," I said.

"That's right."

"But from what you knew," I said, "do you think she regretted not having a family?"

"Maybe." Marty Cardona shrugged.

"That happens," I said. "People don't realize. Then they do."

"Sure," Marty Cardona said. "It's possible."

———

There are things I can tell, and there are things I cannot explain. At first, after Victor, I thought I'd be able to explain myself with time, with distance. A writer friend, Justin, said, "First step is write everything down before you forget, or you'll regret it."

Days followed. I read Modiano novels. "Who is the puppy pot pie?" I said to Cowboy, and "I bet there's a Mr. Helicopter Tail who likes chicken," drifting through rooms. When friends called, I wished I could contain in language what my meeting with Marty Cardona meant, why I felt an event had happened in Victor when the number hunt had been a bust.

"But you did do things," Justin said. "Right?"

What I related was what I'd heard someone I did not know at all did: That afternoon in Victor, Marty Cardona mentioned her daughter Julie, also adopted, meeting her birth mother. The three of them had gone to a restaurant in Korea. Julie was a young teenager, but she had gone with a plan, as I had gone to find a number. That plan—she executed it.

Julie said to her birth mother, "I have thought of you every day of my life."

Julie's birth mother had sat across the table from her daughter for the first time in many years. She heard her daughter's voice, responded, "You have a good life." Something like that. "You live in America. You have everything you need. Everything turned out how it should be."

When Marty Cardona told me this story, she shook her head and looked off at a trash bin stacked with trays of greasy paper. She shook from her lung. That sound wasn't exactly a laugh.

"Julie was crushed," she said, "and my heart ached for her, and my heart ached for the mother. Because the mother was trying to be gracious, I think. But I know Julie, she's my daughter, and she was a kid who needed in that moment for her mother to say, 'I thought of you every day, too.' She didn't."

Marty was fiddling a little piece of paper in her hand, a straw wrapper. She gave an abrupt huff. I could see she wished she had another piece of trash to worry.

"Of course, years later," Marty continued, "when Julie was grown up, her mother wrote a letter, and that broke my heart a little, too."

My throat was dry, but I had said I would be fine when I arrived. I had said I did not need water. "Why?"

"The mother, she wrote this letter. She wanted to come to America to see Julie."

"I see," I said.

"And it broke my heart because she said, 'I know I wasn't there for you, but please let me come. I'll stand behind a plant if you want. I won't tell anyone who I am if you don't want me to, just please let me see you.' She'd realized, but it was too late." Marty shrugged. "Julie, she'd been so hurt, and now she was grown up. She had the power, and she wanted to use it."

I looked at Marty Cardona. She must have been around my mother's age. Her hands held each other, thinking of her daughter's mother, whose realization came too late, and her daughter, whose forgiveness came too early. I considered the image of that plant Julie's mother would have skulked behind, if only she'd been allowed. It was cartoonish. Haggling with desire often is. Maybe it was not a case of wrong time, wrong place, but a case of being the wrong people at the wrong time. And I felt a flickering in me, and I wanted to brace this flickering until it was a spent wick. I was afraid to speak. I couldn't. Then I did.

"I have to get out of here," I said.

"You have a long drive," Marty Cardona said.

"I have to get out of here," I said again.

I got out. In the car, I smoked a cigarette. My face didn't call back straight in the mirror. But see enough that you can scram, that's what I had to do. I blinked once, twice.

A paradox: my vision wasn't clear, but it was clearer.

The detail that renders no additional meaning to that inner flicker in Victor—which I told my friend anyway—is that I stopped for gas an hour and a half, two hours out from that Panera Bread. The sky was an infinite pit, and I'd driven as fast as I could into it, then hit empty. I'd also, it seemed, left my purse about a hundred miles back at Panera Bread.

It was snowing again. It was black and white with winter that early night, and there was nothing to do but pull my hood up and push a screaming impulse down my throat.

"Excuse me," I said a few times to people who did not welcome the approach of a beggar in a mask.

"I don't normally do this," I said.

"Hey, you," I said, and, as a man waved me off, "Jesus H. Christ."

Inside the convenience store: pairs of wrapped cupcakes, dismal light. Made my way to the teenage boys working the register. One wore a pinched white hat and maroon golf shirt that said "Stewart's." I don't think he needed to shave yet. The other was a big boy, but I doubted he needed to shave yet either. "Listen," I said, and they moved away from the cigarette display, closer to the counter to listen. Then: "I'm listening," I said, as they spitballed options I didn't have. They blew air in flummox, and I went to wait for another car to pull up, another person to ask for gas money.

"Hey, wait," the slighter boy said, remembering.

I turned back. He opened his wallet, slid out a ten-dollar Stewart's gift certificate that, evidently, "some asshole" had given him as a Christmas bonus.

"Christmas bonus, my ass," he said. "Who *does* that? I work here."

"You don't want it?"

"I *work* here," he said.

TRACY
O'NEILL

"Only an asshole," the big boy muttered, smacking the air, walking away.

"Think ten dollars of gas will get me to Victor?" I asked.

The kid shrugged. "You can try."

So I did. I tried. I did not have a plan for if the tank ran down, but by some asshole's grace, I made it. Back in Victor, veritable children passed my purse over the counter and called me a poor thing. "Poughkeepsie," they whispered, wide-eyed. "Poughkeepsie." It was their object to send me home with two free chocolate chip cookies and a plastic cup of lemonade. I remembered I'd not eaten all day.

"Are you sure?" I said. "You won't get in trouble?"

"You have so long till home," one of those children said. "You need something."

In retrospect, it's apparent I did learn one thing. I learned to fill the tank before I got on the road. Then I pushed my foot on the gas for a few hundred miles, through the tripped-out blue-black tunnel of night. And I loved those children pumping gas, sneaking freebies, the children who rued there was still so long until home. Their kind indignance in those greasy part-time uniforms, I'd remember. I did not really know them, surely never would, but I saw in the baby fat of their faces that they knew what I needed better than I did.

And I kept going. And I thought of my mother at the ironing board on winter evenings, giving a play-by-play with a wink: "Miles to go before I sleep." And I thought of the last time I saw the house of my childhood.

It had been foreclosed on, the house. All weekend, I had set out my parents' belongings. Strangers came for open season on the trappings of my childhood, as my parents sat inside. The operative delusion, anyone could have seen, had been that if they did not look at their possessions, they could not be dispossessed.

A man arrived to grab up a metal patio set. His car was down the hill of the driveway, angled up. My father must have heard the sound of that engine rev ceasing. I don't know why he called me into the house over these precise items, but he wanted to know the price that this man was receiving.

The patio set they'd soon have no patio for had been haggled down to a figure less than that of Costco membership. My father slapped the arms of the chair, but he didn't stand up. He knew a bullshit number. I did, too. As it happened, by my calculation, it would have cost more to have the patio set hauled off the property than even to give it away.

I watched my father show his teeth and slap the arms of the chair. His hair was white, and the rage was no longer the expansive rage I remembered from childhood. When my brother and I were children, if my father smacked us, he would sit afterward with his forehead in his hand, torturing himself for hours while drinking plastic cups of boxed wine on ice. The day the man came for the patio set, I watched my father slap the arms of the chair with his chubby, impotent palms and put his forehead in his hand in that familiar position, and I was afraid and terribly embarrassed for him, and all I could think to do with the embarrassment and fear was to scream at my father to stay inside, then sneer at the cheapskate, and in the end, the cheapskate said some insulting things before taking the furniture for a sneeze, and my father was angry at my bullshit help, and so was I.

The moment I thought of most, though, on that car ride from Victor, occurred after the cheapskate left, when I stopped my descent down the stairs to the foyer, knowing it would be the last time I'd stand in my childhood home. Upstairs was the window in the closet that had made me hope we would move to this house when I was a girl. I had imagined that window would be my own space, even more mine than a bedroom could be. It was a place a girl could see the world her own way, safely, and from afar.

The last night in the house, I looked at the front door that I'd passed through on first days of school; the night a falling tree killed the family husky; and when I came home from Brooklyn to see my father after cancer treatment, trying to think up how to hug him in a way that would avoid the urine bag that humiliated him. Then for who knows how long I lingered on the stairs, knowing I'd never see my childhood home again. I lingered one last time, waiting to feel something, and I did. I felt a wish, and the wish was that if a loss was coming, I could hurry up and lose this home faster.

"Son of a bitch," my mother gasped. "This is our house."

"It's not yours anymore," I said in my measured, numbskull way. "You have to accept it's not your home, it's just another building, and don't look back."

At the wheel on the road from Victor, I ate my cookie. I drank those children's lemonade. I knew the baked-in fallacies, and still I was not transformed. Still, I was compelled by the disproven proposition that I could salvage something by trying to see the world safely, and from afar. And I predicted I was about to cry because I was. Then I did. Cried maybe because I had been on that road so long. I had been on that road all my life. Time freaked from the famine of road marks on the highway as I made my forward push through the dark. Outside the Outback, the sum total was nothingness forever and bright white saucer lights pulsing off eighteen-wheelers, and in the nausea of the hot car, in the dizziness of hunger I hadn't known I had, when the road still hadn't ended and the delirium of truck lights clocking ninety came for me, I was doomed, I was dying, I would die on this ill-conceived errand of information, and I didn't die, and I waited for it.

The apocrypha would have had these horrible halogen eyes unblind me into revelation, but this was not a road trip story, this was not a picaresque or an odyssey, and I could convert nothing of Theresa Weisberger's death, Julie's mother's blown shot, or that lost window on Corduroy Road into insight. And I was not someone who prayed, but in my chest I was down on my knees.

And all I wanted was to go slug drinks in the throbbing mass of a nightclub, get my arms up and be raised overhead, to be a body punching holes in the night, whipping hair. If nightlife weren't dead by pandemic, I would edge up the temperature and live and live in the anonymous mist of filthy group sweat sparkling up off a trashed dance floor, feel bass twitch my brittle bones. That was the extent of my desire. I couldn't run a sentence in my mind a way where the moment didn't lay a finger on me, couldn't on the way from Victor see how to compose myself or the future.

Because I could not have known on that black drive that Joe Adams would call again. Attitude: Wasn't it regular as a Tuesday for him to chat? I could not have known he would say how much he thought of dogs, which he couldn't say for humans. I would say I had been afraid he was gone. He'd say of course he wouldn't have gone anywhere. I would ask, "But where are you when I don't know where you are?"

"Right now, I'm in a parking lot," he'd say.

"All right, I'll take that. So now what?" I'd say.

TRACY
O'NEILL

There are hours on the Thruway, I told my friend Justin, when you recall upstate New York situates in outer space. That's how much galling nothing you're in. You look out the windshield, and you'd take any sign just to corroborate you're still on solid ground. You're too fast to stop, too slow to have arrived. At the sight of a truck come too close, you intuit the feel of a nine-star cosmic pileup. Only later can you see that the road is less eventful than those hiccups of fear. You surrender coordinates for miles at a time. That's all you can do. You surrender.

CHAPTER SIX

# GIVE ME
# A SECOND

To Brooklyn, Summer 2021

Down around College Avenue, the snow slop clumped everywhere, a disapproving radiator hiss slipping in and out of earshot.
It was ten to nine, or it was half past twelve. It was afternoon
with a chance of precipitation. And whenever it was, I knew the
time, and it was time to take the hint that I might come up short
on the mother who, if not dead, could be dying alone.

Conflating life and literature, I'd jury-rigged the stance that
all I had to do was write a new plot into my life; instead, post-
Victor, I mostly just went jumpy at the sound of a shovel morti-
fying pavement out the window. The scenario of my search had
not become scenes. I did not have my story straight, and this
had not escaped Joe Adams's notice.

Missing was one thing, the lam another. Which is to say, a

fugitive from motherhood might not want to engage, Joe said. I'd better get my head around it.

"She doesn't belong to me," I told him. "And I don't belong to her. I know that."

"So if it's a no-go?"

"According to the papers, she worked at a café," I said. "I'll fly there."

"And then?"

"I'll see her from across the street."

Many in my position hoped to learn that they had been wanted by their mothers, which I considered materially insignificant information. But I wanted to know her, or at least know what it felt like to be near this woman. If it came to it, I'd settle for being near at a distance.

The rub was that Joe had gotten a regional security officer on the phone, and that RSO told Joe the score on the peninsula: the National Center for the Rights of the Child told people like me to get to the back of a line stretching tens of thousands of orphans long.

But Joe figured I should press my advantage. That my desire was not unique meant others had made it to the front of the line, proverbially or not. They found family, following dilatory bureaucratic plays or not. Their moves could be borrowed off books, blog posts, TV. Take a cue.

When, one afternoon shortly after, I watched Korean Broadcast System's reality TV show *I'm Looking for Someone*, the host said, "We have guests today who are looking for their families, and therefore looking for themselves." Then came the gleeful turn, as he told a woman in search of a mother that she and her husband looked so alike—just like brother and sister!

So I was stalled. But no—the case was; and you can live without looking. I had. If there was no movement on the case, then the move was to wait for the case to catch up to me.

Make a break from the first person of my own mind and lose the tail of the past.

What's left then? Be you. Do now. Answer the question of what's next in the language of simply living.

Do not try to force time to pass but mean something. You can apprehend yourself outside endless loops of the same questions, same old hungers.

Recall the poet Randall Jarrell: "The ways we miss our lives are life."

A humble proposition: miss this life of missing missing woman living.

Ergo, one day, you get a vaccine jab. You pack boxes. You eat time finding an apartment where you can hear the Brooklyn-Queens Expressway.

Figure resolution simple; move the body outside the mind's fool habits until the story follows. Be otherwise. Procure a new desk.

———

In Brooklyn, it's clear the thing has heft. You've got a third-story walk-up, a couple hundred pounds of desk, and the wingspan of a size 2 dress. You push. You pull. God grant me the serenity. You will catch a second wind.

You make it five stairs.

But like Joe Adams, you've got people. For this vertical haul, there's the trucker who once got you eighty-sixed.

Cut scene to physics: the hoisting and *hold the door*. The thing to do is altitude. You struggle but together, struggle but up. Cowboy's verbose lunacy reports from the bedroom.

Job done, your trucker friend remembers an item worth mention. "Come Sunday to my wedding. I don't know what time yet, but come. I'll text you."

"You don't know what time yet?"

"I'll text you."

So days trip ahead; then, there are vows with meat on the patio. You drink pink wine in an old blue dress, gawk skyline. Soon after the promises expiring in death finish, a tall man enters urgently, as if he has a favor to collect. The trucker friend says, "You should talk. He is Stalinist, too."

"I am not Stalinist," the tall man says.

"Okay, okay, Marxist," waving, and then your friend drifts off on the promise of someone else's chain to pull, the not-Stalinist following.

For a while, play dumb-face with a local baby. On a table laid with bottles and cheese, hunt coffee. It's early and time for home, you think.

You think that, but there's still the night's sign-off, a cigarette. Your trucker friend comes around to once more present the not-Stalinist in the mode of *here: for you*. The heaviness of this man's shirt does not match the weather, but he's unencumbered. Weeks later, you will realize that quality of personality is, in fact, cocaine. In the moment, the illusion is a man all air and lung.

His name begins with *N*, though he says in Serbia the nickname is Johnny. He does not go by Johnny. Some people riff on his surname to call him boss. He used to move himself up rocks for recreation. Now for cash money he moves furniture. To fund a small Balkan press pushing translations, he snaps up grants.

Say, "You have a boner for Sisyphean things. Me, too." Through the doorway, your friend Hannah's eyebrow catches air.

Night contracts on the balcony. Someone plays a song called "Mama." "Brate," a man shouts, then N offers you a new drink.

You stay. You won't. N says, "You cannot leave. You will leave my heart on the ground by the fire hydrant."

"Are you sure you aren't a poet?" you say. "A bad one, but a poet nonetheless?"

"I'm not," he says.

"O-kay." The skeptic's elongated vowels.

"No okay, bad one," he says. "But no, I am not. I am not writer. I am normal."

"No one's normal."

"I am. I am normalno. In Serbia, I only start publishing house to get the gossips."

N who doesn't go by Johnny says his people are normal. His people are normal, are loud. He states his convictions on the best radio station and his countryman Tesla. To look at him, you look to the sky. Then it's quiet.

"Ask me questions," he says.

"You have no idea what you're getting yourself into," you say.

———

You are not surprised to hear from N; 8:53 a.m., and his name spills outside the night, his name in your pocket, your hand. What, you wonder, did you miss?

No you didn't miss anything,
bunch of drunk talk and spilled
drinks.

                              Ah I like those things.

Anyways I'm glad I met you,
tell me would you be down for
a drink or maybe a climbing
session sometimes? No wait,
coffee, no drinks, like seriously,
never again.

                              Yes we can never again.

Never again ends up tomorrow. He pulls over in a black sedan,
smiling an unconstructed smile, then smears blocks with the speed
of a maniac. He's passing cautious speeds and blurting. He would
like to have a boy child, he says. Jesus Christ was a Serb born in
Niš. He has a friend so pure of heart, this man drinks lemonade. It
is not only sobriety, the proof in the lemonade. It is goodness. This
man is good guy!

The sum total of the ride to the restaurant clocks out a few
minutes north. You case for spots; he'll risk a ticket. "You're sure?"
is the question. "Pa dobro," the answer. That gets you quickly to
the first time you've entered a restaurant in over a year.

That's true, and still this night, all it is is what people have
done into mundanity. It is *what are you thinking of,* where the
answer is food. N was married once. Now he is not. People ask
what's his creative outlet, he's noticed, and sure, okay, he played
drums, but he never had a passion. A few years ago, eureka: his
unhappiness was being broke. So he chased money here, went

there. Couple years did nice-nice long-distance trucking. As a boy, the game was partisans and fascists.

His brother's built like a Hungarian pornstar. His grandfather was his best friend. The grandfather would lie to the illiterate wife about the pension check once a week to buy himself a secret drink, his grandson a secret toy. N went home in February but won't return until next year when he might finally have US citizenship; otherwise he got nothing here all these years, and what was the point of America?

The waitress shows up with spilling oblongs of khachapuri.

"That's it," N says. "Food is here; now I won't talk."

"What will you do?"

"Now I eat," he says, and he keeps his word.

This, then, is silence. The recitation is over. You sit across matching plates. Chewing passes. You aren't sure why you're here. Cut the khachapuri. Drink the drink. The faster you finish, the faster the night does.

But look up, and see that this man eats like he means his hunger. Catch the clump of cheese on the face, piece of leek. Somehow a slick of oil got up under his eye. N pauses, face half-wadded, a cartoon animal. You don't always like people, but you always love animals.

"It's good?" he asks.

You say, "Very."

After, he wants to go to a bar that isn't open. It's no matter. It's Brooklyn. Walking happens. Whiskey does. At a narrow table on stools, say the next day you'll have to lug out the new desk, which arrived damaged.

"You are working tomorrow?" he asks.

"Always, in a way."

Meaning, you say, you are a writer. You write. Even when you aren't writing, you are sure, you're writing. Even now you might in some obscure spot near your neck be writing, as you look not to be. Writing is something the mind does. The narrowed attention.

He says, "I want to kiss you."

"I have to go to the bathroom," you say.

Fall back on an old maneuver. Before S, you'd sometimes head to the bathroom on dates, then slip off. Once, you were caught. A Société Générale banker doused in the most beautiful cologne called your name down the street. You ran as he called your name, and when you could no longer pretend not to hear it, copped an apology. You never found out the name of that fragrance. Now, in the bar bathroom with the verbena soap and low tea lights, you lean over the sink, pause. The mirror doesn't call back correct. There is something terrible about this man who's not Johnny, all babble then vacancy, speed and normalno and viscosity. He runs over, leaking impulse, unchoreographed, then bravado. A stranger swings through a stall. The miniature sunshine of tea lights shakes. And you could leave right now, save for an image stuck like a tick: leek on face, this naked evidence of hunger. There is beauty to naked hunger.

Back at the table, ask, "Are you afraid of dogs?"

"No," he says.

"What about big dogs? What about wild dogs? Dogs named Cowboy?"

———

The afternoon after, a call. He remembers your address. He's come without announcement because he wants to move your desk.

"Move my desk," you repeat. "That a euphemism?"

"Euphemism," he says. "What means?"

It will not be the last time he must ask the question, or you.

Case in point: You say you are not pregnant. He says he hopes you will have a boy. You say you may be too old, and he says the product of your genes would be cute-baby. He can't keep track of what day it is. The shape of time goes no jobs for a while, then nice-nice in the busy. The busy is the end of the month. The end of the month is not when you think it is.

You get sick. He delivers fruit. On phone calls, he specifies his breakfast. When he needs to use the bathroom at your place, he announces he'll be there long time doing pow-pow and therefore will require a full-size bath towel with which to wash his ass. A ping from across the apartment: We will go real grocery shopping tomorrow, that's just warm-up.

"You can tell your friends I take you good places," he says, having emerged from the bathroom. "I take you to Trader Joe."

The Trader Joe's bit is one act in a narrow repertoire of self-deprecating humor, but in fact, you do like to grocery shop. Do like sharing the dailiness. When he asks how you slept, the inquiry is sincere. He is all body, all, "What did you eat?" At brunch, he concentrates on his phone. You ask whether he is reading a book, and he wonders why.

"Because we're at a restaurant."

"So?" he asks.

"So," you say, "talk to me."

N asks, "Why?"

N declares, "There are only so many words I can give and receive in a day."

N says, "We talk in morning. Now I reach my quota."

What he means is his limit.

He has his own language for other things, too. He calls you "b." He calls your bathroom his office. He is long on your couch and out of the blue. At your apartment one night, he disappears mid-film. When the last shots have been fired, the hero killed, you discover N in your bed, say, "You went to sleep?"

"What it looks like?"

"You didn't say anything," you say.

"I was tired. I go to sleep."

In sleep, his feet find your feet, his pinkie your pinkie.

———

Tell friends, "I don't understand this person, but."

"But," they say.

"But," you say. You can't figure out how the clause finishes; still, you mean it.

Perhaps the *but* clause, then, is: but you were going to answer the question—What's next?—in the language of simply living.

———

Some weeks after the wedding, N calls to say, "I won't make it tonight, actually. Actually, friend dies."

You leave Prospect Park and slip a cab to Ridgewood. That night at the ramen spot, there's sushi and Coke, the eulogizing impulse. The dead friend would lend N money for truck parts. Big brother stuff. Deal was pay him back whenever. No one saw it coming. He had a business; his life was unfinished business.

"Are you okay?" you ask.

He says, "People die. What to do?"

And, of course, what to do is the question you wished to put away. Put it away. Buy N a black Oxford. The funeral comes and goes. Groceries. Bad movies about bad blood. He says, "In Serbia, dog like yours would be shot." You say, "We are here." Time passes, and you feel the restless creep of not having, lately, written.

"I've not been writing," you tell N.

"You write, don't write, so what?" he says. "You don't have normal job. You have to feel it."

"Which *it* do I have to feel?" you ask. An honest question.

"Jebiga," he says. "You think too much."

Still, there is, indeed, occasion for you to suppress laughter at the phrase "cosmic orgasm." He laughs at screens all night. He predicts you will think it's funny that "this fat-boy, so cute on YouTube," charges into a kitchen to say, "God bless this house. God bless this family."

"Perhaps," you say, "this is a matter of taste."

He reads books in which old conquerors fall in thrall with virtuous Christian teenagers. You read Saidiya Hartman on the experimental lives of wayward women. The overlap is gangster movies. One day, N says in Serbia he will publish Baudrillard. Your favorite, you tell him, is *The Perfect Crime*, the one beginning: "This is the story of a crime—of the murder of reality."

"The artist, too, is always close to committing the perfect crime: saying nothing," you tell him Baudrillard said. "But he turns away from it, and his work is the trace of that criminal imperfection."

For a few beats, N is the perfect criminal.

Then life returns to his face. All that life in his body. N says, "God bless this house. God bless this family!"

———

There are things to stifle, mainly laughs. He says he loves beauty. Catch him flexing at the improvised mirror of a turned-off television. When he sees you see him, he smooches biceps. He catches you, too. There is, on your desk, a long, torn-off sheet of paper where you've written, *WHO IS TRACY?*

"Who is Tracy?" he teases. "Who is? Who is?"

Take the paper. Call it a note. It is a note for a book you've thought of writing. N makes a face meant to be yours. He asks rhetorically, asks with mock carefulness in his impression of you, "What . . . is . . . words?" Then, "What . . . is . . . writing?"

Short story is the answer one night. The narrator will not be you. "It could be worse," the narrator thinks. "I could, for instance, be the stepmother of three boys who are bedwetters named Nicholas, Henry, and Bellwether, ages seven, eight, and fifteen respectively."

You stop. You start again. Everything itches.

"I want you to be my girlfriend," N says.

"What do you mean?"

He says, "I want to have monopoly."

It's a joke, or it isn't. Or it's a joke, and it is also meant. Perhaps, it's no joke at all. This moment in Brooklyn can reckon with what the anthropologist Gayle Rubin called "a systematic social apparatus which takes up females as raw materials and fashions domesticated women as products"—or you can take N's tone to be ironic and raise the stakes. Decide the punch line is funny.

"I thought you were a Stalinist," you say.

This, too, is a joke, or it isn't. Or it's a joke, and it is also meant. Perhaps, it's no joke at all.

And so for a while you do not chase story, do not chase her. As a moment happens, it is impossible to know what's for a while, what's permanent. What you're doing could be enough, you decide. Decide that as long as you can.

————

A writer might see where this is headed. A reader might. As it turns out, autobiography can't be abandoned as easily as a bad alibi, or a child. At a certain point, the question is not, What will you do next? It is, once more, How did I do what I did?

The next year, I would try to compose myself as I was on return to Brooklyn, when sleep did not keep cheap. When I tried to get at what was most myself, I remembered some of the happiest moments were phone calls with Maggie. She was working too much that summer, as she always had, but she said she liked the Hooters girls on her shift since they reminded her of when I was younger, pushing bottle service bottles like my life depended on it—and for all intents and purposes, my life did.

I thought to write about how, after her double mastectomy, I asked after my friend Treska's new boob job and got in line for the day when we could take it out for a spin. She and her fiancé, James, had taken me in once when an apartment didn't work out and I'd thought for a tense few hours I had nowhere to go. For a whole week, we were happy throwing cut sausage to Cowboy.

The city was itself, yet rawboned and cluttered with make-do outbuildings. I wondered how to write myself in that period when I'd just returned to Brooklyn, write how I'd gotten there off a high-speed chase for home in proximity to a cliff.

At a certain point, though, affairs must settle. When a year had passed since my trucker friend's wedding, I would want N to carry the chapter. "Let's say that was the summer I decided to surrender authority to chance" would be one sentence I mulled. For a woman who wanted to be the kind of woman I wanted to be, this was a terrible confession. The narrative would come slow. N's character would, with its thin spots and antic turns of speed, stone, creature. When I wrote something true, I'd wonder whether the prose suggested that I loved this person or only nearly did.

"What does he have to do with your mother?" Treska would ask.

In my defense, I would say, "For a time I stopped looking."

Such was the defense. It wasn't entirely true. Though the summer of 2021 hauled forward on the fumes of second-person perspective, on the offshoring of impulse, there was itch, there was relapse, there was writerly instinct to advance the plot. More than once, I caught myself red-handed entertaining how to make time pass and mean something.

Watch television, and I'd wager the detective could have been the criminal if things had shaken out different, as my own arbitrary life might have been another. On the walk to the restaurant Reunion, I posited to N that every noir novel is a historiography of the rap sheet. My friend Sean was working on a podcast about dead girls. Over the phone, one back-and-forth hinged on criminal existentia and the letter the Golden State Killer's grown niece had written for the trial.

"He saved my life," wrote this woman, who, in her teenage years, had been taken in by the murderer. She wrote, "I didn't know how good life could be."

Once a "cold hit" matched the Golden State Killer's DNA to a police database, this woman lost a metric on the good life. I did not remember how the killer killed, I told Sean. I remembered that Joseph DeAngelo was loved and that love once kept a desperate girl going. The revelation of violence did not reinterpret her memory. She said, I said, "He taught me everything. . . . I always wished he were my dad."

And when Sean asked about my interest in the Golden State Killer, I'd had to admit I'd been reading about DNA analysis, and at that depth, I could not shrink around the sorry truth that I had not disappeared Cho Kee Yeon from my mind. I could confuse my life for experimental literature with its possibilities of diffuse narrative perspectives, but it still adhered to realism with its science and measuring devices.

And science had proved topical throughout my half-baked investigation. To nearly everyone I'd bothered along the way, if I wanted a location on the mother who did not keep me, I could do worse than spit in a vial.

It will perhaps suggest something of my own confused prognostication, though, to confess my habitual response: The genetic route would work only if Cho Kee Yeon had done a test, then submitted her results to a DNA database. It would work only if she, too, had been looking.

I had said that, and more than once, but as the months ticked on, I'd also read about crime scene residue outing the perps. I read about the newborn found dead in a Sioux Falls, South Dakota, ditch in 1981, tears frozen to its cheeks and still swaddled in a red blanket. Nearly forty years later, the DNA was run. That surfaced a name: Theresa Bentaas, the baby's biological mother. When the game ended with a cold hit, she was a fifty-seven-year-old paralegal. She did not, when they came for her, put up a fight. Instead, she surrendered a motive for killing her son. In her words, the factors were two in that murder. She'd been, one: "young"; two: "stupid."

Young and stupid—I could not say that Cho Kee Yeon had been either at the time in question. She had been thirty-eight and had noticed when her marriage was over. She'd known how to have the last word; she'd disappeared.

Yet even the fraud leaves a clue; she'd missed a track to cover. Since notionally, biologically, and not incidentally, she was one of my mothers, I was that errant evidence she left.

I could want N to carry the story, could want to live in the present outside the old hungers, long questions. I could plan to lock up the fever pitch of the search. But in Brooklyn that summer, sleep did not come cheap, even as the second-person perspective wore itself out, and I'd lie in bed thinking how genetic material loiters, a fact as inconvenient to mouse as opportune to cat, though here the game would not be cat and mouse; it would be mouse chromosomes betraying mouse, like the unconscious betraying its better half in a Freudian slip.

That summer I could not quite get around myself, since I could not get around the errant evidence she left, and when I did take the test, it was not a test at all. It was six.

One night, when N called, I did not pick up. That was the night the sixth test result came in.

———

A bad habit, revision. You can see the allure. In revision, history is not entirely immutable. Writing a chapter, my mind will often wind up to pitch forward. I go back to the scene of the crime, though I know already how it ended.

Shortly before the day the sixth test result came in, there was one night I recall in a little patch of city surrounded by vined walls. It was the place with bad service, good bread. The theorist Lauren Berlant had just died, and I was saying that no one had given them enough credit for being funny.

"Everyone knows what the female complaint is: women live for love," they had begun one book, "and love is the gift that keeps on taking."

I told N that, and I told him about a talk they'd given at Barnard College, where they defined love as wanting to occupy the same time as someone. They'd credited Stanley Cavell with that notion, but I couldn't find the reference in *Must We Mean What We Say?* N interrupted under the dye-job light of that sunset to inquire about my next sentence. Namely, was I going to say that I wanted to move to Serbia and be with him forever? he wondered.

"Of course not," I said. "I'm on the tenure track."

His face blanked. His face repositioned. He shrugged.

"Maybe I so addicted to you, I don't go," he said. "But I can't make promises." I hadn't asked him to. I hadn't asked anything of him, other than to keep up his side of the conversation at brunch.

In the prick of the second, there came in a belch of memory that once, on mushrooms, I'd seen a car with half a screaming family hanging out of it barrel down a Barrytown field, as sheaths of pink and orange sky scissored above. S was with me, and the grass squirmed as though it needed an exit strategy from reality. If I got caught in that day of sunny field forever, I wished I'd be happy. Instead, I was a shivering misery because I couldn't think how to gather every person I loved in one moment and place, and because I could not read my watch. I was petulant with drugs, wanting Ali in Berlin, and Maggie and Treska and Jelly in the city, my brother in Massachusetts and S already here with me, Rebecca in Los Angeles, Crystal in Connecticut, wanting all of them, all in one room, all in the same day—and how could that happen when I didn't even know where I stood in history, could not even read on my watch what time it was?

"Do you know that Anne Sexton poem," I asked N, "with the line, 'It is June, and I am tired of being brave'?"

"I don't know," he said. "I'd keep doing this forever."

"You say that, but when you get your citizenship, you'll return to Serbia, and you won't come back," I said, because I knew desperation for home. I wished that were not the case, but knew, too, that was to wish he were a few degrees off the person he was.

"That was plan," he said. "It was also not plan to have girlfriend. Maybe I go, I don't go. I can't tell you what happen year from now. You can't tell me. I'd keep going."

A few days later, the sixth test result came in unobtrusive as an online coupon. A link to click. A link was clicked. It was afternoon, and I had been planning to work on the new short story. Like each of the five previous tests, the sixth offered no use to my search. The closest relative was a fifth cousin.

Reading the test result, I wanted, when I told N, for him to understand what it meant. I knew he would not because he had not been in the right rooms at the right times, and that was no one's fault, and he would likely never be in the right room at the right time, and that was no one's fault either.

Come night, I joined my friend Hannah and her fiancé at their sublet in a neighborhood of glass, steel, and artisanal everything. The baby took her time going down, then we ate meat and sautéed mushrooms on the balcony. We did not see stars draw up as I said there was nothing more I could do to hunt down Cho Kee Yeon, even if there had not been nothing I wouldn't have. At the table, my phone rang from N's name, and Hannah said, "Go ahead, answer."

I shook my head.

"Why not?" she said.

"I'm devastated," I said. "I don't feel like also being disappointed." She shrugged the shrug of someone who believed other people's natures unstoppable.

As we sat beneath the night, I could see an end already to N and me, and I considered whether it was best to protract or accelerate that end. I could not see the home I was after, but I knew N was not in it, and I'd better see it now, even if he didn't. I knew that, just as I knew I'd exhausted options in my search for Cho Kee Yeon, and I did want to accept things, and I didn't entirely. I had never learned how to accept anything. I had romanticized acquiring ice water in hell, so now I picked miserably at diced onion on my plate.

When her fiancé had started from miniature sleeps already a few times, Hannah and I brought the dishes to the sink. Her fiancé drifted off to the bedroom. N called again. I didn't answer. I was babbling about Cho Kee Yeon, and I'd started crying, and only the personal insight that I was making a corny little scene was enough finally to stop me.

A car arrived to take me back to North Brooklyn. I said my thank-yous, gave my love. The next day, I would apologize to N, and it wouldn't be the last time I'd have to. I would try to explain the sixth test result.

"I have father my whole life. I have mother," N would say. "I am hundred percent father. I am spitting image. I cannot understand."

I would say, "Okay."

"I can't understand," he would say. He would ask, "What means?"

"It means it's over," I said, but his question would keep us, N and me, in motion.

Like a promise, after all, a question can link two people in time. He would ask that question again: What means?

That would be when, late summer, I told him there was now another missing person on my hands. This time I would notice the naivete, though. To call a missing person "on my hands" was, of course, a delusion.

# CHAPTER SEVEN

# BEWARE THE BOAT

Williamsburg, Fall 2021

Missing persons had become my modus operandi, but I didn't have the bona fides to ascertain certain facts. By law, the Portland ER that had admitted Jelly for a mental break prior to his disappearance could not pass information to the likes of an old friend. I was not on-paper family. I was someone who Jelly insisted belonged at Thanksgiving. He was my first friend in grad school. I still remembered an homage to *Endgame* he'd written ten years before.

And this was how our friendship operated: homage, retelling. He liked to repeat the story in which the day trader who funded a literary journal where I'd once been editor-in-chief scolded me that I ought to have gotten better writers, like Flannery O'Connor, to publish in the last issue, and I'd said, "Unfortunately, she was tied up being dead." I liked the one about how when Jelly was mugged, the mugger kept calling him Larry Bird, said, "Bird, I swear to God if you don't shut the fuck up." There was also the period in which I'd briefly moved out of the apartment I'd lived in with S a couple of years before the pandemic, when Cowboy lost his mind, and sometimes on waking I'd find he'd defecated on the bed.

"There's a metaphor there," a therapist had told me, "a metaphor to waking up in a pile of shit."

I'd looked at the therapist, and I'd liked her, and I'd said, "It feels more actual."

This had become a story Jelly would relate at the bar. "There's a metaphor to waking up in a pile of shit," he'd tell a stranger by the jukebox. The more he told that story, the funnier we thought it was, and the less the metaphor felt true to my life.

At the time he went missing, Jelly's father had committed suicide, his mother had dementia, and his marriage had ended. On-paper family was in short supply. Off paper, I recalled him saying, "You have to come to Thanksgiving, pup. You're family."

———

In the wood-paneled dining room of a German restaurant on a September night, N was hollering over FaceTime with drunks in Belgrade when my phone rang. The place had been silent other than N and the long-distance friends, metal pings on plates, but I still couldn't hear Jelly's boss.

Cross the room. Fling the door. I'd been waiting for that call. Outside the restaurant, I took in pimply pavement, scuffed-up sidewalk glitter. Across the street, the quinceañera shop lights were half-mast around explosions of tulle and tiaras with built-in combs. Girls would eat their pineapple cakes and flash nails through banquet halls, and their people would say, of the time before womanhood, "Where did it go?" And where did any of it go, where did anyone go? Time slipped. People slipped. People were lost every day. I had to pinch the flat pearl button of my blouse to hang on to my own voice, as the weather licked my shirt collar.

"He's not going to make it Monday," I said.

"I wish I knew more," I said.

I said, "But he's going to want to know he has a job to come back to, I can tell you that much. What has to happen to lock down medical leave?"

Because when he was found and he was better, he would want to return to that school. I was sure of it. He got a kick out of dazing twenty-year-olds with Žižek or theories of selling out, and in the middle of that dim street, I wanted a promise about when Jelly was found, when Jelly was better.

The traffic light made the obvious next move. Car screech. Jelly's boss named the administrator who'd have a line on the right papers to push. A woman in green came down the sidewalk, voice half a block ahead. I looked to her, arms shot out, Frankensteinian, wrists flapping chiffon.

"Boyfriend is waiting," she shouted. "He wants to order. Come back."

"I'm on the phone," I said.

"Do you hear me? He is waiting! Come back!" N had finished his phone call, and now, evidently, ordering food was urgent.

"I heard you," I said. "Did you hear me?"

"He is waiting!" she cried. "He is waiting!"

To the boss, apologies. From the boss, not to worry. The woman walked off, muttering, "Stupid girl." The phone call went as far as it could, and in the end, bratwursts got ordered, as they always were going to be. Later that night, at home, N and I watched Robert Altman's *The Long Goodbye*. I had not recalled the scene when private eye Philip Marlowe hears a rumor that his friend Terry Lennox died.

                         MARLOWE
             What happened to the body?


                         MORGAN
         His wife's family didn't want it back, for
         obvious reasons. I guess he didn't have any
                    family of his own.

                    _____

That was one day. There were several. At the short end of long college tables, I'd ask, "What does the speculative imagination make possible that realism does not?" then, between classes, make calls to Portland. The gist: updates on no updates until one day a careless cop let information slip.

Jelly had not cut and run. He'd been committed. It was only that the hospital couldn't, to someone not spouse or family, disclose as much.

So I called Jelly's unit until the odds nodded in my favor. A voice came on the phone, heavy-tongued as I stared at the more unrelenting stains on my stovetop. "There she is. That's the pup."

"He's alive," I said.

"I am. I'm alive," Jelly said, "and it's a fucking nightmare. They threw me in the clink. I'm in the clink, did you know that?"

I doddered by the counter with the greasy phone on my cheek. "Well, sure. I called the number."

"Of course. That's right. What a silly, little dancer," he said. Then, "You've got to get me out of here, pup."

In Brooklyn, Cowboy stalked his bear stalk. I paced, a little strangled from the inside out. The first item on the agenda, I suggested, was rest. We pro-conned that, until, as though he'd just remembered, he began to detail grievances. The utmost one was olanzapine. This year, I needed to understand, Jelly had gotten in touch with his healing powers. Also, repressed memories. His mother had disallowed him from joining Mensa, and now, to top it all off, he'd been thrown in the loony bin, when his real problem was not psychosis but snapped fascia—plus that his hair was growing straight into his skull toward his brain. He needed occupational therapy, and it was being withheld. This constituted torture—not least of all by one of the nurses.

And because I knew the books he loved, knew that for years he'd wanted to publish an essay on an aesthetic he called "Keseyesque," I said, "Ratched?"

"Exactly right," Jelly said.

He was safe in body. He was missing in aspects. References remained, but they were no longer references. Metaphor had ceased to operate as metaphor. Something snapping had become some thing snapping.

"I need to tell you something," he said.

A custom-fit omen had come to him in a vision, and it boiled down to one thing. Jelly must caution me against getting on a boat with a man.

"Don't worry. I saw *Titanic*," I said.

"I mean it, pup," he said. "Don't do it. Do not fucking do it. Also, fuck that sellout James Cameron. But promise me."

"I promise," I said.

"Fuck James Cameron, fuck Leo," he muttered. "And stay the fuck away from men with boats."

———

On an afternoon shortly after, N and I went to move some of Jelly's things to storage before they were put on the street. N wadded masking tape to prop doors open, and I went to Jelly's bedroom, where every wall had been filled with homemade shelves stacked to the ceiling. I was certain when Jelly recovered, he would still want the Percival Everett and Robert Musil, John Hawkes.

Back in the living room, I saw N's hands were fast flipping boxes, but they did not flail, and he thought to curl a paper cone and tape it to the wall to catch sawdust snowing off unwound screws. He'd get a big item on his shoulder, run it down to the street, and that gesture suggested that he understood love was a doing; when you chose your family they were who you'd do it for. Whether N would admit it or not, our tie was a terminal case that would end when he left the country, but I could love a person who looked out for the family I'd chosen. This was information worth sharing.

"Hey," I said. "I want to say something to you."

"Now is not time," N said. "Truck is double-parked."

"So but quickly," I said, kneeing up a crate hugged to my stomach.

Then he took the crate from me, said, "Ai, yai, yai, poo-poo,

give me. I am professional. These hands move baby grand piano."
And he was out the door to the double-parked truck again.

———

Since N had never met Jelly, on the way to the storage facility,
I recounted the last Thanksgiving hosted at Jelly's. Jelly had
made awful brussels sprouts. Our friend Joey Passion fussed
the turkey. After dinner we went to their friend David's glass
penthouse, where we all danced to vinyl, and in moments the
moon, I swear, was below us. It had been a family dinner, in
our own way.

"Okay, listen," N said.

"All ears," and I was.

"I am angry this man take advantage of you," he said. He said,
"You are good person, Tracy, but you are not Jesus Christ. It's too
much."

"Don't be stupid. We both know Jesus was a Serb born in
Niš," I said.

"Ha-ha-ha-ha-ha!" Theatrical, startling. Subsequently, a dead-
ening. "I am not joking. That was not small job." He hit the
brake. "Jebiga."

"He's not taking advantage of anyone. He has no family here
to help."

"That was big job, Tracy."

"Sure, okay, but you love your friend, so it's nothing. We're
family. Do you know the term 'chosen family'? We call each
other family. We look out for each other."

"And this friend," N said, "does he know you have boyfriend?"

I looked at him in the driver's seat. He was a big, elegant man
save his small, wide hands. He claimed he'd ruined them rock

climbing. I didn't think they were ruined, but they looked like the least intelligent part of his body, grabbing the wheel. Surely, I supposed, he did not expect me to have discussed *him* as Jelly raved omens from the psych unit.

"I am not jealous man," N said. "But you have boyfriend now, and there is way to act. You are not kid. You are thirty-three, thirty-four-years-old woman. You should know how to act."

"Why don't we discuss exactly what the discomfort is here. What are you afraid of?"

"Sometimes when trucking, I get bored," N said. "All there's to look forward to is when you gonna eat, and you put truck on cruise, watch the movies whole time you're driving, and I call every trucker I know just to say, 'Bro, I took such good shit today, do you hear me? Seriously, brate. No, listen. Such good shit,' because there's no one else. But now? Now I have nothing to say."

"What if I do?"

"You always want to talk. You think too much, Tracy. 'What is writing? What you are thinking about? What means? What means?' I am good. I don't need to talk. I do things."

Only later would I understand that it was that afternoon that I began to look at us perhaps not safely, but from afar, wondering if I did, indeed, wish to occupy the same time as him or if I simply did not want to be someone who always wished to lose things faster.

CHAPTER EIGHT

# RED HERRING

## On the Town, Late 2021

I could testify I chose to halt my searching impulse, but there is circumstantial evidence worth noting. At a wedding in Istanbul, October 2021, a woman who refused to call it a night frisked me down for my natal chart. Information gathered, she declared that given the contradictory impulses of a Virgo sun and a Pisces moon, my life would not be easy. That season, every so often I forgot cynicism long enough to, on off chances, pursue red herrings—that is, email remote relations from DNA databases who stopped responding or never responded at all. I finished the short story begun that summer. The ending involved a tree confiding, "All real living is meeting."

Around the time N and I moved Jelly's things, I befriended a man called Z who said he'd liked my last book and to whom I admitted I'd barely written all year because I'd had my head full up with a woman. Z liked to talk about sublimation, other people's foolish opinions, and his own foolish opinions. I did, too. He turned up at a reading I gave shortly after we met, then another, where he started calling me Big Face for all the predictable reasons men call women anything but their names.

"Look at me," he said, elbow-to-elbow at the bar, and when I didn't: "You won't look at me because when you see me, you're happy."

"Yeah, so?" I said.

"So tell me you love me."

I did not tell him that. I did tell him we probably would have made a go of it if we'd met five months earlier, but instead I was with someone I wanted to be fair to, so perhaps when we ran into each other we could cut out the air of a big, fat operatic love poem. I suppose I talked the talk, but the running into each other didn't stop, and it was often enough operatic.

"You know that Sexton poem, 'The Truth the Dead Know'? 'It is June. I am tired of being brave.'"

"I don't."

I said the speaker of Sexton's poem cut town from her parents' funeral, and there was life on the shore, that I adored the sound of "sun gutters from the sky," and that the dead refused to be blessed; and he listened.

In theory, I was not superstitious. Yet it did not escape me that a *Z* resembled a spilled *N*. So on an occasion when Z and I had a drink, in an attempt to knock off the close mood, I decided to show Z my Charlie Chaplin impression, then tripped pretending to trip. He said he was happy for me, and he also said, "I'm never going to see you again, am I?"

Maybe it was melodramatic for Z to speculate that he'd never see me again, but then again, this was six days after I'd gotten a man named Phillip on the phone.

"She's alive," Phillip had said, meaning Cho Kee Yeon, and by the time I tripped aping Chaplin tripping, I'd already bought a plane ticket to Korea.

CHAPTER NINE

# MIDDLEMAN

In-Between, December 2021

Phillip was my second cousin's father, but he considered himself my uncle once he considered me at all. His daughter Chloe had been my initial contact. She'd asked that I get off the DNA database and email her, then ceased responding. Dates flushed through sequential and anonymous until Sunday, December 5, when, after many weeks spent awaiting Chloe's reply, I told Z I'd probably never know when Cho Kee Yeon died and then, a chump who never took the hint on *game over*, emailed Chloe again anyway. Monday, December 6, Phillip said, "You're the person," meaning the surrendered daughter, and I agreed.

We agreed, anyway, for a few precipitous minutes. Phillip guessed I was the person, but precipices being, by definition steep, he floated, too, the notion of a terrible mix-up. To corroborate, he wanted photographs to compare with those in the possession of a cousin named Won. I could send the photos, and I did, but that Monday, I was only provisionally a Cho, and in that dazed murk, there was no epiphanic elation. Everything was possibly different, id est, possibly nothing was.

So with that vertiginous nonfact, it was somehow still December 6 when, as previously planned, I went to eat sushi on the expense account of a friend who, depending on the specs of her bonus, might soon cut her husband loose. Sitting with her in the Financial District, I had a handle on the terms, but not on what the holdup was. Pale slicks of yellowtail dressed with skin-thin jalapeño came over the bar. Tartar blobs. I had a soft spot for her husband. He was decent and kind, and I'd no clue why my friend was still with him. Lonely had been how she described their life before her daughter. It was just a matter of time, my friend was saying, and maybe I was a Cho.

The aim of my friend was to keep the BMW, or to keep her husband off hovel life. It was hanging on to the house in the good school district, something, something, credit card. I couldn't really follow. I was dizzy a little, and it wasn't the nigori doing it. My friend was the primary breadwinner, and if there was a big chunk of change coming, there was a big chunk of change coming, that was what counted—that and Phillip's suspicions.

*She's alive. Your mom. Your mom is alive. . . . My mom's second sister's daughter is your mom. And then your mom is still alive, I think.*

In the dim cave of the restaurant with the red porcelain and shiso leaf, my forehead stretched off my head and snapped back. A cheerful arrangement of wobbling miniature eggs floated from the chef to a waiter. I was not getting ahead of myself because it was impossible. You always were where you were.

"Look at my stomach," my friend said. "I'm so full."

And a man she hoped to spend time with came. The man my

friend hoped to spend time with jerked his eyes around the place, nervous as a sad, dried-out tweaker, then said actually he should probably get going. When the check was settled, out came cigarette smoke in the black of rained-on city. We hung a forty-five degree angle across the glare popped up from night-dark streets to get to my friend's hotel, where she wondered aloud for an hour or two whether the man took off because she'd gained forty pounds, if this was why she'd not gotten to give him the horchata she'd prepared.

"Or maybe he saw you and felt, comparatively, like a creepy senior citizen," I said.

"You think that's what it was?"

"I think if I were him it would be," I said. "Also, you're beautiful."

We talked in this manner for a while about the motives of the alleged gentleman, as though there were always a clear motive for why someone showed up or left at all. And in the back of my mind a track careened around the bend: maybe Cho Kee Yeon was alive.

"I should get out of your hair soon," I said. "You have a morning."

For whatever reason, though, my friend called once I was home. I had the tap going in a glass. In the corner that passed for a kitchen, I heard her crunching the math again: mortgage, car payments, summer camp. Home calculus. She loved the house, loved her child. Her yard. The husband was very clean and did due diligence on dutiful biannual sex.

"That's good," I said. "Is it enough for you?"

"Of course not."

"You sure you want to put off enough?"

"I love my daughter. Everything I do, it's for her. My daughter has everything she wants."

"She's a lucky kid," I said.

"I wouldn't do anything different, but you know."

"If it had been a childless marriage, it would have been a childless divorce."

"I'd be out of there already," she said.

"And if you'd've cut out?"

"I'm not saying I would."

"Sure," I said, "but you're not the accused on cross here. I'm in your corner. So when you think about it, what do you imagine?"

"I'd drive a hot car," my friend said. "That's for sure."

"Always wanted a white Corvette. What are we talking? Lamborghini?"

"I'd go places. I'd get another motorcycle."

"Vehicles," I said, "that's the theme."

She got into specs, and in my mind I saw the life she missed living and didn't miss exactly, where she swallowed the length of a tunnel in a silver, buffed-up car calendar car, and I wondered whether Cho Kee Yeon ever got to drive a Corvette.

Jacqueline Rose wrote that "it is the demand to be one thing only—love and goodness incarnate—that is intolerable for any mother."

Adrienne Rich: "Most of us first know both love and disappointment, power and tenderness, in the person of a woman. We carry the imprint of this experience for life even into our dying."

Had Rich been my contemporary, perhaps she would not have used the term "woman." She might have said "parent." But she had understood that to have a child was to become a map of how life would be loving and gutting and regular, a map lugged

TRACY
O'NEILL

through to the end—that this was an immense, terrible power, probably beautiful sometimes, too.

I thought of how the mother who raised me had not been afraid of that immense, terrible power. In February 1992, Love the Children had kids, and the deal sealed was simple as this: hand over one more and we'll call it even. She went full bore on becoming a family of four.

When my brother arrived, he had nails the scale of pencil erasers, and his upper lip gaped with a piece of flesh twisted like the end of a Starlight mint wrapper.

"I don't want him to change," I said, because he was beautiful, my brother, though it wasn't as though change was up to us; there were dire aspects to his body.

So my mother looked into options. We had options. We got familiar with Boston doctors. On the car ride to and from Children's Hospital, our song was "Friends in Low Places" with a put-on twang, the lyrics implying that when your heart's hanging like a loose tooth, there's no elegant way to yank it. And we were not elegant people, never knew where to hang our jackets. My mother, in sudden furies of heat, clamored for help pulling off her coat as she kept one hand on the wheel.

Back in those years when we knew what we were doing, we picked up bits of sign language and did not get fluent. Our hands learned to express more than fight. Even so, as a kid, I did have words with merciless children, adults. This was one regular way we said I love you, throwing down over a slight to one of our own. I never did become accustomed to an inane asshole shouting, "Hey, flat-nose!" at my brother. What became habit was finding other words, catching meaning in our hands' clumsy signs. My brother came home with one new face after another.

At a certain face, his mouth could at last move words. In take one, he called anything wheeled "big, red yucks." Even once he mastered "truck," we O'Neills wanted to get a load of "big, red yucks" in the street. We signed. We yucked. We laughed until we hyperventilated.

In those years under the knife, my brother nearly died twice. The thing to do was gift toy hot rods, stuffed bunnies. The jimmies on ice cream, shrimp cocktail. Our spoken consensus was he made out like a bandit. Only once several of my friends had children did I realize babies don't, across the board, cry endlessly. My brother cried endlessly. When he could not stop crying, my father stomped his foot, going, "Jesus H. Christ."

I asked, "What's the *H* stand for?"—wanting my father to feel stupid.

Then, if sorry for wanting my father to feel stupid, I continued, "Harold, Henry—but all his friends know him as Jesus Hank."

By the time he was a child, my brother had learned to keep a stiff upper lip, though at one point he suffered a collapsing face. This was not metaphorical. It was a craniofacial disorder causing his facial skeleton to cave in. It is hardly rocket science that a caved-in face cannot breathe. Still, there was a cure. Cut the skull, pull it apart, scaffold until the bone sets. My mother sang him the regional nursery rhyme: "Ride into Boston, ride into Lynn, you better watch out or you might fall in the drink."

And eventually, we did hit years of lull. Then the lull did eventually end. My brother's face was sinking again. He was a teenager who'd once more need his face sawed, put together. He kept it together, but could he possibly believe the doctors who said that *this* time his face would take? It's difficult to know because he did not speak much, never has. His early memories of forming language were of pain.

"I'm the mother," my mother said. "I'm your *real* mother," she said, with more than a little piss and vinegar, and heart.

I was a little drunk on the phone with my friend who was a mother, a little drunkenly said, "Then again, sometimes you don't do the thing, and you still don't get the sports car."

"What thing?" she asked.

"You're doing the best thing you can think of is all," I said. "You did good."

———

According to Phillip's analysis of the photographs, I, indeed, had a Cho face. It was December 7 when Phillip, now satisfied that I had a Cho face, sent a message: This is just the beginning to your another world.

On December 7, a genuine-article Cho, I rolled through a Marshall's to acquire towels for N's elaborate fecal hygiene. I sussed out the home section, lights shifting in woozy intensities. There were, everywhere, jelly beans bagged in cellophane, candles with pine brush caught in white wax like fossils. My lunch was going to fall out of me, and then I remembered I hadn't eaten lunch at all. Halfway down the corridor where framed labor laws were posted, a woman complimented my hair. Perception slid; I couldn't quite see her. Air fluoresced greenly, and I heard pipes in the vicinity sound their flushing swallow. To catch a fall that never happened, my legs softened. I braced. Then, I ponied up a polite smile, said, "Thank you, I grew it myself."

December 7, I did those things, but I also understood I

could not afford to be stupid with happiness when all I had was a lead. I was close; but I had not found a number, found her. I had found a second cousin's father in Washington State who knew people who knew her. Therefore, I needed to get a grip, or I'd lose that mother again without having comprehensively found her.

From my "another world," on December 8, I got that grip and, from a different coast, caught Phillip heading into work.

"I couldn't talk to your mom," he said.

But he continued, said, "I talked to Won and Won's mom. And actually her name is Wonyi. So, which is *W-O-N-Y-I*."

"That's Won's mom?" I asked.

"No, Wonyi. I thought she has only single letter for the first name, but so instead of Won, her first name is *W-O-N-Y-I*."

"Okay, I see. Won—"

"So instead of Won, her first name is Wonyi," he said. "Since you are a writer, I'm going to be really careful."

I wondered what he meant by "careful," but not out loud.

There was no time anyway. Phillip named names, fell into the winding inventory of who's who. The lowdown: the family had reach. Cho Kee Yeon was one of eight, and of them, the key witness to my birth was a Jehovah's Witness, Young Mok. Phillip had left Korea in 1986 but remained close enough with Wonyi, Young Mok's daughter, to have called straight off word of the DNA match.

"Because I stayed with Wonyi's family for about a month to teach her English," Phillip explained. "She was a high school student at the time. And during that time, Wonyi's mom, and also Wonyi, and also your sister, Inwahn—"

"My sister?"

"Yeah, your sister. Your sister was there."

"I have a sister?"

"Yes, she is fifty years old," Phillip said. "And you have older brother, fifty-two years old, In Hyeong, and then you have younger brother."

Phillip asked me to hold. I could. I had. I did again. Outside the apartment, the alternating ghostly moan of cars and chirping axles lifted off the BQE overpass. A siren. Cho Kee Yeon had not exactly skirted motherhood. She was, in fact, a habitual offender, and my face numbed out, returned to its senses. I needed to come to my senses and stay in them.

Here, then, was what I knew: in Korea, I had a sister, I had two brothers. I had Jelly's explanation of the difference between suspense and shock. He'd said suspense piles when I walk into a room, lay a gun on the table, and say, "Before this day ends, someone is going to say something dumb, and I'll blow their fucking brains out," then sit down to conduct a bit of small talk. Shock? Throw open the door and spray bullets like confetti. I got myself through a bit of waiting for Phillip thinking of that and how quickly in real life your brains could end up in pieces on the floor.

But I could not afford brain on the floor. Cho Kee Yeon was alive, and I still didn't have a location on her, should something go sideways.

Months before, I'd asked a translator named Hannah Hertzog to take a stab at my documents. I'd latched onto a particular line in the amateur job translation of Eastern's Initial Social History Report: "During company they were in much troubles caused by bio-father's untruthful life attitude and disparity in characters." Off that sentence, I could imagine Kim In Kee to be alternately a compulsive liar, a dreamer, a storyteller, temperamental, a cheater, theatrical, two-faced, a sensitive degenerate, indecisive, labile, a gambler, or a flake—an accessory to my person of interest and a man, in any case, of some contradiction. When I called Hannah Hertzog, I'd supposed that if my history amounted to a few sentences, they could at least be deft.

But when Hannah Hertzog translated the documents, fault redistributed. The "untruthfulness" had softened, and the "disparity in characters," once grammatically in the father's possession, had become euphemistically vacant. Between Cho Kee Yeon and Kim In Kee there'd been "points of friction." I got no exoneration or indictment. I got that I'd had more father when he'd been composed of less elegant language. Now, a year later, I could once more end up with less origin story if I wasn't careful.

Phillip was back. Phillip could not be back. It wasn't a good time to talk, but there was later. He said, "I will explain everything that I know. I have nothing to hide."

As far as I knew, people who said they had nothing to hide often did have things to hide. They might be hiding things, for instance, in "really careful" confessions. N was the one person I knew who, when I caught a discrepancy between two things he'd said, replied brightly, "I was probably lying."

———

A ring, and I was Pavlov's dog: alert, prepared. The room blurred out. Phillip asked questions and did not wait for answers. "What is it? How far did I tell you? Inwahn, your older sister," he said.

His voice got a running start. I didn't need one.

"Actually," I said, "do you think that my mom would want to meet me?"

And so: squinting sound, risking no breath, I sensed my stomach was nothing but a steak startling with heat.

"Of course," Phillip said, "and then you know what? Your family gene. They look very younger than compared to their age."

———

On the phone, the burping discourse of family genes kept coming. Anyone could guess the drill. Mothers and daughters resembled sisters in the maundering. Phillip was talking, and Phillip was talking, and for some reason, I was very quiet, as though then my woman of interest would not be taken away.

"So Inwahn," he said, suddenly terse. "How should I explain? Inwahn is trying to tell your mom."

A pause dropped down the telephone line. A damp black olive of dog nose tipped at me. Cowboy had taught himself a way to demand affection mouthlessly, a nose flick jumping my palm onto his head. Other people told me he was smart. I figured him a little stupid, and I loved his stupid face, plaintive eyes, that canine insistence, my animal.

"Trying," I said.

"She didn't tell her yet," he began, "and as you know, there's no mother that doesn't want to meet her own daughter. There's no one like that. But I think Inwahn is trying to give her time, and Wonyi said in the middle this December."

By my calculations, mid-December was a week away, and mothers sometimes did *not* want to meet their daughters at all, and I knit myself solid as though I'd been entrusted to hold the jammy-legged gonzo gravity of someone else's baby. I had better hold this thing right. It had its own squirming physics.

"They worried she's going to be upset?"

"Upset. Why upset? No no no no no no no," Phillip said. "Okay," Phillip said. "Your mom is a good woman. I do know her. She isn't—she is not ill-natured at all. But the thing was, the fact was, she didn't just serve only one husband. She was not faithful enough. We do know that."

In fact what I'd known was that my father was married.

"Anyway, I can tell you one thing: your dad passed away. A few years ago. And then—but your mom is still alive. She's healthy, and she looks very young compared to her age."

So this was it. I had a comparatively fresh-faced mother and an unequivocally dead father. Possibly, he had had an "untruthful life attitude," and now definitively, he had no attitude at all. His "disparity in characters" had been, you could say, resolved. I'd been too late by half. I'd acquired more biography than I could have hoped for a few days prior, and still, possibility had been redacted. Motherhood, fatherhood—they could be surrendered, but there was no way around death. You barely took up any space in this world, then there was the matter of your ashes, and, perhaps, the conversion of meat to ashes didn't much matter. We lived in biology's cartoon. Everyone did it—die. It was common as skin. Kim In Kee's blood stilled, and he did not think anymore.

"Maybe I should just fly to Korea," I said.

"But then if you go to Korea, at this moment you have ten days of quarantine period," Phillip said.

"Yes, I know."

I knew because it was December 8, 2021. Because new daily infections in Korea had hit record highs. Two days before, infections had not yet peaked. N came into the apartment, damp-shouldered, wanting immediately to head to the bathroom, and I'd asked him to wait, told him my mother was alive. "Your mother died?" he'd said.

I knew of that quarantine mandate because though *alive* and *died* could be confused given their slant rhyme, after my own "Jesus H. Christ," I had, in benders of superstition, combed Korean news headlines. Because those headlines took near-exclusive interest in the new Omicron variant. Because as the prose went on, there were speculations regarding another imminent full lockdown in Korea, resulting in my own wild speculations on a border closure, and I had come close enough to finding her that I'd hit the adrenal berserk of something like a smoking gun, but I still hadn't gotten a second look at my congenitally missing person, and she'd be seventy-two, seventy-three—better hurry up.

I knew about that quarantine because I had prepared to go, as though preparation cut the line to a life I missed living.

Meanwhile, Phillip was talking about weather.

If it were up to him, Phillip would schedule my trip during temperate spring. That way, his children could accompany me as interpreters.

But it was not up to Phillip.

Spring was next year. This moment was already too late by half. I had not come this far for some man to decide the time it would suit him for me to meet my mother, and we wrestled over the ways I did or did not need help, would or would not accept it, and finally he saw that no matter what was said, I'd book that ticket. I did. Asiana Airlines, December 14, I'd go to her.

———

The resolution had been to not get ahead of myself, but with that ticket, I was above myself, ascendant. Six days out from the flight, I couldn't stop talking about it. I told Maggie. Told Treska. Our language hit the rafters. Amazing. Incredible. How? This tone kept on with Justin. I don't know why, and maybe the answer was friendship, but I'd rarely heard him happier.

He was in Portland. I was in Brooklyn. Long distance we ran high on the gas of rampant story. We broke out the superlatives and raved our glee-side incredulity. It was *no way, yes way, for real can you believe it.* We went on talking—the effective verb: *overjoy*—right through his admission that he'd got wind that the Korean government facilities for quarantine were "somewhat harrowing." He'd heard the writer Tammy Kim discuss them recently on a podcast, and perhaps I'd want to listen in preparation. Neither of us doubted those harrowing conditions, but we understood that after the long squeeze of pandemic, the line of questioning was no longer whether isolation would ever end and I'd get closer than across the street from a café where Cho Kee Yeon once worked.

"So of course I have to go," I said.

"Of course, you have to go," he said.

"Of course I have to go," I said again. "I'm going."

In fact, during that tear of announcement, it was only N who thought I'd gotten ahead of myself. He was wrapping a move at the time when I called and still had to get the truck back to the lot if he couldn't sneak a spot on Traffic Avenue. To outgun the gusty street din, he shouted.

"Maybe you wait until next year! Doesn't have to be now! You could get stuck there!"

"With what?" I asked. "Glue?"

"They could try to marry you!" he shouted. "Jehovah Witness like a cult!"

"Highly doubt they'll want to pony up three cows, the good silver, and a hope chest in dowry for a woman they've never met."

"What you are saying?"

"Hope chest!"

"Think about it while! Doesn't need to be now!"

"I thought about it, and I'm going."

"You don't know these people, Tracy!"

"That's why I have to go," I said. "Because I don't know."

————

And so: I did not make it my business to fret over the probabilities of getting stuck or harrowing quarantines. I made it my business to listen to Maggie, who had her finger on Korean customs. I bought, at her suggestion, gifts. My selections: New York whiskey, good coffee, and enormous tin drums of Max Brenner chocolate that—it was crystal as soon as I returned home from a neon fever through the city—would never fit in my luggage. I returned the tins, bought striped violet boxes of Li-Lac Chocolates. My sister would need truffles. Cho Kee Yeon, cousin, aunts. Blitz uptown for T-shirts. The rounds ought to have been brief, but all the blood in my head spun out, and I whipped myself into small agonies gaming out the garment size for the mother I hadn't seen since birth, palms adolescently hot. In the store, streaks of blue and green cut across my field of vision, up shuddering walls, and then I heard an unfamiliar hubbub from my new phone.

**Phillip:** Try to name them apart from the 1st to the 8th in order.
Your puzzle assignment to figure it out till we talk again.
1st–연옥 (Yeon Ok)
2nd–영자 (Young Ja)
3rd–영목 (Young Mok)
4th–기연 (your mom, Kee Yeon)
5th–규종 (Kyu Jong)
6th–규근 (Kyu Keun)
7th–규옥 (Kyu Ok)
8th–미정 (Mee Jeong)
Tracy mom's siblings, I see all of them.

In the picture message from Phillip, I saw them, too, but recognized no one.

And so what? In my mind, the countdown to Korea began with those errands, then jump-cut. Shopping to Thursday night. Thursday night when, at a party, I told Z the news, and he grabbed his own head, spun. Though the guest of honor was too sick to attend, light still inflected rocks glasses, and I told a young editor I liked that I was going to Korea, told strangers, told everyone because now I liked everyone. We went to the Scratcher and Fish. Someone snapped a photo I never got. Without ever seeing it, I knew I had the look of a sleepless abomination because I was. I knew it better than what Phillip said to be true, that is, that the person in the family I most resembled was my aunt Mee Jeong. All night, I made statements of excess, a little poisoned and taken with the

TRACY
O'NEILL

mushrooming aura of late hours. In the stink of a smoking circle, we tried Google Translate. "It kind of works," my friend Michael said. Back inside, a man stretched himself in the doorway of the bathroom as I tried to pass, and he smiled a euphemistic smile.

"Do you do drugs, Tracy?" he asked.

"I'm good," I said, and it was twice true. I was good. I was good.

———

It was Friday when I could no longer ignore the paradox: a countdown and a ticking time bomb depended on one's point of view. The chagrining circumstance was that Phillip figured my gifts nonsense. The family did not need chocolate or Roadhouse Blend coffee. We were haggling my imports, and to Phillip, candy would not cut it. The mother who did not keep me would want years of my life. There was only one thing of me that he asked, and it was to bring Cho Kee Yeon childhood photographs.

"I don't know if that's possible," I said.

"You don't know?" Phillip asked.

"I don't have any," I said. "I'd have to get some from my parents."

He did not see what the holdup was about.

And perhaps there wasn't one, a reason for the holdup. The holdup was that a year ago, Marty Cardona had asked, "What do your parents think about this anyway? Your adoptive parents," and I still had no better answer than, "They don't."

And I recalled Marty saying, "They don't want you to do this."

Recalled saying, "I don't know, maybe."

I recalled the way my mother said, "I'm the mother. Me," and how she wasn't wrong. That when my mother said, "I'm the mother, I'm your real mother," it was as much for her as for those who had their doubts, and I saw it pained her to have to say it. When I was a girl, she'd tickle me past fun to extract the name of a boy I liked if I said I had no crush at all. She shoved her thumbs in her ears, flapping her palms—"Nyah nyah nyah nyah nyah nyah"—as she, wanting so relentlessly to be included, sat on me. To stop it, I sometimes fabricated love objects, and she went radiant believing herself in the loop.

I saw that she had lost her fair share because, before we were O'Neills, she was Munier. Muniers rarely died on time; they habitually jumped the gun. In those houses on King Phillip's Path and Corduroy Road, though, the favored term was "rolling a seven." My mother wept not infrequently over rolled sevens. On occasion, she'd mothered them before she hit the airport to get herself some babies.

Consequently, there were tears for two brothers under forty, dead a year apart. The etiological question regarded whether the second death was motivated by grief over the first. When I was a child, my cousin Mandy went back to prison by virtue, it was said, of eating a lemon poppy seed muffin. I did not understand the precise machinations of opioid uptake by which lemon poppy seed muffins led in some instances to incarceration and in others not, but I knew, crucially, that her innocence wasn't picked apart. Only years later, when she died with a bloated, overdosed face and her babies were to be redistributed, did it seem that that pass did require some clarification. The last time I spoke to her, I was twenty-one, and she'd gotten out of prison again, slurring off smack. No, I told her she could not move in with me and my four roommates. Yes, I told my mother, we were going to have a problem if she again gave my phone number to Muniers.

I was a good shot at making my mother cry, even if those shots were accidental discharges.

Case in point: once, I made my mother cry with the observation that Munier bullshit is hiding the good food in the house. It's watching *Silence of the Lambs* ninety-seven consecutive times over cold coffee. It is plucking up the ingenuity to weaponize new toys during a family fistfight in the middle of a street, while the kids look on with empty shopping bags. It is stealing from your family. It is debating the merits of the story in which Mandy's troubles took off with a gang rape—or if the gang rape happened at all. It is knowing the ins and outs of government assistance, and it is also to be failed by a giant, vague notion of an establishment. Munier bullshit is starting a fire in your school.

You do not want to play a board game with a Munier.

Encountering a moron who wasn't a Munier, my mother said, "Sonofabitch." Encountering a moron who was a Munier, my mother said, "That was good medicine."

And Muniers did give looks they were proud could kill, but I could make my mother cry. I did. When she presumed herself to be the overwrought, conventional mother in my first novel, she called to hyperventilate "sonofabitch" as she wept. When a man shot up Asian spas in Atlanta earlier that year, she called to offer unsolicited comfort, which exclusively entailed her own sobbing delirium over the phone, too. There were tears on her face when I was eighteen, as she told me I made her feel like a failure as a parent and threatened to block my return to college after discovering a condom in my jacket pocket; just as on another occasion, after she slapped me across the face with a winter boot, for the first time, I struck back or, rather, threw back. I threw that boot back at her. On braver days, she asked in wet gasps when I had stopped being her best friend. Even as a child, I was her confidante. In jealousies, she'd call me a daddy's girl. She wanted to hold me all the time, and sucking my forearms in ebullitions of play, she'd jabber, "Corn on the cob!" When I began to shirk all that, I suppose that broke her down, too.

On any of the occasions when I made my mother cry, I might have offered consolation, but often it was easier to consider what needed to be done. I inquired whether she required her inhaler. I recommended perusal of the dictionary definition of "fiction." I said there was no reason for me to be more afraid of dying by racially motivated massacre than from an incompetently installed air conditioner falling from a sixth-story window, though it was true I had more reason to fear hate crimes than she. Even as the prescription was "huff the inhaler, call back later," in my hard, stupid way, I loved her. But it was always easier to consider what needed to be done than to say as much.

Days out from the flight, there was no time to dawdle, so how could I explain the holdup to Phillip? In retrospect, I might have told him about a scene from a Jenny Offill novel: as a mother watches her young daughter run down the block for the first time, she screams, afraid the daughter will forget to stop.

———

And in fact, I had not stopped. Though I had two parents who had done everything, I had pursued the case of the one who did not. December 8, I had pursued getting to that runaway mother until Phillip said finally, "They will welcome you so much. Even your mom is going to welcome you. But you have to expect one thing."

"What's that?"

"Your mom was not faithful," he said.

I was going to say something sharp. I didn't. I knew Phillip's voice could fall off the line as swiftly as Joe Adams's had the previous December.

He said, "Other than your mom, those eight family members, right? They were really successful, and also they were really normal people."

"So you don't think they'll be embarrassed about this."

"Not at all, not at all," Phillip said. "Possibly your mom. But even though your mom is going to welcome you, your mom's personality is not that great."

*Not at all. Possibly.* I wondered what had happened to the Cho Kee Yeon who was "not ill-natured at all." But I did not stop.

Neither, it turned out, did Phillip. He said, "Tracy, Tracy," his excitement unmistakable.

He said, "I will tell you this one, too, even though you might be a little bit surprised, because I want to be honest as much as possible. Okay, so I heard from Wonyi that the older children from your mom—you had two brothers and one sister and you, right?"

Phillip was right, I supposed, though I was probably the wrong person to ask.

"All the dads from all four are different," he said.

He said, "Wonyi said, 'Uncle, I don't want to reveal this kind of thing at all, but since you insist on asking me that kind of question . . .' So I just kept on asking or bugging her, and she told me."

He said, "But your mom was a complete exception in the family line."

"You mean about sex?" I said.

"About the dating with the men part."

"I see." It seemed to me we weren't really talking about dating. The puritanical disaffiliation was silly. But pointed expressions of selfhood mattered less than getting to Cho Kee Yeon.

"So Inwahn was kind of raised by Young Mok because your mom was not with her," Phillip said, still not stopping, and I wondered what "with her" meant. "But she's hesitating to deliver the news to your mom because your mom—I need to say this."

"Say it."

"Okay, your mom, tried to take Inwahn's money," Phillip said.

Maybe he was waiting for me to say something. I didn't.

"She just take it away from Inwahn to give a younger brother, that different dad son."

"Okay," I said.

"Other than your mom, it's really good. You cannot imagine! Everyone is really good!"

And perhaps he knew I wouldn't stop even if Cho Kee Yeon tried to clean me out, because he said then, "Don't give her anything at all."

Said, "Even though she kind of acts like she needs money, don't give her anything. If you have to do something in financial way, then try to talk to Wonyi all the time first."

Said, "Because Wonyi is a very honest person and also kind person. She understands English really well, but in the written form. She's not that dumb. She's smart."

"Right, right." An automatic utterance, though I'd never met Wonyi either.

"So if you try to be there in December, then expect ten day of quarantine," Phillip said. "But financially, if you are trying to be deceived by your mom, then talk to Wonyi first."

Of course, the person I needed to talk to first was not Wonyi. It was my mother. If I would not stop pursuing that woman at large in Korea, there was nothing to do other than quit infantile anxieties, confess. I dialed the number and—*you've reached*—but I hadn't. Maybe that was a relief.

The bamboo palm had been neglected. It showed. I frittered away a few minutes in tardy responsibility, rearranged the suitcase. The new phone with the new ring rang.

"Didn't get to the phone on time," my mother said. "How you doing?"

"So look, I have some news," I said.

"Yeah?"

And the conversation went. It went.

As the conversation went, my mother said, "You *what*?"

I said, "I'm going to meet my birth mother."

And, "*Oh*," my mother said, a fat vowel going sideways between us, then a tight: "Good for you."

"So I'm going to leave next week," I said.

"To go where?"

I didn't understand the question. Maybe she didn't either.

"To South Korea," I said. "On Tuesday."

"*Tuesday*?"

"Tuesday."

"Have you been," she paused, and I think she was afraid of being hurt though she probably already was, "looking for a while?"

"I mean, yeah," I said.

And the conversation went, and I got older controlling my pitch of voice, watching my shaking hands. The conversation was not more terrible than anyone else's conversations with their parents. I was not more singular in my concerns, more sensitive. I had not suffered and built character. It didn't work that way, first of all because I hadn't suffered very much, and second, because suffering often just meant you died or did drugs or fucked people who weren't your spouse as though it would make your dead father love you or were unabatingly a little shit to those who did love you anyway. There were studies about this in the *Journal of American Psychology*, maybe.

My mother grew up with an alcoholic father and not enough food or soap. Sometimes, after she had popped her lid, she'd wail of her past, "There was abuse!" or "You don't know what it's like to have fears!" She did long drives, secretarial work, information sessions, raging confrontations, and a lot of laundry, so that under my belt there would be shrimp cocktail, jimmies, skating lessons, Pantene Pro-V, and a college education. A bunch of Munier kids ended up dead or backed into various corners, and by fluke I was in Brooklyn with a rabbit fur jacket and minor fortunes of books, taking a stab at gentleness the only way I knew how, which was to stick to the facts and not at all let on to happiness, and I wasn't happy now anyway.

"Oh," my mother said again eventually.

She was trying. I could hear it.

I could hear it, and I thought of my friend who said everything she did was for her daughter. I thought of Marty Cardona. I looked at the sorry state of the bamboo palm and in the early winter evening hush saw a smudge of mother behind it. That mother would hide behind a plant to see her daughter because she had tried to be gracious once, and like desire, trying to assimilate into someone's life could be cartoonish. Julie had needed her mother to say, "I thought of you every day, too," and the mother irrevocably didn't, and unless you were slapped into another world, you could not request in the fashion of a Borges character to be murdered more logically the next time. Julie's mother had said everything turned out how it should, and so everything had turned out without her, and when I thought of Marty Cardona, who knew what her daughter needed, I saw that I did not know what my mother needed, though I was her daughter or because I was her daughter or because I was a dolt.

"So you'll go teach as soon as you get back, or will there be time between?" my mother asked.

"I hadn't really thought about when I come back, I guess."

And she said nothing, but it wasn't that she didn't respond. She was trying not to cry. Some part of her had always known she was not *the* mother but *a* mother, of course. Endometriosis had cheated her of maternal singularity, or maybe now I had, and there was only one thing she'd ever wanted to be, and that was *the* mother, ratified and unimpeachable, so she broke down in the serrated way of someone wanting not to. Through the phone came the sniffle back of snot. Small damp winds of tissue movement. At my feet, Cowboy passed gas, as my mother made her wet sounds on the other end of the line.

Suddenly, I didn't know why I was having this conversation, or why I needed to go to Korea at all. It occurred to me that she would ask why I was doing this, and I wouldn't have a very good answer. I was compelled, passive voice, even if I had, too, actively compelled this narrative development into being.

"I'll put some stuff together," she said finally. "Just a sampling over the years? Or baby pictures?"

"Well," I said, "I wasn't that cute of a teenager."

"Even *you* had a couple of rough years," she said. "Imagine *that*."

"It may not matter anyway," I said, and perhaps she could be comforted by that. "It's actually unclear whether the birth mother does want to meet me or not. They were waiting to tell her, and they were a little concerned about how she was going to react because she had four children with four different men."

"But they do know who the birth father is?"

"Yeah, they do, and he's dead."

"Oh."

And in that moment, I wondered how the conversation would differ had life and death reversed, if Cho Kee Yeon were dead and Kim In Kee were not. If I were going to Korea to meet that father, what would my O'Neill mother, my real mother, say? Would she offer condolences? Inquire how I felt? As if it mattered.

"But it might be she's a little funny about things," I said, "because as the uncle put it, she wasn't a 'faithful woman,' and I guess she was quite the philanderer. He said she's the only one in the family who's like that."

"They want to put the red letter on her back?"

"They might kind of. He definitely wanted me to know that everybody wasn't slutty."

"Oh, that's awful," and she choked laughing. "It's funny. It's so funny."

"Yeah," I said. "He really wanted to impress upon me that not everybody is a big ho."

"You're awful," she said, and she loved that, that I was awful.

"Sure, but that's what he said," I said, deadpan. "This birth mother was popping kids out like crazy and never used a condom in her life."

My mother was laughing hard now, and though I hadn't even met my woman of interest, I'd already betrayed her. I had betrayed her, and I'd known exactly what I was doing. It wasn't feminist. It was low comfort. Because I was childish, panicked, uncreative, I had selected my words so that the mother who kept me laughed. This meant, of course, that I was betraying a version of the woman I could be, the one who might be less apologetic for wanting, who was stronger and freer and gave fucks, but not when there was nothing to be done other than leveling. But I'd made one mother laugh. And I didn't want it to stop, that circle around us, that laughter, her sense of primacy, sense of us. I didn't know why I was still carrying on the tribal charade, but I was desperate-punchy. I was desperate-punchy and out of hand. I did not mention that Phillip had declared that Wonyi and Inwahn spoke award-winning English—he'd actually told me they'd won awards for their English—but I did say, "He definitely wanted to convey that the *rest* of the family is very successful and normal."

"Of course."

"Only she's a weird one but at least a very good cook."

"Oh," she said.

"A very good cook," I said, "and apparently very good at getting pregnant."

My ear caught nothing. No words. My mother was silent. A silence. Look at my phone: call ended.

"Lost you there," I said, when she picked up again.

"Yeah," my mother said, "you did."

And it was fine enough from there on out, or I have thought so at times since. We remained on speaking terms, and only once after the fact did my brother say I was "practically estrangered" when, during a tense afternoon at the gym, as his limbs noodled on the elliptical machine, he shouted that I "had no respect"—a phrase whose origin I would ponder—for our parents. He was angry that sometimes when my mother said, "I love you," I did not reciprocate, or did not reciprocate right away, or did not reciprocate enthusiastically enough.

That day in December 2021, my mother and I discussed how she'd send the pictures. At the time, I couldn't gather language to explain to her that just as Toni Morrison once wrote of her father and grandmother, "These people are my access to me; they are my entrance into my own interior life," in moments she was mine. One day over a year later, though, I told a friend that someone was about to get dropped like a hot potato, to which it was declared that I was so from the place I was from. But I was not, of course. I was so from my O'Neill mother. This is why I had needed to remember. This is why I was willing to imagine strangers family, because I was so of her.

I am prone to overoptimistic gambits because I am my mother's daughter. I hate overoptimistic gambits because I am my mother's daughter. I am often weak, needy, shitty, and cynical. I laugh too loud. I am embarrassed to win. I am afraid to lose. I lose. I wait to play decent cards, then go all in on a losing hand. I demand love, scorn love. I imagine I do everything for those I love when, of course, I don't. I can be cold when I am hurt. I am often hurt. I ask to be taken back the wrong way, and I always eventually ask for it.

"Talk to you later?" I asked my mother. It was not a cursory question.

# CHAPTER TEN

# A STRANGER COMES TO TOWN

JFK→ICN→Daejeon, December 2021

I got to Korea out of JFK International, but because I tend to privilege interior life and the words that juice it, often to my own detriment and exasperation, the way I remember that I got to Korea was by saying goodbye. For instance, to Joe Adams, to whom I'd not spoken in so long he might have forgotten me. In fact, he, too, was afraid of what I'd forget. His reminder: he'd called me Lone Ranger because in Korea I'd be on my own.

"When you meet these people, go ahead and shake their hands," he said, "but count your fingers before taking yours back, and never forget these guys are strangers."

For the second time in recent days, the call dropped, but only momentarily; soon his name reappeared—a FaceTime. Perhaps he wanted to see my face in case it went missing, or actual wires crossed, or his curiosity tipped.

From this new view, his beard was white in the car, and he had big hound's eyes. I'd once read he resembled a fit Joe Pesci, whatever that meant, but what I saw was that he was sadder than I'd expected, sad in the way someone who wants things to turn out all right and has seen a lot of unfair shakes, or worse, looks sad.

"I hope I don't disappoint," he said.

"Of course not," I said.

And I said goodbye to Treska, to Maggie. Gave my farewell to Justin, who kindly said he was good for a call to "COVID jail." N was in a mood. I didn't know what it was about, but we did our goodbyes too. This was outside the airport terminal, when I'd kissed Cowboy's forehead too many times already.

"Wish me luck," I said.

"You'll be fine."

"Wish me luck and wish me fine, then," with a swift tug on sweatshirt drawstrings.

"Okay," N said. "All the best."

"You have keys. You have the vet's number. You and Cowboy have a twenty-day membership to the boy's club."

"Opa! Boy's club! Exactly," N said. "Me and papi puppy: hanging, farting, eating junk."

The wind was going, and my hair had made it up over my head. "The dream," I said. "You guys have fun, but don't let Cowboy party too hard. He's only ten."

"It's not boy's club without cocaine, booze, and girls," N said. "So okay, fine, no party. Only farting. But please, do me a favor. Come home; okay, poo-poo? Don't let the Jehovah marry you."

"You're a conspiracy theorist," I said. "And probably a religious bigot."

"It's normal. *Noooooor*-mal," he said. "Okay, bye."

"Okay, bye," I said.

"And remember," he said. "Come home or else."

"Yeah, or else what?"

"Don't be piece of shit," he said.

"Oh, I'm just trying to fit in around here."

"Okay, be piece of shit, *my* piece of shit," he said. "But just come home, okay? Come home, or I'll kill you."

So those goodbyes were how I got to Korea, as was the float of flight attendants down aisles, wearing gauze robes. The plane vibrated a small horror straight into the atmosphere. As a consolation prize for turbulence, neat nests of bibimbap and miniature bowls of skinny, tangled fish dropped down on trays. Fourteen hours, thirty minutes passed almost entirely by counting fourteen hours, thirty minutes.

Otherwise what travel looked like was trying rather belatedly to pick up a handful of Korean words, paging through the introductory note on the translation of a Robert Walser book—"Sometimes there were words that continued to resist their efforts, and so some of the texts contain lacunae"—and not-sleeping to the tune of several questions regarding the spikes of grace Cho Kee Yeon had discovered not settling down. Finally, a great gray cloud swallowed a pink, yellow, and blue sky. Red flashes quick-bathed the plane interior. As I turned off the seat-back movie, an actor said, "Nothing's gonna make up for Luther." Hitting earth, the plane's slowing seemed at first an acceleration. It was just shy of 6:00 p.m.

That first sight of Korea since infancy came in rows of striped wings. They were the most beautiful planes, planes were beautiful, planes moved, and the very project of them was moving, too, that they would take you where you wanted to go, close gaps, that they would not let the lacuna stand. Maybe that was sentimental. I was.

My sentimental interpretation was that I'd gotten to Korea with a tough crowd, since no one on landing applauded the safe arch drawn by that avian bullet from Queens to Incheon.

———

I cannot explain how, in Korea, I came to be excused from quarantine. I can explain how Phillip fantasized that it would go. Prior to my departure, something had gotten into the Chos, and they cooked up a letter requesting isolation at Wonyi's apartment. I wasn't eligible to self-isolate as a non-Korean national, but in their scheme, when interrogated by Immigration, I was to flash four family members' addresses and the credentials of Wonyi's husband, a well-regarded surgeon. There was Wonyi's husband's respectability, which counted for something, and there was lineage, but then there was also "the human aspect," as Phillip referred to it. To adhere to his scheme, when it came time, I should profess that I had flown to Korea to meet my mother, imply I'd not booked a return flight, and as I locked in eye contact turn on the tears.

"I don't know how to do that," I told him.

"Just try," he said. "Think of something sad."

"I do that all the time," I said, "and I can assure you I don't walk weeping through life."

"That's okay," Phillip said. "But just give the human aspect. Sometimes it helps."

"But I told you I don't know how."

"Then practice," he had said. "It makes perfect."

By the time I landed in Korea, I had not made perfect, and I didn't have any plans to. I was not bothered by the possibility of quarantine at all. I expected it. I didn't think I was anyone special or that being special bore any weight in the matter of viral transmission. So I did like everyone else. I followed crowds through the assailing shocks of coruscation and pillowy lines of black parkas. PCR check. Sticker. Scan the finger. Signs declared entry into the country required the download of the state tracking app, I suppose for contact tracing and so that the government could surveil us forever. Here's a lanyard of unspecified import, someone indicated. Stand like so to snap the shot. Go there to—and to do what wasn't said.

Then someone pulled me from the line to a room down a hallway, gleaming and spotless, and the man in the room who said he spoke English studied my documents. The impression was a well-organized body, no rangy gestures or poked-out limbs. He looked up only to say things like "Why are you here?" "What is your Korean name?" "Who is your family?" "Give me the necklace."

"Excuse me?" I said.

"Give me necklace," the man said.

In that gleaming, spotless room, a new possibility made itself known: I'd not be let in the country at all. I had the Korean name. I had the family, but this man was soliciting a payoff. He could fabricate a barrier to entry. He could be the barrier to entry. I would not cry, but I was not above caving to extortion. I had not come this far to turn back. I would give him what he wanted, I decided for a few hairs of second. Crucially, though, I couldn't pay off this man, at least not in the fashion he proposed, because I wore no necklace at all.

My mother in Massachusetts had given me the one necklace I'd ever worn with regularity, a gold medallion etched to say

I AM A CATHOLIC PLEASE CALL A PRIEST—instructions in the event of my death. That necklace ensuring I'd receive my final blessing went missing in college, and that was only right; the other side of the medallion showed the bust of Saint Anthony, who, as any good Catholic would recall, was—besides the patron saint of pregnant women—that of shipwrecks, amputees, animals, animals who were sailors, and Brazil, as well as lost and stolen things. Now, an immigration official was playing a suborning backdoor game, and I had no necklace to speak of. I looked at him, in his trim navy suit, those calmly bribing eyes behind wire frames, and there was no time to, as Joe might have, find the horse in this man's heart.

"I would," I said, "but I don't have a necklace. You can see that."

"The necklace," he said.

Joe Adams, I recalled, had on hearing rumors of the fall of Yugoslavia, traveled to Croatia under the name John Black. Any time he had a job in a new country, he chose a different color. A journalist once asked him about that selection of *Black* for Croatia. "I ran out of colors," Joe said. I, too, had run out of colors, some code to easeful passage, and I had better recognize that I hadn't come all this way to win a hand against pay-to-play, only to lose the game.

"I think you'd like to help me, and I'd like to help you," I said. "How can I do that?"

"Give me the necklace," the man said.

"Maybe I forgot to remove my necklace from my wallet," I said carefully. "Does that sound right?"

An odd little sound came from his lips. He cranked his neck away. Returning my gaze, he pinched his fingers, got them going like pistons. Up and down. Up and down. I watched those hands. Perhaps he wanted me to name a number, but I'd no idea what a nice kickback for someone on a civil servant salary in Incheon was, or whether I had it in Korean won.

"I am here to meet a mother," I said. "That is priceless. You can help me. That, too, is priceless. So I will listen very carefully. I will cooperate."

"Okay," he said. "Okay." But now he was laughing. I stared, as he made a motion as though drawing a hood over his head. I reached for my purse.

"No no no no no no," he said. "Look."

And when I looked, his finger was pointed at me. When I looked, his finger was pointed at my chest. My dumb, nervy heart was there, as was some lint. So was the lanyard I'd been given by airport personnel earlier.

"Lanyard?" I said.

"The land-yard!" he said.

An hour or so later, I could see how foolish I was, but I was foolish and in a car to Daejeon. It was only in that car, watching streaking city light, then furry black mountain ranges like litters of sleeping dogs, that, for more or less obvious reasons, in the back seat I had a messy cry in my face mask.

———

It wasn't quite opaque, that moon peeped through taxi window, giving off gradient radiance. My eye kept on it as though it were a prayer bead, this moving rock that looked, to a naked eye, squat steady in the sky. Then I put my phone close to my face.

"Can you pull over somewhere so I can buy tissues and wash my face?" I asked, and Google Translate translated.

The narrow silhouette of taxi driver did not understand.

"Can you stop the car?" I said. "There a rest stop or something around here?" and Google Translate translated.

He did not understand. I wished I could see his mouth, but even if I were in the front seat, he'd be wearing a mask.

I wanted to tell him I needed to pull myself together. I wanted to tell myself I needed to pull myself together, and for that self to get with the fucking program. But of course there was no program, there was no dignity in back-seat weeping, and my face was swampy; my jacket collar was.

The best tack to take would be simplicity. The app had been easily confused when we practiced at the party before I left. The effective approach was a robot's syntax, an algorithm's—and to speak slowly. My language should skimp on cause and effect, figurative turns, and there was absolutely no room for subtlety. It was not a time for the winding elaboration made precise by qualification, the one with its own turns of intensification and denouement or emphatic surprise. It was a moment for dull instruments that knocked the block off, or got you a Kleenex, anyway.

"I need tissues. I need water," I said. "Where can we go?"

He pointed over his shoulder to a pink cardboard box in the back-seat footwell and two bottles of water. When I'd told Phillip I didn't speak Korean, he'd asked whether I meant that I spoke a little Korean or that I didn't speak Korean at all. "Wow," he'd said in response to my "not at all," and because I had learned a wowing dearth of Korean, my slabby sentences thunked down in the wildering palaver.

Wow! I thought. Wow! Wow!

And of course I didn't understand Korean or even much about Korea. As a girl, I'd no idea, exempli gratia, that North and

South Korea were ideas invented not by Koreans themselves but Americans and Soviets splitting the country. Nor did I know that Kim Il-Sung, the North Korean leader then, considered the "invasion" of South Korea by North Korea a reunification effort. Such ignorance did not require any special selective amnesia, since no attention was paid to the Korean War at all in public schools in Marshfield, Massachusetts, or Amherst, New Hampshire.

What I did know then was that it mattered very much that I had been born in South Korea, not North, that my mother's emphatic pronunciation of "South"—"Born in *South* Korea"—constituted a pass. That I did not know what I got a pass *from* was irrelevant. I was free, I thought.

In this way, I think I was very American. We are forgetful. We call the Korean War the Forgotten War when we remember to speak of it at all. And worse, of course, was that my first thought when I thought of Korea was the war, as though what made an event crucial was American involvement.

Around the time I began looking in earnest for Cho Kee Yeon, while doing research for a piece on veteran disability benefits, I read about children of Korean War veterans born with spina bifida, with congenital heart disease—with cleft palates and cleft lips like my brother. These conditions were linked with Agent Orange. The toxic by-product of weaponized herbicides remained in soil for decades, meaning the cause of these conditions remained in the soil for decades. Veterans now sought VA benefits for their grandchildren who had not seen combat but had been ravaged by herbicidal traces in soldier bodies.

I did not know whether American dioxins from the Korean War caused my brother's condition. In the official history, toxic defoliants were used only within 350 yards of the DMZ, though affidavits from American servicemen state that they were sprayed, too, along roads in South Korea. We likely would never receive answers. We were meant to accept fewer answers, less history, in exchange for the ease of innocence.

"I was born," I tried again. "My mother did not keep me. I went to America thirty-four years ago. Now I am in Korea. I cried. My face is wet and dirty. But tonight I will meet my family. I would like to wash my face before I meet my family. I would like to buy tissues. Then I will have tissues if I cry again." And Google Translate translated.

"Ohhhhh," the driver said, flapping his hand. "Okay, okay." He pulled down his mask, lit a cigarette, and in the hotbox nicotine stink waved a smoky hand at the horizon, said, "Next one."

———

My time in Daejeon began with a small throng crowding the taxi in the parking lot of Wonyi's apartment complex. An old woman garbling words through sobs grabbed me as I opened the door of the car. Her wailing agonies were obvious if unspecific, and she clung for a long keening, and I was startled that I was willing to let her. I hadn't settled on my position regarding souls exactly, but I was not in my own body. I was over my head, looking at my own snarled hair. This woman grabbed my face, then ran her hands over my cheeks, squeezed my arms, and began to moan again until a woman with short, curly hair stepped in and said, "Tracy. I am Wonyi."

I learned that the sobbing woman was Young Mok. I learned that these people were Inwahn and Wonyi's husband, Kim Je Ryong of the Breast and Thyroid Clinic at Chungnam National University

Hospital. No one bothered with the muscular man, heavy face drawn in worry. Wonyi led everyone inside, then poured water, and we all sat around a table in Wonyi and Je Ryong's kempt apartment on the sixteenth floor. Two little white dogs came. "Cookie," Wonyi said. "Choco."

"You baby marshmallows," I said. "Who are the good, sweet marshmallows?"

"Fat one eats all the other one food," Wonyi said.

"Who's a greedy marshmallow?" I said.

"You are hungry?" Wonyi said.

"A little."

"What do you want to eat?"

"What food do you have?"

"What food do you like?"

I did not know what food she had and considered likely culprits in the kitchen. "I like fruit," I said.

For a while, we ate sliced persimmon. We ate apple. Young Mok tore open a foil tube of ginseng honey and by way of instruction mimed squeezing it into her mouth. She grabbed my wrist with incredible strength, then broke out in loud anguish again, muttering, and shaking my wrist to draw my attention to it.

"She says," Wonyi said. "So skinny. You are so skinny."

"Immo," Young Mok said, slapping her chest.

"Word for aunt," Wonyi said.

"Immo," I repeated.

"Immo," Young Mok said again, assaulting herself with conviction. "Immo. Immo."

"Immo," I said.

"Immo! Immo!"

I didn't know if she was going to begin crying once more, so we kept on saying "immo" to each other until she nodded, somewhat aggrieved or tired or something else.

I was the provincial who spoke no Korean at all, so after a while, rather than addressing each other, we mostly spoke to translator apps that then projected, machine-toned, some version of what we'd said. They favored Naver Papago. I kept on with Google Translate.

"Are you marry?" Inwahn asked carefully, and I looked at her face. She was pretty and stoical, and she had a long delicate neck. She held her shoulders quite still. Her hair was cut in a bob.

"No," I said. "Are you?"

"Yes," she said. "Will you get marry?"

"I have no idea," I said. "Is that your husband?"

"Husband?" she said. "He is my brother, In Hyeong."

In this way, I discovered that my sister and older brother were not married to each other.

Inwahn was quiet for a while. She'd slung a long camel overcoat on the chair behind her and with an upward gaze solicited my attention, then got the translation app going again.

"Godzilla is alive," her phone said, and Wonyi giggled. In-wahn tried again.

"Even John will die someday," her phone said.

"Yeah, well, we all will someday," I said.

"Say again," Wonyi said. "Slowly."

"We all will die someday," I said.

Wonyi was an incredibly cute person. She was something like fifty, but her face was as rounded as that of a teenager, and when she smiled, her entire face exploded with smile. This was not one of those instances. She widened her eyes.

TRACY
O'NEILL

"It was a joke," I said. And Google Translate translated.

"Ohhhhh."

"It wasn't very funny," I said. "In Korean is there a term 'dry humor?'" And Google Translate translated.

"Dry?" she said.

"Yes, like," and I patted my arms, my neck, my face as though toweling off.

"My sister is very skinny," Inwahn said.

"Tracy." Wonyi said something in Korean.

"My mother is working," Naver Papago said.

"I thought Young Mok is your mother," I said, pointing. I had no idea where Je Ryong had gone, but now my brother In Hyeong, who was not married to my sister Inwahn, was pacing. "Young Mok is working? Young Mok is here."

"Tracy mother," Wonyi said. "Tracy mother is working. Why she is not here."

"Got it, got it," and I must have pressed something incorrectly because Google Translate repeated, "Got it. Got it."

"Saturday she comes. But call now."

Inwahn placed a phone on the table with her long, beautiful hands. She could move her arms and hands very quickly as the rest of her remained still. I liked her elegant manner, with isolated intensity and a composed torso. Her face was pearly, tended but not done up, and she was intent on the dial tone, on the phone. A raspy voice came off speaker phone.

"Eh?"

"Eomma," Inwahn said, then, "My mother," and flicked her head to me. "Tracy."

"Annyeonghaseyo," I said, *hello*. It was one of six words I'd picked up on the plane.

And on Wonyi's phone, the blue backdrop of Naver Papago jittered lines of white words like an emotive stock ticker:

I'm sorry I am didn't die I didn't know I'm sorry sorry face they took I didn't know but I am love oh my god forgive my mother thank you for growing up well I'm sorry I'm sorry I love you dead dead dead you hate me you hate but I didn't alive know my mother was god oh my god understand grow healthy I'm I'm sorry I didn't know die die always my mother I want I love I hate I'm I'm I'm sorry I love say something my daughter say something are you there if you are there say something. Is my daughter there? Say something. Please say something to my mother.

"Talk to Tracy mother," Wonyi said.

She was crying. Young Mok was. I had seen those words burped from the phone translator, but I hadn't understood in the immediate, hadn't quite experienced Cho Kee Yeon's speech as they had, with particular words emphasized or connotations thickening meaning. All I knew was that they had heard something to which only someone heartless would reply nothing. Je Ryong was patting Wonyi. Wonyi was patting Young Mok. I shifted in my seat, searching for words.

"Gamsahamnida," I said—*thank you*. "Annyeonghi gaseyo"—*goodbye*.

That night, I slept in the room belonging to Wonyi's daughter Jeesu. I wasn't sure how fat the moon was, whether it was sunken. The quiet of the house was the whole sky. My cousin's daughter's white teddy bear ran the length of my body beside me on the bed, and I heard the miniature dogs' claws patter on hardwood, thinking all I could say to the mother who gave birth to me was thank you and goodbye. Only someone heartless would have failed to respond. I could show little heart, though, because I had had little language to return to this woman. It was as though I'd heard a storm roll in, so in turn I'd poured a glass of water.

All those months that I could not find her, I might have been learning Korean. Now, according to Wonyi, I had a matter of days until Cho Kee Yeon arrived in Daejeon. On my phone, I studied phrases until I fell, open-mouthed, asleep, words still forming. Arraso: I understand. Joesonghamnida, ihae mot haeyo: I'm sorry, I don't understand.

Annyeonghaseyo: hello. Eomma: mother.

I would call Cho Kee Yeon "eomma." She was not my mother, but she was my eomma.

———

The next morning, I woke to messages.

N asked, Did you landed?

Then there was Phillip: By any chance, never violate your quarantine rules for 10 days. Everyone is tired and excessively sensitive, especially government officials. You'll be deported immediately once it's caught on the scene. Ask Wonyi to order all kinds of Korean dishes for you and enjoy those food for those 10 days to gain some weight. Your sis says you're too skinny.

Phillip: Don't go outside the house for sure. Remember that.
Me: Yes, I can see them tracking my phone through the app.
Phillip: Yes, that's it. They have tracking device. Some people go outside leaving the phone home, but guess what?
Phillip: They call your phone at random, so don't risk anything.
Me: Ok good tip.

In the living room, Wonyi allowed me to feed the dogs boiled chicken by hand. It was true that one wanted to eat the other's food. He was afraid of this dandelion puff of a bitch and preferred hunger to fear. To feed them both, I had to toss chicken for the larger one across the room, then feed the little one while the greedy one went after the big game.

Wonyi said, "Tracy is Cesar Milan. She is dog," and this one she needed to look up. "Whisperer? She is dog whisperer."

"It's not me. They're no knuckleheads," I said.

"Say again?"

"Your dogs are smart," I said.

"No," she said, shaking her big, wonderful smile.

**Phillip:** If you get a call from them, you need to answer it for sure.

**Phillip:** It'll prove you're following their quarantine rules.

But in fact, to follow the rules, I needed to violate the quarantine. I was required by government mandate to take another PCR test, so Wonyi drove me in her compact car to a nearby facility on a hill lined with four seasons trees, resembling stands of hirsute green mushrooms. The queue ran most of the red paved lane shot down the hill, and the government tracking app vibrated with a warning. The app registered that I was not at the designated address for my isolation, though it did not recognize that I'd been ordered to leave Wonyi's.

I could worry. I wouldn't. I did not know why I felt so calm in that winter fog, but I was doing as I was told—doing one of the things I was told, at least.

"Very long," Wonyi said, pointing to the line.

"Ne!" I said—yes.

"Oh," she said, hitting roughly four octaves. "Ne! Very good."

Children were skipping and being scolded as Wonyi and I chatted carefully through the app about her children who attended pharmacy school in Boston. We two had gotten wise to a technique quickly enough: speak into the phone, then raise it, screen out, for the other to read as the phone uttered its toneless business. Should there be only one word to translate, we'd do an internet search. When Wonyi knew how to say what she wished to, she went without the phone. I could go without the phone to say "coffee," which was "keopi," and "water," which was "mul." I could say "computer," "keompyuteo."

"What does my cousin want to eat today?" Wonyi asked.

"Keopi! Mul! Keompyuteo!" I said.

"My cousin is," she said, then typed at her phone. "Joker. My cousin is the joker."

"Your cousin is American and ignorant," I said.

"You like pija?"

"*Pija?*"

"Yes, *pija*." With the phone, a visual was produced.

"I like pizza," I said. I had not yet read that there was no *Z* sound in Korean.

"I think you like the *pija*," she said. "I love *pija*. Very delicious."

For a while, there was nothing to do and everything to ask. I asked about the dogs, the dumbbells I'd noticed at home by her television. I asked about the countries she'd visited and the music she favored. She showed me vacation pictures from Turkey, and I told her I'd gone there to see my close friend Ali get married, then again for the wedding of my other friend, Eda. Across the street sat a mountain in the mist with thin trees and tangles of wild grass.

"It's pretty," I said.

"What?"

"The mountain."

"That?" Wonyi said. "No."

"I think so."

"It's okay."

"What's it called?"

"I don't understand," Wonyi said. "Again."

"What is the name of the mountain across the street?" I asked Google Translate, and Google Translate translated.

Wonyi said, "It is a just small mountain without a name."

"Really?"

"Really."

Someone waved, and Wonyi gave an underhanded flap of the hands. We went to a long row of windows, where she spoke a while to someone with a clipboard. When she made an ostensive gesture, I moved closer to a window. An arm reached from beneath glass, thrust a swab up my nostril with a merciless little spin. The test was done, notably without anyone from the Korean government making an arrest for the violation of home quarantine.

CHAPTER ELEVEN

# HEARSAY

COVID Jail, December 2021

We did not eat pizza, but we did eat fried chicken and turgid squares of chewy white tteok with miniature forks. Or I did, and Wonyi picked. The apartment pointed quietness, stillness. I could hear my own teeth, the only things going anywhere. I was hogging the chicken, and at this point I had a compact gravesite in front of me. Wonyi had only one bone. "You don't want to eat more?" I said.

"Finish," she said.

"You don't like chicken?"

"I like," she said, "but I was skinny like you. Now I am fat."

"Aniyo," I said—no.

"I am fat," she said emphatically. "I was skinny but then," she popped her arms out and puffed her cheeks.

Usually, went the explanation, she ate only once a day. She sat with her husband while he ate breakfast, and maybe nibbled a fruit. Then, she waited until Je Ryong came home to eat dinner with him. I wondered whether he had told her she was fat, but I didn't know how to ask delicately in the English I spoke with her. In the English I spoke with her, nothing was delicate. I clobbered her with room-sized sentiment. I was not the same person in Korea because, of course, I didn't speak the language. I was made baby by my ineptitude, or else, maybe I was simpler than I knew in the tricked-out language of my mind. I liked things. I wanted things. I was sorry. I didn't understand.

"Look," she said. Then she showed me three pictures on her phone, in which she looked like a dried fruit. "I was like you."

"Oh," I said. "Those are nice pictures. I like you now, too." I said to Google Translate, and Google Translate translated.

She said. "You like the tteok?"

"Ne," I said.

"This is first time?"

"Ne," I said. "Baby's first tteok."

"Tteok," she corrected me. "Tteok. Like," drawing a letter in the air, "*D*."

An appalling, infantile voice announced itself in my pocket: *Kakao! Kakao! Kakao!* This meant that I had messages on the preferred Korean chat application, KakaoTalk. It was Phillip in a group chat to which he seemed to add strangers every day.

**Phillip:** Wonyi & In Wahn, feed Tracy with Korean varieties.

**Phillip:** Tracy doesn't know the names of them, so just feed her with various kinds. We'll see which one she likes.

**Phillip:** Make sure she gains at least a pound a day.

**Phillip:** Inwahn worries Tracy is too skinny.

"Who are you talk to?" Wonyi asked.

"Phillip."

"Phillip?"

"Yes, Phillip," I said. "My second cousin's father."

"Second," she said. "Cousin," she said. "Father."

"He says in Korea I would call him my uncle. Phillip. He called you. He told you I was alive," I told Google Translate, and Google Translate translated.

"Oh, Seokgyo. Korean name is Seokgyo."

"Seokgyo," I repeated. "He said you're close."

"Not really."

Wonyi lifted herself out of the chair to a wall, fussed with the thermostat for a while. Her finger was determined, punching buttons. "I think you get cold"—she consulted her phone—"Easlily. Ea-si-ly. Easily. I think you get cold easily. And sick."

"That's true. How did you know?"

"I can see," she said. "Before I stay home, I work as the pharmacist."

"Do you miss it?"

She shook her head, scrunching features. "No. Why?"

I shrugged. "Maybe you liked your job. Or maybe you hated your job, but you liked talking to people. You liked knowing where you were going in the morning. You liked having somewhere to go that wasn't home. You liked not knowing where your day was going."

This was too much for the translation app, but Wonyi already knew her answer. Perhaps at points she'd considered being feckless, but it turned out deep down she had a lot of feck. Or else, it was the opposite. She did not waffle. She did not keep running the numbers on her life.

"I like to stay home," she said. "Take the Korean red ginseng for the health. It will keep you warm."

"Gamnahamsida," I said. "See, I'm learning. How do you like my Korean?"

"Korean is very hard. I think you don't want to learn."

"Actually, I do."

"It is very difficult."

"I like difficult."

For a while, then, Wonyi drew Hangul characters in a notebook. She tapped these characters, and she exaggerated the shapes of her lips for my benefit. There were little raps at unseen cymbals, connoting the registers she noticed I didn't notice, and she leaned her body into stressed syllables, in the fashion of steering skis.

"You're a good teacher," I said.

"No," she said, shaking her hands.

"You are. Take my job."

"No no no no no. Here. Your mom name," Wonyi said, writing. "Kyu Yeon."

"Kee Yeon?" I said.

"Kyu," she said. "Is different name than Kee. Name is Kyu. Kyu. Kyu Yeon. Cho is family name. Then Kyu Yeon is Tracy mom name. Cho. Kyu. Yeon. Cho Kyu Yeon."

"Kyu Yeon," I said. "You're saying that's my mother's first name."

"Yes," she said.

"I was told Cho Kee Yeon."

"Kyu," she said. "Kyu. Like the English letter," and a circle was drawn in the air, then slashed.

Wonyi had met this missing woman. I had not. There was no reason not to believe her, but over several calls Phillip had specified that he, too, had met my eomma once years ago and her name was Cho Kee Yeon, same as in the documents from Eastern

Social Welfare Society. The documents stated Cho Kee Yeon had been "delivered of her baby." Not Cho Kyu Yeon. The heat in my forehead enunciated the name. Kyu, pronounced "cue" or "queue" or "Q" as in *query*, not Kee like *key*.

Now, I looked at this name, written on the page: 규연. Not 기연. I imagined writing these two names. I tried to catch the feel of what my hand would do if I wrote, for instance, 기연 instead of 규연. As I imagined my own hand recording the characters, the difference between characters did not strike me as accidental. There were left-facing angles of sorts at the beginning of each name, but *Kyu Yeon* required two small vertical lines beneath the left-facing angle and one horizontal line. There was only one vertical line in *Kee*, and it stood to the right of the left-facing angle. And there was no horizontal line to speak of. I continued studying the names as I said, "Does my sister, Inwahn, like my mother?"

Wonyi laid down her pen, eyes still on the handwritten Hangul. She reached for her phone, unlocked it, said something slowly into Naver Papago. "Why does Tracy ask the kind of question?"

I looked up from Cho Kee Yeon's name. "Why not?"

Wonyi's face exploded with smile when she smiled, but she was not smiling now.

"I wonder why my cousin believes I know what someone else feels."

"No reason," I said, and Google Translate translated. "You know my sister better than I do. Maybe you know something I don't."

She wasn't a lip-licker, I noticed. I was. People always noticed that I licked my lips, and I did now, watching Wonyi keep her mouth closed and dry as she considered what she was to say.

"Who doesn't like their mother?" Wonyi said into the phone, and Naver Papago translated, and I was never going to get anywhere with this. She was never going to give me a straight answer. Why, I could only speculate. She wished to protect Inwahn's confidence. She wished me to have fewer doubts about not–Cho Kee Yeon. She harbored real theoretical doubts about how with crude huffs of language we were ever supposed to transfer a thought or feeling to the Other Mind, perhaps.

Except, now Naver Papago continued with its dead-voiced noises, with its text held up beside Wonyi's blank face: "Who doesn't like their mother? Who doesn't like their mother, even if she's a con artist?"

And that dead cellular voice shot somewhere above my lung. And it gave away nothing in tone. It was the best we could do, Wonyi and I, or else maybe that was optimistic, to believe our best was what was happening. I couldn't know the intention behind that question, nonplussed in the smartphone's even keel.

"Is my mother a con artist?" I said.

Wonyi looked at me, calm as milk. Her face was flat of affect, but there was something turning beneath the surface.

"What does Tracy think about her mother?"

"I think she liked sex," I said, "just like anyone else."

Wonyi raised her eyebrows, tilted her head.

"Okay, yes," she said. "I think you are right. Your mother is strange."

"Do you mean mentally ill?"

"No, not that thing."

"Phillip said my mother took money from my sister."

"Your mother was taking from a lot of people."

TRACY
O'NEILL

"She's a crook," I said. Those three words: a statement, but we both knew it was a question.

Wonyi searched the internet for a definition of "crook." Her lips were twisted to the side like the flopped-over top of a drawstring laundry bag. A sandbag-weight sigh. She was doing something on her phone.

"I don't know Tracy mother well. Maybe she is different now. She was doing the bad things," Wonyi said. "Long time ago."

"What kind of bad things?"

Naver Papago said, "My mother was a private money lender."

"Your," she said. "*Your* mother. Tracy mother."

"Like a loan shark?" I asked.

"Like a loan shark?" I presume Google Translate asked.

"Say again," she said.

"Loan shark. You lend people money. They have to pay it back with interest. If they don't—" I slid a flat hand across my neck, the horizontal kill of a knife in cold calculation. "It's deep trouble."

Wonyi looked at my phone to parse what Google Translate had said. I regretted the phrase "deep trouble." I should have just said "trouble." I had twenty days, and I was wasting ten of them on my own automations of vernacular. If I wanted to cut to the chase, I could not say things like *cut to the chase*. I needed to speak trimmer, to spit clean air. "Ne," Wonyi said. "Okay," Wonyi said.

"Some things I heard from my mother," Naver Papago said, pausing where Wonyi had paused.

Then, "Maybe your mother is different. It was a long time ago."

Naver Papago said, "Your mother hurt a lot of people. She borrow some money. She borrow a lot of money. But she didn't give it back."

The white tteok had been topped with a mysterious sweet crumble. Between two fingers, I rolled a loose piece of whatever it was from the table.

"According to the papers, my father did that. He borrowed money from my mother, then didn't return it."

"Paper?"

The rip of notebook paper, a shake. "I have documents," I said.

"That is true," she said. "Your mother borrow money to Tracy father."

"Borrow?" I said. "Or lend?" We did a short jig involving hands and fruit plates to indicate the difference.

"Lend," Wonyi said. "So your mother wasn't with Inwahn and In Hyeong."

"Because she was working."

"No."

"What was she doing?"

"She was obsessed."

"Obsessed."

"She was obsessed to trying to get money back from your father."

"There is information about my eomma and appa. There is a story about them. The papers said my father had 'an untruthful attitude' and 'a disparity in characters.' Do you know what that means? Is 'disparity in characters' a common phrase in Korean?"

Wonyi asked to see my phone. "No," Wonyi said. "I didn't hear before. But your father was a gentle man."

"That's not what it sounded like."

"Say again."

"The documents," I said, and Google Translate translated.

"There are words in the documents about my father. The words are not positive. 'Gentle' is positive."

Wonyi asked, "I can see the papers?"

———

In Jeesu's room, I graded papers, then studied Hangul characters. The mnemonics were the character for *B*, pronounced *M*, resembled a bed; *D* resembled a door; *G*, pronounced *K*, resembled a gun. There were others, too. I took in symbols, covered them. Repeated them in whatever part of my mind was learning the rules of this game. Ladder. Sea. Teeth.

My name began *Teeth*. My mother's name, 규연, began *Gun*. My mother's name was 규연. Not 기연. My mother had written 기연, not 규연. Or someone had. Someone had misheard her, as she'd dictated. I might have misheard things too. I was jet-lagged. But of course, that was a false rationalization. I had not misheard, and now all I could do was wait while Wonyi reviewed the papers from Eastern.

*Kakao! Kakao! Kakao!* That awful babyish cellular voice again.

**Wonyi:** After reading the adoption documents, Facts and lies are mixed.

**Wonyi:** It's true that your father is tall and muscular.

**Wonyi:** But your father is not a scammer.

**Wonyi:** It's true that your mom and dad gave birth to you.

**Wonyi:** Your mom and dad lived in the same neighborhood and met together.

**Wonyi:** I heard your dad was a very humane personality.

**Wonyi:** It's not a good thing for a man with a wife to go out with a woman other than his wife.

**Wonyi:** Your father's behavior is wrong, but he's not a bad person.

**Wonyi:** When you were born, my mom and your dad were next to you.

**Wonyi:** Your father never wanted you to be adopted.

**Wonyi:** But since your mom already promised to let you go for adoption, At the adoption agency, The adoption agency took it without showing your face to my mom or your dad. My mom was really upset at the time. My mom asked me to tell her.

**Wonyi:** I'll walk my dog and tell you the rest of the story.

———

I wanted to hear the rest. Instead, I fell asleep out of jet lag or elaborate psychosomatic avoidance or the massive energy suck involved in digestion of a few pounds of fried chicken, spelled here "chikin." When I woke, I saw that it was near four in the morning. I also saw on my cousin's daughter's desk a flat burger patty, a small blue carton, and a yellow paper bag. On the paper bag, Wonyi had attached a pink Post-It note: "This cookie has a lot of protein. Eat it as a snack." On the carton: "This is a drink made with almonds. This is also good for your health."

In that room, with my cousin's daughter's childhood stuffed animals, it was very late or very early, and I ate the burger, the chemically nauseating biscuit. I'd been in Korea little more than a day, and I had managed to work myself into an odd stammer of feeling, fits and starts of softness and quease. I looked at these pink slips of paper with the squat, spaced letters, and it was as though a sopping brush mussed pigment in my chest, this softening, this dilution. This was what people meant when they said they were touched, this watercolor feeling, new translucence. But then there was also a mental pounding, or a pounding in the head anyway, and my vision was too sharp. Ground meat caught in my gums, and I read from my laptop about Korea's loan shark problem.

One man interviewed referred to "murderous interest rates." Actually, that was a phrase I saw more than once. The richest man in the country had signed his organs away as collateral to keep his pharmaceutical company running during the early aughts. In Seoul, the Mapo Bridge went by another name, Bridge of Death, owing to the statistical reality that hundreds of people had thrown themselves off that bridge, reputedly over debt.

I thought of these people leaping out of life. I thought of Theresa Weisberger bagging her own head. I thought of the institutional documents in my possession and the memories preserved by Wonyi, by Young Mok, by the eomma I'd still not met.

And something of the hour and place, its silence, was outside time. Or I was. I was outside the time of my life, and of course, this was what I'd been after, what any investigation was meant to do: Get you outside the time you knew, outside your story. Break into another life with more knowledge and loot it. The routes of my routine self were elsewhere because I had asked to go elsewhere. There was no reason for alarm at the feel of imminent upchuck.

How goes? A message from Ali.

**Me:** They're adorable
**Me:** Family goal instantly became making me gain weight
**Me:** My sister called my uncle in America to talk to him
about it at length
**Ali:** Wonderful

**Me:** He now is demanding photos of all the food I eat

**Me:** Haven't met mom yet

**Ali:** It's conspiracy

**Me:** That happens Saturday

**Ali:** You excited?

**Me:** Yes no

**Ali:** Ooooh

**Ali:** Emotions

**Me:** I'm maybe quitting smoking here

**Me:** It's been two days

**Ali:** To gain weight?

**Me:** The cousin hosting lives on the 16th floor of an apartment building and won't give me a key. I think she's worried I'm going to spring for it. The Korean government has a tracker on my phone

**Ali:** Oh wow

**Ali:** They are reading this, aren't they

**Me:** Yes they have already called 3, 4 times

**Ali:** Korean intelligence knows our gossip

He liked that, my friend. I liked that he liked it, and I was lucky he'd sent his messages from Berlin, because in Daejeon, the sole reminder of the size of my own shoes was the long-running language between friends. We were people who favored ironic little verbal plays. That was who we were, even if I could not be that person here with any of the family.

In fact, I had entered into other games of language, too. There were messages that I'd missed on KakaoTalk. I was up to my neck in text. Phillip, Inwahn, Wonyi, the youngest aunt Mee Jeong, and someone named Rachel had been messaging all day. Slowly,

I transferred the Hangul characters to the translation app. Most added up to Phillip's commentary on my relatives' abilities and looks, but the ones that struck me had arrived later in the day.

Time is the bullet, Phillip said. Take a lot of pictures and give them away, and be careful because you don't know which page you will be on in the next book of Tracy.

I had not replied in the KakaoTalk thread for several hours, and who knew whether Phillip had forgotten I could see these messages. Who knew whether the warning was for my aunts, my sister, my cousin, or me. It was then, in that thought, that N replied to the picture of the almond milk, the burger, and the cookies I had sent him shortly before:

I LOVE YOUR FAMILY
TELL THEM I SUPPORT AND IM A BIG FAN
SHOW THEM THESE MESSAGES
!!!

———

And who was this family? Exhibit A: Immo Young Mok appears December 17, 2021. On her person: pajeon, shrimp, tofu, rice, red foil bags of ginseng drink. She rubs aloe serum on the face of a stranger come to town, unzips her own down vest and pulls it over the shoulders of said stranger. She hands over the goods: boxes of more ginseng drink and a pair of floral slipper socks. She weeps holding the stranger's wrist beside hers, comparing circumferences. She cannot master the translation app. She speaks too quickly, too much. Translation applications are a young person's game. "So skinny," Wonyi says.

Exhibit B: a letter found on the kitchen table of an apartment in Daejeon that same day. Letter totals one sheet of Morning Glory brand spiral-bound notebook paper, liberated from its binding:

Tracy!

There's something wrong with what I said earlier.
I talked to <u>Inwahn</u> on the phone.
(your sister)
And I talked to my mom on the phone too.

Your dad ran a Ginseng business in Geumsan.

Your birth mother lent (a lot of money) to your birth father.
Your birth mother didn't receive the money lent to your birth father.

Your birth father's wife gave your birth mother some money and asked her to erase the child in her womb.

Your mother didn't erase you and raised you in the womb, but your mother had a miscarriage after eight months.
Your mom thought her child was "Dead" because she was miscarried.
Your mother didn't promise to send you to adoption.

I think my mom and your dad had a plan to send you to America for adoption. They decided not to kill the child but to send her to adoption.

My mother believed that an unborn child should not be killed because of religious beliefs.

TRACY
O'NEILL

(At the time, my mom should have cooked for several family members. At least 9 people.)

At that time, Both your brothers and sister lived in my house. (including great grandmother and four aunts).

Tracy
↓
And Your father couldn't raise you because his wife was against you.

My mom and Your dad decided to let you go for adoption, but When you were born, they must have wanted to see your face.

My mom had No choice but to watch you get adopted. After sending you like that, my mom cried a lot. My mom was very sorry for you.

The gynecologist Song lived next door to (me.) → my house

I only remember talking to my mom & Song gynecologist's wife. I don't kow know what they talked about. But my mom and his wife were very close.

That's all. I know.

Writer of letter is not to be found on the premises at the time of discovery. Upon reappearance, letter writer presents: Exhibit C: green decorative tray with three types of baked goods, two Jeju mandarins, one bowl of strawberries, stems removed. Pink notes attached to food read as follows:

*Emergency food*
*Eat it when you hungry.*

*I'll take my dogs for a walk.*
*I'll be right back.*
*Pick up when the health center calls you.*

Letter writer's oral statement: "I thought you sleep."

———

Since I was not asleep, I resigned myself to miming. The bulk prose of it was hitting me. I could see that I was going to keep getting hit by words. That's all there was in this world of one quarantine-permissible Daejeon three-bedroom apartment—words—and I was desperate for something else, some system in which what I meant was not represented, where I had more than the metaphor for what I meant that was language itself. But there was nothing outside representation, evidently, so what I had at my disposal was miming, and in that miming of my own birth, my body represented that of Cho Kyu Yeon. As Cho Kyu Yeon, my knees were wide. The swing of my arms was meant to model the ejaculation of my own newborn body from between my-as-Kyu's legs. I was my birthing mother. I was my being-born self. I was life becoming itself, in the form of flung forearm.

"Are you sure you mean miscarriage?" I said, pointing to the word in her letter. "Not stillborn?"

"Still? Birth?"

"Stillborn. Did you mean stillborn? Not miscarriage?" How, precisely, I could dance out the difference was anyone's guess. Instead, when Wonyi passed me a notepad, I wrote STILLBORN.

Wonyi consulted her phone for a few minutes, recited the dictionary definition. "Not the stillborn," she said. "Miscarriage."

"It stretches the imagination," I said.

"Imagination?" A theatrical cock of the head. Her eyelids flipped up like a doll's. She, too, was miming in a way. But she wasn't miming labor.

I had not come to Korea to litigate my birth. I had come to meet a woman of interest, my woman of interest, and I liked Wonyi. I did. I thought of the almond milk. The notes. I thought of how she wanted me to eat protein and Korean red ginseng for health. She was good company in a line. She'd flit her head very quickly in refutation of a compliment it pleased her to receive. She liked pija and boiled chicken for her dogs. She worried that her son was not happy in Boston. He wasn't strong like his sister Jeesu, whose bed I'd slept in two nights already and whom Wonyi missed terribly. I liked my cousin very much.

We could get on just fine, if she'd quit pushing this narrative, or if I'd drop my suspicions. The story could be chalked up to the impulse to spare me grief or to diminish an embarrassment, whose I could not say. But I did not mind a story in which Cho Kyu Yeon had not wanted a baby, who happened to be me. I minded not knowing Cho Kyu Yeon.

That Wonyi's narrative was not true meant I knew less of the person who'd always been missing to me, always missed, maybe, that woman who was not five foot seven and who had not had a miscarriage in Seoul. I knew Wonyi was lying. Wonyi knew Wonyi was lying, and each lie took Cho Kyu Yeon away a degree more, though there was not enough of her even to be present. I'd come not for a consolation story, but to see what my woman of interest did with her life, to know her before it was too late and only the long lacuna would stand.

"I'd like to believe you," I said.

"You don't believe?"

"I don't see it. Walk me through the process. Let's go step by step. I'm going to need your help to believe this story."

"I told you already. My mom arrange adoption, not Tracy mom. Proof is my mom always pronounce Tracy mom name wrong. And name is wrong on the paper."

"Okay, sure," I said. "I can believe your mother has a speech impediment. But she also doesn't know how to spell her sister's name?"

"Say the word again."

"There's a screaming human excreting from her genitals, and she thinks it's a miscarriage?" I said.

We were at the kitchen table. The dogs had been fed for the second time that day. There were still wedges of cut fruit on the table from the morning. Once more, I tried to do the play-by-play. Here is Kyu's stomach. Here is Kyu's vagina. There is Tracy's head. See how it screams for air? Now Tracy's shoulders emerge. Now her stomach. Her legs. The screaming continues. It continues in a hospital bed at the Song Obstetric Clinic. My arms formed the walls of the hospital. My arms did the baby's dramatic entrance again. What baby doesn't bust out in a wave of histrionics? I was person. I was people. I was medical theater, and what I absolutely was not was something that could be mistaken for a miscarriage.

"The noise is right there," I said, pointing to the space between my own extended legs, V-ed off a chair. "I am screaming right there. Optimistically, we've got three feet between a screaming mouth and a set of ears." With my hands, I showed the distance. Then, hands still at that remove from each other, I stood that measurement away from Wonyi, said "birth," and screamed. "Loud, right?"

Wonyi's jaw scooched. Wonyi's eyes blanked, a perfect counterpoint to my daft enactments, and her chin tipped up, dignified. "Do you have baby? Have you give the birth?"

"No," I said.

"You did not give the birth. You are not a mother," Wonyi said regally. "Then you don't understand."

"So obstetricians who don't have uteruses," I began.

"There is so much blood and pain," Wonyi interrupted. "There is very confusing because the drugs. A lot going on in the birth. It is confusing. Because the pain, take the drugs. You don't know what happens. It could be miscarriage."

"Okay, let's presume that's true," I said. "The drugs, they turn down the commotion. But you're saying an ob-gyn administers an epidural for a miscarriage?"

"I don't understand."

"Naturally."

"You aren't a mother." Wonyi shrugged. "You would not understand."

"If a newborn falls out in the forest, and no mother is around to hear it, et cetera, et cetera," I said.

"Say again."

"It's nothing," I said. "We just have an expression in English about trees falling."

"Trees?"

"It's fine."

"I think you are very different person."

"Different?"

"Yes, different. Your questions are sharp." And she pretended to stab me.

"They're direct," I said. "Questions are only sharp when you're trying to maintain a soft view on factuality."

We might have done the translation app song and dance then, but Je Ryong returned home from the hospital, and for a while we moved into their domestic routine. This included watching maudlin songs on television. The courteous question was what I wanted to watch, and Wonyi smiled at me, said in a flirtation with irony, "*Colombo!*" In the living room, Je Ryong spoke about K-pop and Luciano Pavarotti. There were occasional exclamations at a hit high note. The screen was big and blue and crooning, but my mind was on the conversation with Wonyi, the mania of labor, mania of drugs. There would have been blood. There would have been a body. Something was ringing, and the body, mine, would have been appreciably alive.

"Your mother," Wonyi said, extending the phone.

Cho Kyu Yeon's voice was, as I remembered, raspy, hushed. According to Google Translate, she said, "You're pretty, tell me, my groom, thank you, my daughter, she's pretty and has grown up well."

"Gamnahamsida," I said.

To Google Translate, I said that I'd heard my mother was a good cook. Then the app suggested that we cook when I saw her, though I had a genius for burning pasta.

"Yes, tell me right now, my mom has a taste of hand, hand, hand, hand, hand, so if you cook it with your hands, you'll be fine," Google Translate said on behalf of my mother. Like Young Mok, she spoke too quickly, softly, and naturally for the machine's brittle ear.

"Joesonghamnida, ihae mot haeyo," I said—I'm sorry, I don't understand—and "Annyeonghi gaseyo," goodbye.

Call over, Wonyi and Je Ryong idly spoke to each other in Korean, snickered. The voices on the television arrived: alien, auto-tuned. In another life, I'd know whether these songs expressed the delusions of love or disappointment, whether these songs related how the singer thought she'd die without someone until she got strong enough to survive.

Instead, I'd grown up in Massachusetts, in New Hampshire. So I watched the performers beneath stage lighting, sat with my cousin and her husband having a hoot in the privacy of the language I'd not learned, and was untouched by the songs. I watched Wonyi's simpered lips, and I did not know what I was doing with these people. They were snickering and, even without language, I could see they were only pretending not to want to laugh. In this sixteenth-floor isolation box, I was the only one who didn't see what was so funny, who saw instead the jellyfish undulation of the boundaries between objects lit, psychedelic.

Je Ryong apologized at last. He realized that I did not speak Korean, so he'd fill me in. They had been speculating, he confided, that my eomma had not yet come to Daejeon because she was ugly now. Though she was a rich woman, Kyu Yeon had gotten cheapo cosmetic eye surgery, and you could see the price tag on her face.

"She is ugly. I think she doesn't want you to see. She used to look—" Je Ryong searched. "Normal. She was fine." He and Wonyi bobbed their heads, shrugged. "But now." Wonyi waved her hands, shook her head. "She is ugly."

"So she does not come to Daejeon because she doesn't want you to see she is ugly now," Wonyi said.

"She said that?"

"We think," Je Ryong said.

"Against the Freudian odds, I didn't come to Korea to find out if my geriatric mother is attractive enough to make a pass at," I said.

Je Ryong reached for his phone to translate. Wonyi said, "Slowly, slowly."

"Never mind," I said. "I'm tired. I'm tired. I'm tired."

I was. I wasn't. I went to Jeesu's room, temporarily my room. The dogs followed with the twinkling sound of their collars. I couldn't remember my own shoe size, and I'd better do a habit of my life or my forehead would crack open and I'd waft off. The internet tab on the computer was still open to a shitty photograph of the Mapo Bridge, from an article about a public service campaign intended to stanch the flow of bodies into the Han River. "Have you been eating all right?" and "Let's walk together," signs on the handrails said, and there were horrifying bronze statues— for instance, a life-sized bronze friend gripping a life-sized, suicidal bronze man that Samsung Life Insurance and the PR firm Cheil Worldwide designed to convey to potential jumpers that people were willing to help.

I'd not come to Korea with a plan, but I could complete my end-of-semester grading work. I could go to bed. There were piles of final essays to grade—but only virtually. *Title: What does the speculative imagination make possible that realism does not?* Three-headed aliens with blue tits, a smart aleck might write, but I didn't have any smart alecks in the mix.

No smart alecks. I could see that. I could see. I could clear out the psychic attic. But in the wonked physics of that condominium aquarium, the sideways gravity sucked my mind crooked, and I realized I was reviewing the scanned Eastern documents I had in my possession once more.

The order of operations had been that I had first seen a phone screen refer to Cho Kyu Yeon as a con artist, then Wonyi had read the documents. Wonyi had, after, sent a refutation on KakaoTalk, followed by a revision in the form of a handwritten letter.

Notionally, the letter had been written because of the problem of real-time translation. But a letter also avoided the problem of real-time questions. And I did have questions now because she'd missed a detail in the Initial Social History report, under Section Three, heading: "History Birth and Admission":

*"Period of pregnancy:———,"* I read. *"Delivery Type: Using Pitocin. Birth weight: 2.6 kg. Any Medication During Pregnancy: None."*

That had been the original English translation provided at the time I'd been shipped to America. But Hannah Hertzog had translated the documents differently. In her version, the delivery type was *"Used a labor inducer."*

After all, the synthetic hormone Pitocin, I'd learn, was, indeed, used to induce labor or to perform an induction abortion. And so, the art of translation was not an esoteric matter alone. Because I was not a mother, not an ob-gyn, because I did not yet know from WebMD that "Pitocin® . . . helps imitate natural labor and birth by causing the uterus to contract," the art of translation was how I concluded that someone in that family was lying.

CHAPTER TWELVE

# ON
# SUSPICION

Kyu's Route, December 2021–January 2022

It was December 18. It was a day of little velocity and fewer faces. COVID-19 had miniaturized life. It took yogic torque to get a jumpsuit on in Jeesu's room, and the conditions of the world at large were not far off what they were the year before, but for me they were. Though it was a year of social distance, I was going to meet someone named Cho Kyu Yeon who had been the only person to give birth to me, using Pitocin, at the Song Obstetric Clinic, following a relationship sexual in nature, with a married man who was or was not humane, though by all accounts well-muscled.

I could not at that moment think about N calling earlier to rave about Cowboy throwing up on the bed the night before. I could not think about whether he had or had not understood what to do when I told him the location of the cleaning solution. I could think of one thing: today I would meet Cho Kyu Yeon.

*Kakao! Kakao! Kakao!*

**Phillip:** Tracy, I'm out of all the rooms of our relatives. There's minute conflict among us in communication. Talk to me directly if you have specifics to share. I'm always on your side in your trip to Korea. Don't try to know details too much on what has happened to your mother. Just enjoy your current situations with them.

I had not told Phillip I was trying to know any particular details about my mother. I had told him that I hoped to meet her and to obtain a photograph of my birth father, Kim In Kee. My hands expressed heat at "don't try to know details."

**Me:** I'm sorry. Did I do something?

**Phillip:** Not at all. No worry. I tried to gather as much info as it exists, but it has worried a few.

**Me:** I keep getting different stories about her. I know people probably want to protect both of us, but I don't have any personal investment in the idea that my mother was a saint. She clearly wasn't.

**Phillip:** Is Wonyi at home next to you?

Eggs scrambled high in my abdomen. A burgeoning sense that something was about to be spilled whisked me up.

No, I'm in my room, I replied. Yesterday Wonyi kind of reversed the story she told me. Suddenly the story was that my mother thought she miscarried . . . I feel as though she and Young Mok decided to change the story to make this easier, but it's not easier because I'm not an idiot.

**Me:** I like Wonyi and my aunt tremendously
**Me:** But this story is deranged
**Phillip:** Let me call you.

The sit. The wait. What Phillip had to offer was this: despite the nearly bureaucratic volume of KakaoTalk messages I'd seen, at some point another group had formed in the messaging application. In the splinter thread, conversation turned to Kim In Kee, my birth father. My aunt Mee Jeong got on a roll about how handsome Kim In Kee was, how all the women gave him the eye, so on, until my sister Inwahn declared that this man had destroyed her family, a detail this family could bother to remember. That was strike one for Phillip, who'd gotten Kim In Kee's name back in Cho mouths again.

The second strike had occurred when Wonyi told Phillip that I'd been asking an unfavorable number of questions. She had admitted to fabricating elements of my origins story because she wanted "everyone to be happy," and so she was tired of Phillip asking about the photographs of Kim In Kee I'd requested; tired of his endless questions, not dissimilar from my endless questions; and tired of Phillip generally, because he was annoying.

Phillip thought I should know why I wouldn't see his participation in the KakaoTalk thread anymore, and he thought I should know that Wonyi had lied through her front teeth.

———

And what could I do? I did push-ups. I shoved luggage to the perimeters of the room where a child I'd never met had grown up. I got down, but not on my knees. At breathless, I leaned against the magnificent white stuffed bear, still half-dizzy, thinking of Wonyi wanting everyone to be happy. I was not happy.

Because I was a beginner on the subject of Cho Kyu Yeon. For so long, I had wanted to begin again. To begin again, I had allowed myself to believe all I could do was surrender myself to experience, and I couldn't now, or I'd never be more than a beginner on my missing person. I'd get passed counterfeit mother.

"Go ahead and shake their hands," Joe Adams had said, "but count your fingers before taking yours back, and never forget these guys are strangers."

And so to count my fingers, as it were, I told myself flowers did not have teeth. I told myself Daejeon had existed during the past five minutes. These statements were true. I must remember what I knew to be true, because as any philosopher knew, the duck-rabbit was not only a duck. As far as I could tell, the story looked like a duck, walked like a duck, talked like a duck, but it was also a cock-and-bull rabbit.

So I would need to stay vigilant. I could not afford to go swampy in my jacket, as I had in that taxi from the Incheon International Airport. Admit I had stupidly relied on my new—or was it old?—family to translate. Now I wouldn't. But I could not do this myself. Cho Kyu Yeon would arrive in a matter of hours. I had only a few hours to secure an interpreter who was not my cousin Wonyi, whom I liked so much and who lied. She could fictionalize what my mother said, and for all I knew, Cho Kyu Yeon could go missing from me again.

I could bank on only one shot to know something real of her.

This, then, was the familiar adrenal thing. This, then, was *call for a quote*. I called for a quote, for quotes. "Yes," I said. "When I say 'today,' I mean today!"

I did the thing universally acknowledged to screw a head on straight, which was breathing, and after the homeostatic efforts, I did the thing that near-universally was acknowledged to be of suspect relevance, which was stick myself up with nicotine patches. To know someone was to betray the image they wanted you to receive. I knew them, in this regard. This family, I'd begun to know them a little.

———

I couldn't be late in self-quarantine, but my eomma was, was the word, owing to snow. She was coming from Seoul to Wonyi's in Daejeon with Young Mok on the bus, and the apartment fell into a strained quiet. I'd lost track of Je Ryong, but I notified my cousin that I'd reserved time with a phone interpreter.

"It will be simpler this way," I said, getting my eyes straight in hers, "less work for you."

She gave a deferring, diagonal nod, because or as though she accepted my decision—or perhaps because we both knew what I knew. The motion was made to sit, and whether she worried I couldn't parse, but looking at her kind face, a heavy sack swung behind my breastbone, until the judder of a speed bag, until the counted fingers of my hand became a fist.

I still liked her, and I didn't trust her as far as I could throw her.

I drank water. I drummed fingers on surfaces. In the waiting, Wonyi extended a here-and-there remark to urge a smile. So I met her home-cooked gaze, but all I really wanted was to pet my own beautiful dog. Treska once noted that my dominant genre of self-portraits documented me holding Cowboy who was, she pointed out, as big as me, maybe bigger. "It's a probability thing," I said. "Because I do spend a lot of time holding him." I couldn't

TRACY
O'NEILL

help myself. He had a worrywart face and a sense of humor with a ball. When frightened, which was often, he rubbed his nose against my legs or tried to climb onto my lap, and I think this was a sign he let me love him. It comforted me to comfort him, to feel the anxious pump of his stomach slow beneath my hand as I spoke tender gibberish: "Who loves comfort? The beauty bear loves comfort. Baby stinko's safe."

"Your mother will bring the food," Wonyi said. "Tracy mom cooks very delicious. Even for a job she was chef."

"I heard," I said. "Where?"

"This I don't know," Wonyi said.

Her little white dogs connipped at the door. That got Wonyi up. I was sitting at the kitchen table when Choco and Cookie got loud, and of course the ruction announced Cho Kyu Yeon's arrival, and I didn't stand, didn't look. It was happening. A wooze of foreign sense swelled in my orbital cavities: the woman, my woman, must be removing her shoes by the door.

And I held my own hands like a prayer, or maybe just holding on—and to what? I did not remember when she became missing to me, this eomma, after all, but I suppose I screamed, screamed right there, optimistically three feet between us, then more, then an uncountable distance, across which I had been afraid she was afraid to die alone, though I did not remember her ever having held me, did not remember her face. I could not. I could not remember this woman who induced me into life, though I must have called to her before I had language and though in some organ south of my neck that calling may have been too regular a historical feature of life as I knew it to be noticed. You felt anomalies. You did not feel the routine of existence. You did it. You kept on until you didn't, even if beneath the polite routines and set silverware persisted a wild scream, just a protracted tongue of aporetic instinct: I could not *be* without her I am without her I am.

"Tracy-ah! Tracy-ah! Tracy-ah!"

I stood. I turned. From the two phone calls, I recognized that smoky rasp that had never said my name. She wore a long, black down coat, and soft gloved hands thwapped away. She was clapping like a toy monkey, elbows out and chest-height, at each utterance: "Tracy-ah! Tracy-ah! Tracy-ah!" She percussed like so and by some sentimental trick of the eye floated across the room, a small woman, hair more than a hint of mad cherry red, like a half-rinsed paintbrush above lit eyes: agrestal, possessed, and absent a few screws.

She launched. I caught. I had all of her in my arms. I was not accustomed to holding someone smaller than myself. She was so much smaller than the archetypal mountain of her in my mind, smaller—but she had a bone grip on me, hard through the mush of coat. It was unmistakable, the bushed vitality in her arms and cries. She shook, so bound in her clamp we shook, as a sharp scent of urine grabbed me by the face.

This might have been the moment I understood the inimitable bond of mothers and children. I didn't. I held this woman like a metal music stand wrapped in a packing blanket. Her ammoniac smell fastened over me like an assaulting mitt, and I did feel as though I might cry, but not any more than on watching a conventional movie that went for the cheap blows. I let my eomma babble and hold, babble and hold, and with dumb hope, I held on longer, as though then the ineffable would come: a recognition of some unimpeachable link, some shared compulsion to want more, or else a love prior to election in a world of hard choices. I held her. I did, though there was no way out of the truth: I was nothing but a stone-cold cardboard cutout of stranger come to town in the iron clench of a shuddering old woman with a red dye job. She'd missed a handful of hair at the back of her head, I noticed.

"Tracy-ah, Tracy-ah," she whispered, like a question.

"Ne," I said. "We've met once before."

Then, for the second time in my life, she let me go.

———

I looked at her: rounded, detention-postured. She wore a gray sweater on which red, white, and blue rhinestones spelled NISSY NISSY HEARTTHROB, and she had almost no eyebrows to speak of. Sporadic hairs startled off thick tattooed stripes, ancient pigment fading milky gray. Her eyes were light, almost orange as they seized on a small square of table. Her hands did not shake. Before I could ask a question, Cho Kyu Yeon had begun marathoning throaty mumbles, somewhat dumb to the demand of conversation to be heard. I clocked twenty minutes—with occasional questions in Korean from the interpreter—and she hadn't stopped. I still had no clue what a NISSY was.

Scads of words. Young Mok pulled the socks off my feet before I could stop her. I was enamored of my eomma's endless voice, but in my stomach, miniature hands bounced off hot stove. I wondered what had happened to those eyebrows. I wondered precisely the mechanisms through which my eomma collected on loans that might make plunging off a bridge the more humane option. The interpreter asked that I tell her she needed to speak up, speak slowly, as though I'd need him at all if I'd facility enough to do so.

She was still staring down that square of table with her eyes—perhaps, as Wonyi and Je Ryong had predicted, ashamed. She was not ugly, as they'd said. She was startling, hurt, and visually incoherent, and her strange, blank eyes didn't blink.

When I'd disclosed Wonyi and Je Ryong's theory that my eomma was ashamed of her appearance, N had said, "Fuck that." He'd said, "Who cares? You are old. You are bald and have wrinkled dick. It happens. When I am old and children grown, fuck everyone, fuck wife, I go to monastery and fart in peace. I'll meditate and don't give two shits what I look like."

"You give three now," I said.

"What you are talking about?"

"You kiss your own biceps."

"Come on, poo-poo, that's normal. Noooormal. I am Serbian Spartan, baby!"

Now, across from my eomma, there was no use in paying attention to what she said in another language, but it was the second time in my life I'd met her and the first I could remember. I should remember. I should keep my attention in the room. Every so often I heard "omona," a Korean interjection something like "oh my God" or "Mamma mia."

"Yes, hello, miss?"

The interpreter—let's call him Gunter—didn't realize that once Cho Kyu Yeon repeated her story three or four times, I'd already heard it four or five, owing to Wonyi. According to him, according to my eomma, innominate people of shadowy origin had snatched her baby away. Someone had written 기연, not 규연, and she'd never given permission for it. She'd had the distinct impression she had a miscarriage—that was the alibi, other than when she declared the reason for her choice was that she'd been too young to take care of a child.

"Is that all? She was going for a long time."

"Basically, yes." Given her verbosity, Gunter the interpreter could not recall.

At Wonyi's kitchen table, I wanted better words. I wanted to trust that this man would accurately convey that I wanted to talk life, not birth. I'd tired of discussion of the latter event and, anyway, I'd been there for it. There was nothing to forgive in the choice not to mother. There had been nothing to forgive until she began to alter the story. My instructions: Tell her this was not an interrogation. We were just here to talk. I'd come to Korea to know her. But know *her*, the real her. It was she who was of interest, not the illusion of wanted fetus.

"I'm not angry you didn't want another kid," I said to Gunter, as though to Cho Kyu Yeon. "But let's be clear you were thirty-eight. Let's be honest."

Then, without consulting her, the interpreter said, "But you must understand age is relative."

"Okay," I said, counting in my mind.

"Sure," I said, and I could not do this conversation alone. I knew that.

"Right," I said, and I didn't manage to stop myself. "During the Middle Ages a thirty-eight-year-old would be dead."

Gunter and Cho Kyu Yeon conferred. Her voice was throaty. He cleared his throat, then made a long flatulent noise presumably vis-à-vis brute force through his nose. I thought he was done. He wasn't. Another trombone whole note. "Are you there?"

"I'm here."

"She says she's telling the truth."

The truth: I wore a size six shoe, sometimes five and a half. Had I been excited? *Yes no. Oooooh. Emotions.* These things were true. But that story was not. She was not five foot seven. I was not miscarried in Seoul. Still, the mythology rocketed.

After what my eomma thought was a miscarriage, the interpreter said, she prayed for her daughter, wondering where that baby was.

I'd not noticed when the old heat came to my face. It was there now. I lost track of the disinterest in litigating my birth, then went cold, and I was shaking a little.

"Okay," I said. "So ask her why exactly she was praying that I was okay if she thought I was dead. What's the aspiration? I'd not go to hell again?"

The interpreter emitted a bizarre honk, then said, "The important thing here is that your mother said she loves you."

"That your editorial opinion?"

My aunt reached for me once more, so I sat on my feet. Her hands slid under my thighs anyway. She wanted me in red flowered slipper socks. I wanted to slap somebody. If my mother had, in fact, been praying I'd not return to hell, we'd come up no dice.

The interpreter went on chastening. I went on asking questions never passed on. Young Mok's face turned tight, other than her slack, circular mouth.

"This is how it works, right? I say something. You interpret. Therefore, I ask a question. You ask the question."

"Miss," he scolded, "miss."

There was a crinkling noise. A silence. He muffled complaints regarding a bad connection. I waved the phone, then poked speakerphone on and off. He repeated that we had a bad connection, to which I said, "You're telling me."

Young Mok had become a forty-five degree angle. My mother had. And, as it happened, they were as abstract to me still as geometry.

"I flew halfway around the world to talk to this woman," I said. "Are you telling me that you won't ask her the question?"

"If you're dissatisfied with my services," he said.

"I am."

"Miss," the interpreter said. "Miss, your mother loves you. That's what you should focus on."

It was a nice thought, and of course so, too, was the one that love was patient, love was kind; but I was hot, I was cold, I got cold *ea-si-ly*, not yet having tried the Korean red ginseng cure. I was vibrating with recognition: My autobiography was not mine alone. No one's was. But also, no one who could help me wanted me to know anything about this woman.

And this man was eating time. Or she was. She was hoarding time so there'd be no time for questions.

"Please, miss, will you say it again?" Gunter said.

"Fuck," I said.

"I'm just doing my job."

"Then ask her the question," and I began shouting. "Ask her the question! Ask her the question! Ask her the question! Do you hear me now? Ask her the question!"

It was then that Young Mok got her arms around my neck, and I was so keyed to a mad, maddening force in the room, which happened to be my own tantrum, there was no time to fight it. Strung between her hands: a ropey thing. Her shadow domed over me.

"This is real freshwater pearl," Wonyi said for her mother, as the necklace settled on my chest.

---

Young Mok patted me. I did not want to be patted. I'd hung up on the interpreter, and someone decided to heat the food Cho Kyu Yeon prepared and brought from Seoul.

They served. We ate. Before us: steaming pork bulgogi, beef bulgogi, japchae, kimchi. Everything was red with spice and sweet umami, and it was rich. It was so delicious, I was sick. We defaulted into a decent impersonation of family doing dinner, and I sucked down a gagging impulse as Young Mok poked chopsticks of beef at my mouth. She poked, determined or a little demented. I couldn't tell.

"Ah ah ah," she said, mouth demonstrating how to open up for the airplane.

I had a half foot on Young Mok, or in my shoes I did, anyway, but I still ended up waving my palms, thrashing face left to right, infantile. I anticipated vomiting. I didn't. "Aniyo, aniyo, aniyo!" No, no, no!

"You don't like Korean food mom is wondering," Wonyi asked. "But I tell her you like Korean food. Why don't you eat?"

"I like Korean food okay," I said, when Young Mok had retracted her beef. "I didn't like that interpreter."

Down the table, my eomma was so small, quiet. A vigor in her was obvious, but she ate in portions suggesting she was embarrassed to exist. She was already done, a prognathic moue on and plate empty as her eyes. She was there. Right there. And the

TRACY
O'NEILL

impression she gave was of an idling Xerox machine. To reach her seemed impossible.

Nonetheless, I recalled a scene in *The Long Goodbye* when Terry Lennox said he didn't know what to say, to which Philip Marlowe suggested he could try a good old-fashioned "Come in."

"I didn't like the interpreter, but he certainly did want to talk to *you* a lot," I said knowingly to my eomma, and Google Translate translated. "I think that man was flirting with you." She cocked her head, and her forehead shrunk, alarmed maybe.

"That was a joke, kind of," I said.

"That was a joke, kind of," I guess Google Translate said.

Wonyi turned out of her chair, made for her bedroom. "I have an idea!"

———

Wonyi's idea: get Jeesu on the phone from Boston. Her English was fluent. It was three or four in the morning her time. But Wonyi had the mother card. She pulled it. The girl's sleep-confused voice rose from the table, metallic but still round-edged, gentle. She wanted to please her mother out of love; I could hear that seven thousand miles away.

By the grace of that unquestioning daughter love, I learned my eomma did not know why she abandoned Inwahn and In Hyeong as teenagers, other than that she was trying to reclaim money from my father, Kim In Kee.

Nor did she know what she liked about him.

She did not know his favorable qualities. She wanted money from him; then she liked him.

"There must have been something," I said.

A pause. He was masculine and quiet.

Cho Kyu Yeon did not know that she'd kicked up thrills any different from those she would have rooted to one family—she didn't even like adventure.

She did not know why I'd heard there'd been four fathers to her children, when there were only two. It wasn't clear to her, either, why the marriages didn't last, though she asserted she was actually widowed.

This was a lie. The family and Eastern papers had divulged the divorce, and according to both Wonyi and Inwahn, the first husband died years later. Hyeong Min had a different father than Inwahn, In Hyeong, and me, respectively.

For some reason I was very tired now, and I had the sense that I was deep in an onanistic endeavor that I ought to have predicted would end up just as numbingly navel-gazing as sitting in a one-bedroom apartment with drop-ceiling tiles downing Popeye's, holistic medicine, and self-pity had been. And under my eomma's hushed lull of a voice, I skipped out. I mean that my concentration lagged, and I remembered suddenly a veteran I'd interviewed the year before for a piece. When I'd asked about his life after war, he'd said he did research. This entailed cryogenics videos on YouTube, primarily. He planned to freeze his head, since it cost "only" eighty thousand dollars. I'd inquired about the appeal of immortality, what he'd do with eternity. In his explanation, he wanted to see the end of time to prove infinity a foolish misapprehension. His wife took no interest in freezing her head, given her belief that in death she'd be reunited with her ancestors. But there was nothing he could do. Fantasies were one's own—he got it—and she'd follow hers right into death, even if there was no one there waiting for her, as he would laugh

TRACY
O'NEILL

at time's end alone, too. And I didn't know why I was thinking of this man now, as my mother carried on mumbling, except that some eerie chill on my shoulders recalled the interview with this man planning to pack his head in a freezer.

My eomma, Jeesu said, did not know what she hoped for out of life when she was young, but she wanted it to be good.

Nor did she know her own thoughts on what good was.

I wanted to ask what she *did* know.

I wanted.

But though I heard Cho Kyu Yeon, without common language, I would not say I listened to her anyway. I searched her features for clues to her, really her in good faith. A cauterizing anesthetic helmet had settled on my head. Numb, I tried to suss out whether my eomma understood these questions to be curious or designs on her eventual self-indictment.

"I know she isn't a saint. That's why I was interested in her. I figured her free in ways women with more traditional lives might not be," I said. "This is why I ask these questions."

After another conferral, Jeesu asked, "Do you still?"

My eomma braced. I could see it. Her hands did not shake, but she'd assumed a concave, defensive posture like a chihuahua sizing up the odds on fight or flight. All evening I'd not seen her teeth once, and her eyes remained unstocked cabinets. I looked at her ridiculous dye job and the incomprehensible glitter NISSY NISSY, then concentrated on her equivocating lips. Once I'd gotten Jeesu on the phone, I'd reverted to interviewing my eomma as though she were anyone at all I'd been assigned to cover as a journalist.

"How could I say?" I said. "We're strangers."

Now Cho Kyu Yeon stared flat as platitude at me as she spoke, though it was Jeesu, on the phone to her left, my right, who would understand.

"She says if you get married, she wants to come," Jeesu said.

"I see."

"She wants to know if you have a boyfriend."

"Ne," I said.

"She wants to know if you'll marry him."

"Yeah, well, that's a question."

"So will you?"

I thought of N curling paper cones to catch sawdust off a drill, thought of N declaring he was a professional—these hands moved baby grand pianos! For whatever soft-brained reasons, there was something touching to me about his arms extended in the hokey fashion of an old uncle when he saw me at a distance, but I was troubled that he also believed in an incontestable code for how women thirty-three, thirty-four years old were to act. He didn't know what would happen. I didn't either. I knew longing for home, and he wanted to name his son Stoja. I'd not had the heart to tell him his grandfather's name was homophonically also that of a popular North Carolinian pornstar.

N was a big man, and he didn't forget it. He was never reckless with his strength when he held me, but he did follow his impulses without apology. N considered himself a socialist, but he talked endlessly of ways to squeeze money out of people. He easily felt cheated. He had a taste for "world music," Christian history, ćevapi, but he predicted I'd like *The Knick* because lots of self destruction cos of the stress induced by work. Steven Soderbergh was the director, he'd written. Then, no, he had a joke: Steven hamburger Hhahahahah.

TRACY
O'NEILL

"Probably not," I told Jeesu.

A quickening. My eomma had gone intent: all wireless fidelity, plaintive, skin aureate with a pink scarf around her neck. Her knee pointed to the side of her body. We played telephone on the telephone.

"Your mother says she hopes you'll get married," Jeesu said.

"Okay, copy. I'll think about it."

That I took to be the end of the discussion, but Jeesu wasn't finished.

"She says she hopes you'll get married, because she doesn't want you to feel alone."

And something in me dropped. Something dropped in the instant, stomach-deep lowdown: my eomma had said it because she *did* feel alone. The self-inflicted ruse had been that I'd come with no expectation at all, but of course I had wanted her to toss a child off and keep going, no regrets. I had wanted to see what happened after that parting shot down the road to the horizon, when a woman was of interest enough to herself to skirt the norm with its chalk outlines marking the limits of certain unfortunate lives with their obliged meanings. The norm: where you do not want to be someone who, traversing the Mapo Bridge, cannot be stopped because the sole interested party is a handrail commissioned by Samsung Life Insurance, suggesting, "Let's walk together."

I had hoped to see that in the universe in which she killed off certain conventions, her life had unspooled with beautiful control and art to it, that everything had turned out as it should. The story had straightened. Instead, whether she knew it or not, she'd sounded an admonitory note: *do not introject, do not become me.*

I had never beheld a parent's body as oracular spectacle, interpreted a parent's story as, somehow, vatic. I didn't now either, exactly, but some squalid corner of myself had been ransacked, and I knew it.

We hung up on the call with Jeesu. Hands of unknown origins pushed napkins. The entire apartment was bouncing on my head. There was motion, leaning, and in the grating furniture movements, it seemed perhaps now Cho Kyu Yeon would leave. So I called out, though Young Mok and Cho Kyu Yeon could not comprehend what I meant, "Wait."

Cho Kyu Yeon was a scammer and a shark. To give her preferred account, she'd given me the slip all night, and I had to believe the dutifully morose mother was a con, too. It was not as though you ever really got to the bottom of anyone, but there was more to this woman. There was more. There had to be. I fumbled phone, slapped one hand down on the table. I saw startled faces.

"Eomma, wait," I said to Google Translate. "What makes you happy?"

It was sometime after ten. Her needled-on eyebrows didn't move. One of the dogs had peed nearby, but it was little dog pee, and it was easy enough to stay blind to it until your foot was wet, as with anything else. As a result, Wonyi and Young Mok remained at the table, watching. That long pause, I could see even then, would go on forever, even when it was over, just like any other memory.

After that long pause, from a screen running Google Translate, I learned that Hyeong Min's dog made my eomma happy—actually no, her dog.

She was happy, too, that I came to Korea.

She was not being polite. She had missed her daughter.

TRACY
O'NEILL

All those years ago, you see, she'd chosen a name: Yu Min. Yu Min, not Seon Ah. She really did like that name, Yu Min—liked it so much, indeed, that she gave it to the dog.

"Do you believe in God?" I said, and Google Translate translated.

"Aniyo," she said, no.

And though she would not understand, I said, "Thank you for your prayers."

CHAPTER THIRTEEN

# USE OF FORCE

Virtual Reality, December 2021

The day after Cho Kyu Yeon came to Daejeon, when Z inquired about the visit, I said: Her hands didn't shake. I said, She also told me to dump N, keep him as a friend, and find a good man I'll marry.... So she's at least a little incorrigible.

That's good, he said. You expected her hands to shake?

I said, Yes, mine do.

Yet you regularly restrain Cowboy who might soon outweigh you.

It's true. If he gets any bigger, I'm gonna teach him how to pull me on a sled to Poughkeepsie, I said.

Get rid of the Outback, I said.

Go for a Charger, I said.

And because he sensed across the distance I wanted to laugh, the reply went: You can enter him in the Iditarod.

I talked to Maggie about Choco and Cookie, how they looked like adorable wet rags with bug eyes and vicious personalities. We talked about what she and her mother were going to eat and that it was disappointing her mother didn't want to eat at one of our favorite restaurants, Hot Space, where we always ordered the hot tray of fish bathed in red chili oil and the waitstaff provided plastic bags to protect our jackets. We talked about Cho Kyu Yeon.

N was the person I dreaded speaking to the day after I met my eomma. N was also perhaps the last person to ask about it. This was not the first time I anticipated he would not understand me, but it was the first time he wouldn't understand because I could not bring myself—from quarantine at Wonyi's, at roughly seven thousand miles remove—to admit the inner pits related partly to telling Cho Kyu Yeon not to bet on N and me making it for the long haul. Off his first impression of my voice on the phone, he asked if I'd been physically harmed.

"Physically? No. But all she wanted to know," I told him, "was whether I was getting married. I died a little, and then I learned symbolically I'd died and been reincarnated as a dog. I could say it was depressing, and I am."

"Listen, poo-poo. It's normal. She is different generation, and it's not first world country. I go home, and grandma makes me food, then asks when I am getting married and she gets grandkids. That's it. What to do?"

He wasn't half-wrong. My eomma had asked me a peremptory question and extended a peremptory hope: marriage. It was not personal—personally hers or personally mine. It belonged more to the long social atmosphere, but I agitated my own bouncing heels anyway. I thought about cigarettes. I thought about not smoking cigarettes. I said, "Actually, Korea *is* a first world country. And I was fine until she said she doesn't want me to feel alone. Only then I lost it."

"Are you afraid you will be alone?" N said.

"Not really."

"I would marry you," N said. "It's actually very practical. Then there are two incomes and you have each other when you're fat, old, taking two-hours shits, and your children only see you every five years."

Out the window of Wonyi's apartment: residential buildings like children's blocks, an actual child, a father chasing. There was fog again, gray again. My eomma would return that night, and if the desire to take a walk outside could kill, I'd be buried. I wanted to get somewhere, and fast. I wanted to run.

"Right, insurance on rides to doctor's appointments."

"But it's true. You get sick. Someone is there."

"Didn't you say your retirement plan was to desert your family for a monastery where you could suffocate in your own farts and never look in the mirror?"

"Well, pa dobro."

"Pa dobro," I said, "indeed." But I couldn't get the chill off my shoulders. It had been days since the sun had hit my face, and soon the call ended courtesy of a fight about, of all things, the sensible date for N to commence a coding boot camp.

I was cold, too, that evening, when Phillip called Wonyi's from Washington to tell my eomma that the Song Obstetric Clinic records in my possession declared I'd been born by induction, and when my eomma insisted, pointing backward at me, "She was dead! She was dead! She was dead!"

TRACY
O'NEILL

So I was the prodigal daughter but also risen. The prodigal daughter continued to close herself off in her borrowed bedroom once Cho Kyu Yeon returned to Seoul. The risen one considered the vacant warehouse behind that woman's eyes and suspected they expressed damage. The prodigal daughter was debriefed by the half-exiled uncle, Phillip.

**Phillip:** Tracy, Inwahn wants me to tell you what she has heard from your mom.

**Phillip:** I will just translate what she wrote to me.

**Phillip:** Yesterday, I interviewed my mother . . .

At that time, the birth mother wanted to have a child born and raised with her, but the biological father and his wife were against it, and it was the aunt who played a role in the adoption process. Your bio-father couldn't refuse to Young Mok's suggestion due to his situation.

Though your mom wanted to keep you in 10 months, she had no choice but to go through induced delivery in 8 months due to forceful environment at that time. Your mom thought that the child could have died from earlier delivery before due date, but she was told she delivered a baby girl from your father.

The prodigal daughter was under the impression pregnancies ran nine months. The risen one recalled Korean age counting began at one, not zero. Eight months equaled labor at seven months. The prodigal daughter was sick of personal history, wanted to hop a ride anywhere else, but she took the call from the uncle anyway.

The uncle had heard more, namely that Cho Kyu Yeon had done her best to get pregnant, on the weak supposition that a baby would impel Kim In Kee to leave his family. He didn't. She had lent him roughly $650,000 and come up empty-handed. The abortion had been the condition of Kim In Kee's wife for the repayment of around $35,000 Cho Kyu Yeon had borrowed from Young Mok to lend her lover, but Kim In Kee's wife was not uncompromising. Since no doctor could be found to abort a seven-month fetus, they could split the difference. The negotiation landed on inducing a two-month premature birth which, given the likelihood of complications, might accommodate the baby's early death anyway. Inwahn, the uncle said, believed Young Mok to suffer from Ripley syndrome, a form of antisocial personality disorder named after the murderous Patricia Highsmith character Tom Ripley.

And though Phillip was excited by the prospect of Ripley syndrome, the prodigal daughter, because she could not help but keep her nose on language, asked, "In Inwahn's letter, what does 'forceful environment' mean?"

"Forceful environment," went the explanation, meant Kim In Kee had tried an old folk medicine remedy: kicking the fetus in Cho Kyu Yeon's abdomen.

"But then you lived. And your mom and aunt think, 'Okay, wow, this is strong baby,'" the uncle said. "'This baby wants to live.'"

Risen daughter, indeed.

———

At Wonyi's apartment, I mostly stopped eating. My instructions from Wonyi were to help myself to my eomma's food on the counter, and though much of the world ate days-old un-refrigerated meat, indeed would consider unfettered access to sitting trays of beautiful pork and beef a windfall, I was afraid it was turning. My throat pulsed at the scent of my mother's food's real or imagined spoil. I predicted I'd need N's elaborate fecal hygiene should I eat my mother's food, and alas, the Korean convention was to dry off after bathing with hand towels. Maybe an analyst would have asked what exactly it was I couldn't swallow.

As a result of my own princessy abstinence, days fell dizzily into each other. Conversations collided, and I didn't know what I did between them anymore. I numbed out in the lightheaded periods between talk. I showered and trembled as I patted myself with small towels. That vertiginous wobble was real, but it was real, too, that sense had been made.

For instance, I understood now why Wonyi had suspected I got cold easily. "Temperature control problems" were one long-term complication of preterm birth, and mine was considered a "very preterm birth." According to the Mayo Clinic, other complications included breathing problems, heart problems, brain problems, digestive problems, blood problems, metabolism problems, immune system problems, cerebral palsy, trouble learning, vision problems, hearing problems, dental problems, behavior and mental health problems, and "ongoing health issues," though there was also a higher risk of sudden infant death syndrome. The latter, of course, had been banked on.

I understood, too, Young Mok crying as she held her own plump wrist to mine. It was credible that labor had been induced two months early because, of course, she'd been weeping over the disparity between our bodies, over evidence of what would be done for $35,000. Or maybe what would be done for a man whose only help was an unsuccessful bid to beat a fetus loose.

It was all so logical. There was so much sense. But what was the use of sense? What did this clarity offer, with many days in Korea remaining? I did not know how many more times I could hear the story of my birth iterate. I was sick of the beginning of myself. It seemed I'd been quarantined in that apartment for months, and I was dying for world, any of it.

World, as it happened, was not dying for anyone to be in it, though. Omicron was on a tear, and one day, Justin sent a message. There'd been an announcement; the residency in New Hampshire where we were meant to teach when I returned had been canceled.

**Me:** I thought we all agreed we were down to die in the snow, happy

**Justin:** I know I'm so bummed out.

**Me:** Are you still coming to the city?

**Justin:** Haven't canceled my ticket yet but I guess I probably won't come. Everyone there right now seems terrified and is self quarantining.

**Me:** Are we heading into Our Winter of Discontent Pt. 2?

**Justin:** Yes

**Justin:** It's gonna get worse and worse until about Jan 15 I think

**Me:** What happens Jan 15?

**Justin:** Everyone who got infected over Xmas will be sick.

And so the sudden fear: I could end up stuck in Korea.

The voice in my own mind had split off. Exactly one part of myself was the naïf; the other was resigned to the thought that investigation was futile and was compelled to continue anyway. I watched conventional Hollywood pictures like *Se7en*, in which inevitably the two detectives had it out over the use of investigation.

                    SOMERSET
        You meant what you said . . . about catching
           this guy. You really want to believe that,
                        don't you?


                     MILLS
                 And you don't?


                    SOMERSET
                (laughs, very tired)
           I wish I still thought like you.


                     MILLS
        Then, you tell me what you think we're doing.


                    SOMERSET
           All we do is pick up the pieces. We take
           all the evidence, and all the pictures and
           samples. We write everything down and note
                what time things happened . . .


                     MILLS
                 Oh, that's all.

> SOMERSET
>
> We put it in a nice neat pile and file
> it away, on the slim chance it's ever
> needed in a courtroom.
>
> (pause)
>
> It's like collecting diamonds on a desert
> island. You keep them just in case you ever get
> rescued, but it's a pretty big ocean out there.

But there was no rescue in this case. My eomma's narrative was an ocean. I wasn't going to escape from it, no matter how many of my questions prompted Wonyi to stab the air or how many versions of equivocation I collected. I could wave papers, say I had papers, and what would I do with my neat pile? Nothing. It was time to forget the beginning of my life.

In the wakeful silent night, I practiced Korean. Eopsseoyo: There isn't / I don't have. Bogo sip-eoyo: I want to see you / I miss you. Ige mwoyeyo: What is it?

———

Cho Kyu Yeon wanted a word. Phillip wanted to ferry those words. A time was set, and I went to Wonyi's son's room, where the internet signal shot out, full dignity. Phillip's face filled the Zoom window, but Cho Kyu Yeon hadn't gotten a handle on Zoom and was, as a result, a black box. That talking black box spoke to Phillip. He spoke to me.

From that degree of remove, the talking black box insisted that once Cho Kyu Yeon and Kim In Kee had been in love. He told her he loved her. He did. His love came out of his mouth, and an assurance he'd leave his family to marry her. The problem with thoughts, though, was that they didn't stop. Second ones followed. Kim In Kee had two daughters and a wife. They held weight, if not enough to end the affair. By the time those second thoughts manifested, though, Cho Kyu Yeon had already dropped her husband for the man who met her secretly in fields of ginseng.

She knew what she needed to do. She got pregnant. In the small town of Muju, it didn't take much for Kim In Kee's brothers to hear who was with whose child, for the wife to. Cho Kyu Yeon had been lenient on my father's debts out of love, though she claimed, too, she did not normally have people beaten to persuade repayment. This left the balance at Cho Kyu Yeon: divorced, with child, and near destitute after lending Kim In Kee nearly everything she had—as well as Young Mok's money. Eating was not an assured daily activity.

"After you were delivered and sent to the orphanage, even though that thing happened, your dad didn't leave your mom yet. He was comforting your mom. He didn't leave right away. He was next to your mom," Phillip said for her.

Phillip said, "She doesn't know exactly how long, but your dad stayed with your mom."

Phillip added, "Tracy, your mom is saying after you're sent to the orphanage, he was next to her. And then she waited, and circumstances didn't work out for them to stay together, so she had to leave the town."

A narrative was forming. Perhaps Kim In Kee had loved my mother. Perhaps he hadn't. Perhaps he'd made promises. Perhaps he hadn't, and had watched Cho Kyu Yeon run out of town into starvation. But the story didn't ride on him, really.

The story was that *she* fixed to particular details. The story was that Cho Kyu Yeon, decades later, still insisted that a man had stayed with her who'd never really been with her. She'd licked crumbs off the floor for love and years later wanted a witness to that love having meant something.

"She felt some kind of absence after the relationship was completely over, but somehow, at the same time she felt some type of anger because it didn't work. . . . She did her part and then your dad didn't do his part," Phillip said.

My eomma was just a stranger in a black box. I was aware of that. And I'd heard some stories, seen some things. I'd seen a man burned so bad his lips had melted off, the pope, a scared man beat a scared animal. A family friend cleaned up off smack, then died of HIV complications when her daughter was six or seven. My friend's husband left her and their son shortly after emptying the bank account to buy the mistress a pet shop. People said, "Fag, no offense." I'd seen a father say to a little girl that if she didn't stop crying from pain, he'd pull down her underpants and hit her harder. I'd seen a mother wail, "Stop it." Locals poorly tipped bartenders with whom they flirted. An unhoused man on the train told me that if I took him home, he'd make love to me and sew for me. I'd seen a small child say to his mother, "Girl, I've had enough of your bullshit." A friend's father killed her mother. Another friend's father killed his mother, and in a dispute over money, his roommate tore the sole remaining picture of that mother up. I knew a woman who never allowed her child to attend a sleepover because of what her own family had done to her at night.

But for some reason, it still wrecked every wised-up surface of me to hear that my eomma had wanted love to be fair and like a child believed it would be, that she starved for it, while all signs pointed to a good fleecing. She had thrown every bit of herself at Kim In Kee, perhaps because a pinhole aperture opened and she thought that rough-and-ready fling led to the ineffable. Perhaps she'd gotten into a love where there was no way out, or maybe she, wild-eyed, got caught up in an unnameable current that declared none of the low bits of her biography mattered much anymore; she could go fugitive from her history as long as she wanted enough to, and all that mattered for the four crazed years leading up to a procedure at the Song Obstetric Clinic was the sweet-talking majesty of going the whole nine yards and two inches past earth to begin again.

After that, she'd had to begin again once more.

Cho Kyu Yeon never fell in love again after Kim In Kee. There were other concerns. To eat, Phillip said, she eventually married a man who turned out to be "helpless financially." She gave birth to her son Hyeong Min, then separated from the father, and without him, she, in a fashion unspecified, became not helpless financially. She declared she now had five to six million dollars.

"Five to six million. She has five to six million! Wow! That's a lot of money in Korea," Phillip said.

I supposed I was meant to be impressed, and I had no idea what I was supposed to say about her account balance.

"She has gathered five to six million!"

Phillip, it seemed, viewed this as a happy ending. But I was stuck on Cho Kyu Yeon's repetitions: he stayed with her, he was next to her, he didn't leave right away. I thought only someone very lonely would three decades later still insist upon these distinctions.

"She told me she doesn't want me to feel alone. Tell her I don't want her to feel alone either," I said.

"Your mom says, 'Don't worry about me. I'm okay,'" Phillip said. "Your mom's current worry point is you found out a lot of different things this time, so she's worrying about when you return to America. She's worrying you would never come back."

Now, Phillip began crying and flapping his hands at himself. I looked at what appeared to be a finished basement, this windowless room in his home. I'd no idea what my eomma was doing. I had flown around the world to see a black box insist upon a story. She had plowed herself straight into abashing, incomplete love; was conniving, pathetic, and a crooked liar who didn't see the liabilities of a discount eye job; and like anyone, she wanted to announce her life had, in moments, meant more than anyone guessed.

I supposed Cho Kyu Yeon was familiar with the view in which he was a bad guy and she was a fool. She understood what she looked like: desperate, esurient, careless. And she could be. She understood what he looked like: abuser, cheat, adulterer. He could be. And they were other than that, too. She wanted this remembered.

Because their stolen moments snatched at life askance of prescribed obligations—even as she admitted she was angry that he'd done her dirty. There was no justice in this love, but astray was the place where life livened, lost the script, where she could be more than a failed representative of respectable womanhood as she recklessly grabbed at whatever she could. No one understood the huge, insubordinate good of ephemera. No one understood a woman unwilling to surrender to subsistence on beaten-down desire. In her ploys for more, Kim In Kee was a double-crossing accomplice. But he was *her* accomplice.

And because she had let me know the story she needed, I could imagine that in a few days, once my quarantine ended, I would go to Seoul and know her more. I would be a part of her life, as she'd asked. I could believe this. I could believe it because she had not yet advised, for instance, that I "forget little by little" Kim In Kee in a way that made me question what she had to hide about his death.

Before I knew it, I had assured my eomma that I would not abandon her. I thought I meant it at the time. Maybe Kim In Kee had, too.

# CHAPTER FOURTEEN

# LAST STAND AT DAEJEON

Neither Here nor There, December 2021

The last days in Daejeon arrived as more or less disconnected conversations and images. One morning, I sent Ali a text message: Today PCR, tomorrow my mother comes. Didion is dead. I'm going to see where my father lived and have practiced asking my mother if she likes coffee, vegetables, and books. We read Didion at each other for a while on the phone. Then I reread the beginning of *Salvador* by myself.

From N came a photograph of Cowboy flopped sideways with sleep on the couch, message: We partied hard last night. My boy is hangover. So I sent a photograph back of Choco and Cookie: If I steal my cousin's dogs the first time I'm meeting her, do you think I'll still be allowed in this family?

**N:** You wont be

**N:** That would be your death sentence

**N:** Speaking of blood, Merry Christmas.

It wasn't yet Christmas.

Merry Christmas, I replied anyway. Don't work too hard today (for Jesus.)

**N:** Ok if it's for Jesus I won't

And though it wasn't yet Christmas, Treska had a gift of sorts to send, too, an article: "When Breast Implants Drop & Fluff: Phoenix Surgeon Explains," describing the process by which breast implants settled.

**Treska:** This is happening to my boobs! Weird and good!

**Me:** Drop n fluff!

**Me:** It's like how you gotta snap the pillow case when it comes out of the dryer

**Me:** How a casserole needs to settle before you cut it

**Me:** Etc etc

**Treska:** My boobs are asserting themselves!

**Treska:** "Like a casserole." It's perfect.

It was. It was perfect to talk to these people. Shots of outside—better, shots outside myself. When I wanted world for a crunched-down quarantine eternity, they slipped me what they could.

And on the last afternoon in Daejeon, after another PCR, Wonyi began to laugh.

Hahahahahaha, Google Translate said.

Google Translate said, as she did, Stop it hahahahaha stop it stop it.

This was perfect, too.

I didn't trust her on the matter of Cho Kyu Yeon, but in every other way I wished Wonyi and I had more time together, or that we'd had it before. I hadn't gotten handle enough on the linguistic apparatus to tell her that I regretted I hadn't known her when she was a young woman, a new parent, that I hadn't snuck cigarettes while minding her children. So there was cooking shrimp for her, and there was, as I held up taffy-sized cylinders of foil-wrapped butter, shouting, "More beoteo!" There was—when, in wide-eyed alarm, she asked, "More?"—calling out, "More! More! All of it!"

It was Christmas Eve. Designs happened without my hands. Contrary to what I'd told Ali, someone had decided that when my quarantine was over the next day, I would hitch a ride to Seoul with my sister Inwahn. Though Inwahn and I had said scarcely a few words to each other, there would be the long ride, lunch, and sun again, too. I would see my eomma's life outside language, outside representation of the past. It would be a fresh start. And I imagined that when the next day I stepped outside, the air would pour down my throat, cool and bright as just-popped seltzer.

"More," I said. "More. All of it."

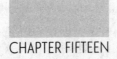

CHAPTER FIFTEEN

# THIS MIGHT BE A ROAD TRIP

Daejeon→Muju→Geumsan→Hanam, Christmas 2021

My entire impression of Inwahn prior to that day was that she favored camel-colored clothes and that she slinked. One day the week before, she had come to Wonyi's, and, in Jeesu's room, I'd not even known she had arrived until she left; perhaps she'd wanted it that way. On occasion, in the family KakaoTalk thread, she'd gone silent only to type suddenly: ㅋㅋㅋㅋ, the Korean way to indicate something was ridiculous, and she hadn't been wrong. Inwahn was more composed than Wonyi, quieter, but we had the translation app, and we could go without it if we kept talk simple. We made it a few miles on her weekend activities (the spa), her children (two), and which music she preferred (yes).

Now, she'd pulled off the highway. I followed her gaze up a small hill surrounded by bushes to a pale brick building, decorated with candy pink squares, a translucent blue cylinder that ran up one tall spine containing small round balconies. Two stars had been etched on one wall, as though someone had begun a pattern and tired of it. Black tangles of flora surrounded the place, and the structure towered, leaning. The palette was eighties. The material was, I guessed, cement. It looked like a child's toy, a child's toy abandoned at the scene of a crime, but a child's toy nonetheless.

"Your father's hotel," Inwahn said.

"I didn't know he owned a hotel," I said.

"He had the ginseng business," Inwahn said through Naver Papago. "At first, he didn't have so much money, but then he was rich. He bought this place but with a few other businessman. Now it is closed."

Inwahn was clutching herself and squinting due to the temperature. Only for a moment did I wonder whether she had fabricated this story. Only for a moment did it occur to me that she could bring me to any derelict pile of bricks, say it had belonged to Kim In Kee, and I wouldn't be the wiser. But belief would cost me nothing, and if I did believe, this day could mean something.

In the offense of subzero wind, I looked at the building, and the experience passed through me without a trace of scent. Had I lived another life, this building might have meant something to me, but instead I'd become someone who'd stood on the stairs of my childhood home wishing to lose it faster. Maybe I would not be someone who wanted always to lose faster, in that alternative life. Maybe the quality was essential, and I couldn't be trusted to say what of me inhered. It wasn't as though I'd cultivated any proprioceptive expertise to radar out which elements of myself preceded experience, other than a clawing animal instinct uncowed by my appa's lowlife kick.

Now the air bit our faces, my sister's and mine, as we loitered, gawking concrete. I lifted my phone to snap a picture, as though the hotel would become memorable for having been remembered. Now, perhaps it would touch me. A tautologist's boob optimism. I'd told my friends, "Of course I've got to see a picture of my putatively hot dad," and this would be the closest I'd come.

"Okay," I said.

"Okay," Inwahn said.

"Ready when you are."

———

Outside the car, it was all blue sky, pom-pom trees, and clean-as-a-whistle everything. Behind it all, the bumpy green of mountain spread. We passed short building after short building. The radio wasn't on, but the length of the town would have topped out at less than a single song.

"Now we go to Geumsan," Inwahn said. "Where your mother born."

We passed S Oil. We passed a gorgeous white Hyundai pickup with a chubby cabin and wall-eyed headlights. A garland of flags lifted and rolled on air. A sign said: 오구쌀. A sign said: 핑크. A sign said: 테마, and I quit efforts to read Hangul at fifteen kilometers an hour. Crossing a bridge decorated with yellow flowers yanked the other side of my appa's hotel into view. From this angle, it seemed to sit, rather than tower. We were gliding far up off water, far up off the brambled hill on which it leaned.

"You met my appa," I said to Inwahn. "Was he quiet?"

"No, your dad is sociable."

Inwahn did not look like our eomma. I didn't either. Cosmetic surgery supplied an obvious answer to that divergence, but there was something else. I could not imagine Cho Kyu Yeon considering things. Inwahn, it seemed, considered. She was couth.

"Why does my sister ask is dad quiet?"

"Because eomma told me he was quiet, but documents from Eastern Social Welfare Society said he had an 'outgoing personality,'" I said to Google Translate, and Google Translate translated.

"No, he is sociable," Inwahn said. "He could be quiet. But he likes party. Not party. But have some drink and talk to people."

"That," I said, "sounds suspiciously like a party. You can trust me with the password to the speakeasy."

"Tracy?"

"I'm just being not quite funny. I wish I could be funny in Korean with you."

"Why?"

"To make you laugh. To make me laugh. To have some drinks and talk to people like a sociable person."

The momentum broke. "You think you are like your dad?" Inwahn said finally.

"There are obvious differences. For one, I'm not dead. Two, I'd never do business with our eomma, let alone the rest."

"Wonyi says you want a picture of your dad."

"Ne, do you know where I can find one?"

"No, but your father died ten years ago."

If I'd come eleven years ago—but eleven years ago, I wouldn't have been able to afford a plane ticket to Korea.

"My sister likes to laugh?" Inwahn said.

"Of course," I said. "But once, I didn't laugh for almost an entire year."

"Why?"

"Last year," I said. "The pandemic. The only times I laughed were when my friend Maggie came to visit, when I spoke to my friend Ali on the phone, and then when I talked to a detective who said my face was an inconvenient quality. I wanted him to find eomma."

"And you did find her," Inwahn said. "Now what do you think about your mom?"

"She lies a lot, but she doesn't lie well."

"Okay, ne."

"I debate whether she just threw herself down like a rug or if it was a gambit gone wrong."

"I don't understand," Inwahn said.

"She gave up almost everything for my appa. I know that. But I can't tell if she was pathetic and not taking the hint," I said to Google Translate, "or if they were both con artists, but he was a better con artist. He knew she loved him, so he made promises he never intended to keep, then pressed his advantage."

Although Inwahn's face stilled, the car moved, as did an intelligence behind her eyes. She concentrated, but she did not squint.

"The second one you are right. I think my sister is smart."

"Not so smart," I said. "I'm just familiar with going all in on a losing hand. What is In Hyeong like?"

"In Hyeong."

"Yes, the older brother. We didn't speak much when I arrived. But you grew up together."

"In Hyeong," she said like a question. "In Hyeong." Her quick hand plucked up her phone to open Naver Papago again. "In Hyeong is a very introverted, quiet personality," it said. It said, "He can also be angry. When he is a teenager, he is a runaway."

"He was angry with eomma."

"Sometimes, he is angry," Inwahn said. "Sometimes he is scary."

"Scary?" I said. "Or scared?"

"Sometimes he is violent."

"Scary," I said.

And, God help me, I wasn't afraid. I thrilled to hear all this ugliness, presuming the ugliness meant Inwahn was not lying to me.

―――――

We kept on our path parallel to the guardrails, and the glare went increscent against expanded blue. The piled-together buildings had made way, and streaming through thrown-open space, I caught the visual half-rhyme of American farm towns. To my right: green mountains and, below them, stretches of plastic bubbles. To the left: hip-roofed shacks and then rows of gold things buttressed by spare wood railings.

"Ige mwoyeyo?" I said—What is this?

"The ginseng field," she said.

We parked. We crossed the street. Up close I saw that it was not plastic bubbles I'd seen but steely mesh veils protecting the crop. Turning back toward the side of the street with the press of houses, we passed a shack's lean-to where dried flowers and pots hung over a mess of plant pots and hoses, and that was all it took to get winding through the village. It was hardly more than a cluster of twelve, fifteen short homes. My eomma wore rhinestone sweaters now, but someone in the market for a rhinestone would be disappointed here. Inwahn swung an ornate gate.

"This one," she said.

It was brick on one side, cement on another where paint peeled off, butter yellow. A stuffed armchair and couch had been left out in the dry, miniature yard under a tin-roofed lean-to. The clothesline was still up, a single hanger swinging in the breeze like a just-struck, silent musical triangle. Inwahn turned through a door, no key at all.

"They leave the door unlocked?" I said. But there was no they. No one lived here anymore.

We moved through a sliding glass door. A microwave had been left, some cups, hand sanitizer, a space heater. In one white room, there was still a black couch and a chair, floral pillows. I saw a column of leaf wallpaper. I glanced, in a mirror, another dusty wallpaper of giant pink flowers. The ceiling hung low in that small three-room house, and I could not conceive of eight children in it.

By degrees these piles of brick and dusty lodgings betrayed my eomma's biography more than any inquiry face-to-squirrely-face. Seeing this place, an itinerary clarified. Marriage had been my eomma's ticket from village to small town. Disgrace had been her ticket from small town to small city. And whatever she'd done to become a millionaire, whether or not it involved the Bridge of Death, it *had* bridged the gap between the small city of Daejeon and the big city, Seoul. In this home, I could see the beginning of her tour of striving.

At the age of seventy-two, my eomma had never traveled outside Korea. Now, hers was a Korea that included 4B, the Korean feminist movement. These activists had agitated around the call to bihon, the refusal of marriage, and bichulsan, the refusal of childbirth. They'd protested their own second-class citizenship and the tepid punishment of femicides, of which one report stated that

31 percent from the past five years had been "brutal," begging the question what precisely about the other 69 percent of those murders was *not* brutal. The answer was that "brutal" looked something like the man who stabbed, 145 times, the woman who tried to leave him. The women of 4B took to the streets. They staked out their demands and shouted what was intolerable. The activists weren't afraid to spit at convention; in their view, there was more to fear in the everyday prescriptions of womanhood.

But there had been no 4B when my eomma was a girl or a mother of two in Muju, no 4B when she was a mother of three living off the good graces of a friend in Daejeon. Korean inheritance law was not reformed to provide for the equal distribution of family estates to descendants, regardless of gender, until 1991. The fact was, even recently, Korea had been ranked 127th of 153 countries in terms of equal economic participation between genders, and the Korean Ministry of the Interior publicized a birth rate map, displaying the number of childbearing women by district. The point: identify regions in which women shirked their civic responsibility to breed.

Still, the Korea I'd begun to know was far more beautiful than the most prominent impression of it I'd received as a child. My mother's brother Paul had fought in Vietnam, and never having forgotten his time in the Pacific, wished to educate me on "Oriental" customs when I was three or four. He'd confided, "In *your* country, people pick their nose and eat it," demanded I do it, then told the family to check out this sick little nose-picker.

According to my mother, this was his sense of humor. It *was* his sense of humor, and so when I was older I held my breath when Paul addressed my brother. I didn't have it in me to see my brother shamed for his body more.

"On holidays, it's Paul or me," I told my mother after one Thanksgiving dinner when I was in my twenties.

"I don't care if he's your family," I said. "We chose you every day of our American lives."

And then, though it was pathetic to beg for love, "Choose us."

In the moment, there had been profuse demonstrations of my mother's misery, but I forgot such moments for weeks at a time, for years even. Paul got holidays I relinquished and vice versa. I went on to forget whether my own felonious rage had to do with war or Boston lineage, Chrysler-high expectations of mothers, or something else. There were other fights to pick. There were novels to work out. Groceries got urgent again. The day-to-day trash haul. Press of words. A friend from Massachusetts and I discussed the corny prevalence of novels in which fictional male writers' morose cunnilingual gestures replicated the alphabet. In our impression of residents of the town of Revere, Massachusetts, the line levied at liberals was: "Go back to BU, you fucks." That sort of thing.

"What does my sister thinking?" Inwahn said.

"It's a house," I said, stupidly.

She said, "Are you hungry?"

———

We passed a three-story gold statue of a humanoid ginseng holding the hand of his ginseng child. We passed a sign displaying a man in a high-flying Taekwondo kick. We did not pass any cars because Inwahn was a careful driver.

"What do writers do?" Inwahn asked, eyes on the road.

"Oh, you know, drink too much, talk too much, think too much. We think too much of ourselves or too little, and as a result self-pity too much. Then sometimes, on a wing and a prayer, we write."

"Say again."

"Sometimes writers drink too much. Also they write, even though it's a questionable bet."

"Question? Of? A? Bet?"

"Questionable bet," I said to Google Translate, and Google Translate translated. "Act of faith."

Then: "You have to be a little delusional. I'm a little delusional. Every book, you hope to mean something more than yourself, though you know you'll fail. But you follow all the clues in yourself to a better story, every experience and thought you've ever had as though they'll become more than the sum of the parts, and you have to believe the book that doesn't exist yet is a crime against all the dreary stories that already happened. It's just a matter of solving how the crime went down. Does that make sense?"

"Arasso," she said—I understand—and maybe she did understand a certain pitch of voice or a walnut-ish forehead in concentration. "My sister enjoys to drink?"

"Sometimes."

"Sometime I drink the beer so I can sleep. Do you sleep bad?"

"I don't sleep. I dance horizontally in the dark."

"Again."

"No. I move too much."

"You don't sleep well. Maybe this is the family gene."

"Okay, sure."

"My sister thought my mother drinks whiskey. Why?"

I said, "I do."

She thought it was funny that I'd brought Cho Kyu Yeon whiskey from America, but she did not, as Je Ryong and Wonyi had, tell me it was a man's beverage, not an appropriate gift for a mother.

"Do you want to drink whiskey with me someday?" she asked.

"Ne."

"I would like to drink whiskey with my sister someday," she said.

"You trying to get me drunk, eonni?" I said, invoking the word for older sister.

"Drunk?" she said, a little shocked.

"Yeah, I'm talking to you, and I think you're trying to get me drunk. You want me to spill all my tawdry secrets," I said. Then, "I'm teasing."

She could smile a little at that. She did. "Drunk? No. But I would like drink whiskey with you."

"Is that what occupational therapists like to do?"

"I don't think so."

"Why did you want to do that anyway?" I said. "Occupational therapy."

"I did not want."

"So what happened?"

"I went to school, and my dad want me to do the job."

"You wanted him to be happy," I said.

"Yes."

"I bet you're good at it, though," I said.

"Why?"

"You have perfect posture," I said. "And you're kind."

"No."

"It's true," I said. "You could teach me not to hold my body like a T. rex when I write. See?" With that, I curled my shoulders and drew my arms to my chest, paddling my hands to type chimerical keys.

"You don't look like."

"That proves it. You're kind."

"Usually, I am boring," she said.

"You aren't boring."

"My life," she said. "My life is boring, but now my sister is here. I'm exciting. Excited. I am happy Tracy comes to Korea."

Outside the car window, highway receded. Inwahn was beautiful beside me, copper-bobbed and glowing in a long dark coat. The fur lining of her hood bopped a little with the heater's blow. It had not previous to the moment occurred to me to desire a sisterly drive, but now as she pulled off the long stretch of road, it hit me: I wished for nothing more than that we remain on the road together, no destination in sight.

———

There was a destination in sight. We got there. Our eomma lived in a three-bedroom, luxury high-rise building in Hanam, a city adjacent to Seoul proper that many considered part of Seoul nonetheless.

On arrival, walking—or was it creeping, for whatever reason?—through the apartment, I saw two dark bedrooms remained completely empty. This was no mere matter of minimalist aesthetics. There was nothing in those two rooms at all. Not a chair. Not a desk.

Even my eomma's room had been furnished only with a twin mattress on the floor, a single pillow, and a basket of mysterious blackened sticks in the corner. This would be my room temporarily. Another borrowed bedroom.

For an instant, a bizarre notion: Cho Kyu Yeon did not live here at all.

Keep going. Walk normally. In the bathroom, I found a squeezed-down tube of putrid, puce toothpaste, which the label identified as ocean-flavored. Unscrewing the cap, I inspected a moist worm of it, and I didn't know why, but I was afraid.

———

The next morning, Inwahn was to leave. Before taking off, she removed a gold necklace from her throat, then strung it on me. She'd already given me her own compact of powdered sunscreen after I observed she didn't look a wink sleepless for someone who'd slept on the floor and relied on the soporific property of Cass Fresh Beer.

"For Tracy," she said.

"You don't have to give me anything," I said.

"I want," she said. "You are my little sister. I love you."

Our eomma was shouting, "Yu Min! Yu Min!" in pursuit of her toy labradoodle. The objective was to work the leash clasp on the collar tucked under his Supreme sweatshirt, but he'd clocked an opportunity to play hard to get. Eomma chased him around the living room, bent and reaching, ape-like. "Yu Min!" The name that nearly got away.

I guessed Inwahn was waiting for Cho Kyu Yeon to do full farewells. The pinch of impotent wish was on me. I didn't want her to go yet. By the door, Inwahn gathered her bag. My sister was looking carefully at me, and I was thinking of the tube of lurid toothpaste in the bathroom.

A stoic's glance off the perch of my sister's long neck. I watched her watch our eomma piddle after Yu Min. She'd now worn the

NISSY NISSY HEARTTHROB sweater four out of four days I'd seen her. I held my sister's necklace similarly to how I'd been taught to hold the rosary to beseech the Virgin Mary as a child. Inwahn had her long, dark parka on already. She had sons to return home to, a husband. I clicked open and closed the half-used compact. I wanted to say, *Don't leave.*

"Keep the necklace," Inwahn said. "Then you remember me."

"Please," I began. Then I stopped because my throat had closed.

"Ne," she said.

"Eonni," I tried again—sister.

"Ne," she said.

"Joesonghamnida, joesonghamnida," I said—I'm sorry, I'm sorry. But that wasn't what I meant. I may as well have said, "Koepi, mul, keompyuteo."

Look down. The cartoonish girl painted on the compact appeared in a thrall of her own hair, marble-eyed and coquettish. Cho Kyu Yeon had finally gotten Yu Min leashed up, and now she cradled his squirming body like a baby. My canine near-namesake had taken a few small, hard dumps by his bowl. To tease me, I recalled, Maggie had sent a text message declaring that Yu Min's hoodie and irregular peeing tracked with that of his human counterpart, which in her own way conveyed that she hoped I'd not experience my eomma's cathexis as an indignity. Now, I wanted to say something to Inwahn in her own language. I wanted to speak in the codes in which my sister daydreamed and lied to herself as anyone did, the one in which it was a given that our eomma's name, 규연, began *Gun*, and the fancy to drink whiskey flipped on, and things registered as funny.

"Drive safe, eonni," I said. The bit: steering hands for *drive*, crossed arms—*safe*.

TRACY
O'NEILL

"Okay," she said. "Gamnahamsida."

And I didn't know how to conjugate future tense, but in fact, it didn't matter.

"Bogo sip-eoyo," I said—I want to see you, I miss you.

Then, when she was gone, I asked our eomma: "Where do you put the dog shit?"

# CHAPTER SIXTEEN
# THE HOUSE THAT EOMMA BUILT

Hanam→Seoul→Hanam, December 2021

I did not make good on my promise not to abandon Cho Kyu Yeon. I—who had booked a mere twenty-two days of my entire life to spend in the country of the woman who gave birth to me, of which only thirteen would involve her presence—ultimately decided I'd overbooked my stay by five days. I did this even though I wanted my promises to be more than promising. I did this after everything.

That early departure could be chalked up to a series of events, but the truth is I can be a leaver. I left. Go back far enough in the long habit of myself, and though I do not know my first word, my first steps were (1) out of a room and (2) occasioned by my father whooping, "Shit!" over a Patriots play gone wrong. I mean that my first walk was walking away.

What I remember now of my last days in Hanam is a near-premonition. I can see how in a strictly mental sense I first began walking away from Cho Kyu Yeon after Inwahn left. Verbatim isn't the way of memory, but more than any animal, vegetable, or mineral, what I trust of my recall is this: the moment my sister departed, my eomma's apartment rushed with emptiness, and the air had the quality of a starved-down stomach. In that new, abrupt reality, the place was an awful sky-high basement gaping around the soul of a dog, a senior citizen with a taste for street-wear, and a sleep-short husk.

I recall that I paced to do something. I inspected the squat table, the toothpaste, the rice cooker. I looked again at the single pillow on my eomma's friendless mattress. Stand close enough to the doorways to the vacant rooms, and a two-inch bar of cold could be felt off cracks to the unheated space. This was a lonely home for a lonely woman.

In theory, I ought to have been thrilled. I had wanted so much to know this missing woman, and now I could see where she slept and gutted fish, where she dressed her little dog. But you could be suffocated by the comfort-ciphered air, and the whole place spooked me.

That peculiar atmosphere challenged fathom at the time. The first night in Hanam, my aunts Young Mok, Mee Jeong, and Kyu Ok had come for dinner. For a while, the place had been full of women, full of chatter. I'd not slept a full night in at least two weeks, and everything was strange and soft as dreaming, and in an ambience of impossible déjà vu, my eomma cooked. Her sisters touched my hair as my phone spat text:

She has the father's hair.
It isn't from the mother.

It is complete him.

Yes, that is from the father, the hair.

The father's hair. She has from her father.

In these sounds, I entered a sphere of givenness. My hair was a given, given. Their remarks were a given, given. Father, hair—these near-mantras didn't extend farther. They were simple and res ipsa loquitur as natural instinct.

Isn't it the father's hair?

Certain from the father.

I see the hair belongs to the father.

Now I think it was because she sensed everything did not quite belong together, though, that my eomma gave me a papery drawstring LG bag. It was the sort that usually comes complimentary with a cell phone purchase. I presumed it to contain slipper socks like those Young Mok had dragged me into. These, after all, were Cho preoccupations: warm feet, cold bodies. But the contents were not footwear. Instead: one million Korean won, roughly eight thousand American dollars.

And I thought: Your mom—I need to say this.

Thought: Financially, if you are trying to be deceived by your mom, then talk to Wonyi first.

But Wonyi wasn't in Seoul. I was. What did Cho Kyu Yeon want from me? was the first question. It was also the last question.

"I don't want a dime," I said to Google Translate, and Google Translate translated. "Why are you giving me this? What do you want?"

"I want to give my daughter something," Google Translate said for my eomma. "It's a million won. Count it!"

My ears were ringing. Her eyes were somehow flat but euphoric. Time went large and jiggling as psilocybin, swift as uppers, and two parallel tracks had opened in my mind:

*If you are trying to be deceived by your mom.*
*Your mother hurt a lot of people.*
*Everyone likes their mom.*
*Is she a con artist?*

*You said you would not leave her.*
*Begin again.*

*Even if she's a con artist.*
*Even if she's a con artist—*

Suspend judgment.

I did. I wanted to.

There were other concerns to attend to, anyway. Chiefly, there was the matter of how to get a pram full of Yu Min on the subway ride to Kyu Ok's two days after my arrival, since transporting the dog by pram was nonnegotiable. My eomma noticed no obstacle. She had on her side a manic vigor that sprinted her geriatric body down the street and a cunning belied by an utter lack of self-consciousness.

As a result, my eomma was not delayed when Yu Min left his urinary signature on our route from her apartment to the luxury mall below to the street. She found marble-side, station-centric, escalator-located, or any other canine waste evacuation about as much fun as anyone could have without spending money. She slapped herself with hilarity. She shook with comedy. Then my eomma caught the sound of a close-coming train, and we ran for it down the subway stairs. We would not miss it, and in a hiccup of feeling, I could love this goony brawn, this dumb determination, her dash at stealing a little more un-waiting life. I'd said I would not abandon her. I would not abandon her. I ran harder and let her smack my hand away from the pram. She didn't need help. On sight of the train gateway, she shook a white card, zipped it in the air before tossing it back to me, and we made it out of Misa Station just in time, gasping.

"Keep it," Google Translate said she said, as I passed the card back. When I looked down, I saw that it was imprinted with a name: KIM DA HYE.

I did not know who Kim Da Hye was. Nor did I know how my eomma had gotten this card. I could have asked whether the card was stolen. I didn't, for some reason complying with a sudden confused etiquette in which one did not interrogate whether the origins of an item were theft, fraud, or impersonation if there was not time to discuss the matter privately at length. Should I be caught using this card and then questioned about it, I would not know what to say about it.

Soon my eomma was charging over the gravel shoulder of the road from the station to Kyu Ok's anyway. We passed metal fences. Abandoned lots. The pram bounced from the small rocks, until the terrain, as it were, ceased to cooperate with her authority, that is, the whole kit and caboodle fell, including Yu Min. The dog was not hurt, was bushy-tailed. My eomma wailed as though she'd taken a bullet.

"That's an okay patootie," I said to Yu Min. "You're A-okay, right?"

No matter. My eomma, nonverbal and resiling from one delirium in favor of another, now had the pram and Yu Min jumping back up and over the side of the road again like popcorn. Yu Min leapt. Yu Min with his Olympian gastrointestinal speed once more squatted. For the first time, I watched my eomma clean up his excrement, not with a bag but a piece of refuse picked up off the street.

She slid the newspaper wad of shit in her pocket.

If ever there was a moment to leave the shit where it was—as she had on the marbled floors of the mall, for instance—it was here outside. But, it occurred to me, this was a person who had changed three of her children's diapers. Such was one explanation, and the one I elected, since I had told my mother I would not leave her; since I admired her peculiar defiance of viability and imbecile's vim; and since we were, I found myself delusionally believing, in the process of faking it until we made it on the count of mother-daughter relations. Some people would let shit lie where sleeping dogs did. Some people would find a waste bin. But she had gripped a lot of shit in her long career as a mother, my eomma. I told myself that. She gripped shit like an expert. A pocketful of shit was nothing at all to a well-versed shit-gripping matron!

———

On arrival at Kyu Ok's, Kyu Ok and Mee Jeong got up off their knees from floured newspapers, where they'd been rolling dough for mandu. In the light of day, anyone could see that my eomma did not look like her sisters. The other Chos were plump, sturdy women radiating health and comfort. My eomma looked, comparatively, ill in a vague, amphibious way. I'd the instinct to put her in a blue phototherapy Tupperware like a jaundiced baby, then tend to her.

For a while I chatted with Tae-Hun, Kyu Ok's husband, who knew a good deal of English from his business travels. He and Kyu Ok's son and granddaughter showed up, so I played school with the granddaughter—which is to say, she taught me numbers, and sometimes I said them right and sometimes I said them wrong, but once I noticed she preferred when I got them wrong, I commenced a magnificent idiot spree to extract shrieking noes elongated by the fun of violating adult authority. Then for reasons no longer memorable, it was time for Kyu Ok's son and granddaughter to go.

We set to eating. Kyu Ok and Mee Jeong had carried trays of mandu the size of fists and iceberg salads to the table, ramekins of kimchi, radish, sauce. My eomma grabbed rice with a sheet of seaweed—and was it me or did it resemble the newspaper of dog shit? She meant to feed me by hand. I ran defense. She started in a stricken way, and I was ashamed of my disgust but no less disgusted.

"Koreans are very friendly," Kyu Ok's husband, Tae-Hun, said. "We give the food."

"Okay, that's valuable cultural insight. I could stand a little less friendliness with my lunch, though. We can shake hands or something."

"Tracy!"

Kyu Ok stood. She rifled through items on a shelf. I understood she wanted to give me something. On producing a sheet of paper, she ran a finger down a table displaying each Cho, spouse, child, birthday. "Your family."

Kyu Ok, I saw, had penciled in a revision of my eomma's birthday. April 21, 1949, had become April 26, 1949. Not even my eomma's date of birth was simple, and Kyu Ok had transliterated some names differently than the other versions I'd seen. For instance, my brother was Hyung-bin, not Hyeong Min. It wasn't lost on me that in this genealogical document there was no Kim Da Hye to speak of. Hyeong Min's surname was Lim, not Kim, so Kim Da Hye was not Hyeong Min's father.

TRACY
O'NEILL

"You have nothing to worry about," Tae-Hun said for Kyu Ok. "Your family is very healthy. There is no cancer in the Cho family. You are lucky. Not even one person with cancer at all."

"And what about my father's side?"

He asked.

"Your mother don't know about that."

"Well, what did he die of?" I asked Google Translate, and Google Translate translated.

"Cancer," my eomma must have said in Korean.

"Cancer," Tae-Hun said.

"I see."

I wondered what Yu Min was doing.

It was quiet. Moist mouth sounds. Sounds of masticated dough thwapping. I found my finger fidgeting a screen.

"Do I look like my father?" I said to Google Translate, and Google Translate translated.

"No, not like your father," Naver Papago said for Kyu Ok.

"Only like your mother," Naver Papago said for Mee Jeong. "Not like the father at all."

"They say not even a little," Tae-Hun said.

"Really?" I said. "Most people look at least a little like both of their parents."

The aunts' voices stacked. The aunts' voices stopped.

"Really," Tae-Hun said. "Just like your mother. You only look like your mother. Not at all. Your mom was a farmer. Did you know that? At one point she owned ten thousand chickens. She had a hard life. She had to do everything herself. Now she is rich."

"That's a lot of poultry," I said.

Then: "And how exactly did she do it herself?"

In her story, Cho Kyu Yeon did not use muscle to prompt

repayment. In Wonyi's, she "hurt a lot of people," and she stole. In her story, my eomma lost a great deal of money as a result of her lenience, and not only to my appa, because she was "not a traditional lender." But in the story I'd lived with her, without a bashful lick, she'd told Jeesu that she'd wanted Kim In Kee's money before she wanted him, and I doubted she'd let debtors off the hook without a slap around or something harder. I didn't particularly care if she was a criminal, but I did want to know her.

"She says real estate," Tae-Hun said.

"Like my father."

Tae-Hun conferred the message, to which Cho Kyu Yeon said, "Aniyo," no.

There was no point in bothering. I bothered. "Ne," I said. "He owned a hotel. What do you mean? I saw it with Inwahn."

"You saw?" Tae-Hun said.

"Ne."

"Well, your mom says no hotel."

| | |
|---|---|
| *And Inwahn could've fabricated.* | *I'd not caught Inwahn lying yet.* |
| *I wouldn't be the wiser.* | *I was not stupid.* |
| *I had been stupid.* | *If I believed her, this trip could matter.* |
| | *Maybe I didn't.* |
| *If I believed her, this trip could matter.* | |

"Okay," I said. "Whose hotel did I see on Christmas?"

They discussed. I watched. I caught an "omona." My eomma left the room with the phone to her ear, making a call.

"I wonder how she kept track of ten thousand chickens herself."

"She counted," Tae-Hun said.

"How time-consuming."

Cho Kyu Yeon was not gone long. She returned, muttering. She sat on the couch, where she hunched like an overcooked shrimp and talked to her knees. By way of Tae-Hun, I learned that suddenly my father had, indeed, owned a hotel. Before I could ask more, the doorbell rang, my aunts having, evidently, ordered pork belly.

The group went cross-legged again around a short table, then returned to that local industry of mass digestion and cutting down fat-striped pork with scissors. I didn't see how I was supposed to still be hungry. I'd not slept a full night in weeks now. Even my teeth were tired.

But I had only twenty-two days in Korea, twenty two-days in which my current participation could be described as "non-." To participate, I roboted my learned lines. "Mandu mashisoyo," mandu is delicious; "kimchi mashisoyo," kimchi is delicious; absent the Korean word, finger toward the pork, "mashisoyo"— one could get the picture.

"Mashisoyo! Good!" Mee Jeong said. "Good Korean!"

"Mashisoyo, annyeonghaseyo, bogo sip-eoyo—" I said, then Google Translating, "I've learned a lot of -yo things."

"Also is salanghaeyo," Mee Jeong said. "I. Love. You."

"Got it," I said.

"Now you can tell your mom," Naver Papago said Mee Jeong said, "I love you."

"Oh," I said.

"Tracy! Tracy!" my aunts said.

"Now your turn. Tell eomma I love you!" Naver Papago said.

"Tell her!" Naver Papago said.

"Salanghaeyo, Tracy-ah," my eomma prompted.

"Say it!" Naver Papago said. "I love you, eomma! Eomma! I love you. Say it."

"Eoooooooomma. Salanghaaaaaaaaeyooooooo," Mee Jeong said. "Salanghaaaaaaaaeyooooooo, eooooooooooooomma."

They were staring. Their heads had gone huge, leaning at me in encouragement. My lungs shot down a flume. The chanting kept on, and I stared at a small bottle of soju on the table. I counted lettuce leaves. I shrugged. "Salanghaeyo."

"Salanghaeyo!" my aunts shouted like a toast.

Only Mee Jeong was drinking, but the whole room was fucked up on something.

And on whatever we were on, I watched Kyu Ok feed Mee Jeong in that friendly, Korean way. I watched my eomma play with white daikon radish, iceberg lettuce. It was quiet. I picked at soggy scraggles of kimchi and, as the dishes reduced down, reviewed the family tree once more to do something.

| | |
|---|---|
| *I did not know these people.* | *These people did not include Kim Da Hye.* |
| *I did not know these people.* | *I did not know these people.* |
| *I did not know these people.* | *I came to know these people.* |

"When will I meet my brother Hyeong Min?" I asked finally.

"Say again," Tae-Hun said.

"Hyeong Min," I said. "When will I meet my younger brother Hyeong Min? I met Inwahn. I met In Hyeong. When do I meet Hyeong Min?"

My mother waved her hands like a crossing guard. "Aniyo, aniyo, aniyo."

"Your mother says you won't meet."

"I caught that," I said.

"You understand, Tracy?" He laid his chopsticks down.

"I understand 'aniyo,'" I said. "Why?"

"Your mother says you won't meet Hyeong Min," Tae-Hun said, "because he don't know about you."

———

For stints of an investigation, knowledge resists. You don't know when the next fact will come. You don't know how to look. You call a man who paid for his Corvette with the proceeds of training contras and hold on for dear life to dubious prospects. This wasn't one of those. In a fathoming snap, everything else died down and I saw it: I'd decided that I could abide my eomma's dirty secrets when, as it happened, *I* was the dirty secret she could not abide.

My eomma had said she was worried that knowing the truth, I would never come back to her, and I had wanted her to see that I would. But I could not return to her. I could return only to what of herself she did not care to protect from me. This would not include what and who mattered to her most.

———

On return from Kyu Ok's, my eomma watched *Doll Singles* on television. I couldn't follow. There was a premise. I didn't care. "My daughter pretty everyone the family thinks so," my eomma said; Naver Papago said.

"Okay," I said.

"Understand? Pretty pretty beautiful."

"Sure do."

Because, after all, the previous week, Wonyi had told me that Hyeong Min was my eomma's favorite child. I'm sure my eomma did love Hyeong Min, but also she could treasure their narrative. She had not abandoned that child, and she did not want to surrender a shameless story of motherhood. I probably wouldn't have, either.

And I sat beside my eomma on the floor watching *Doll Singles*, and I knew I could wish my eomma wanted differently, but I could also leap to another track, and there I'd see she was willful about protecting her narrative and willful generally, recalling from my reading of the feminist Sara Ahmed that to be a willful subject is to refuse to be willing to live the right life. To be willful is to be seen as a perversion. It is to say, "Work on my marriage? I'd prefer not to." It is not to strive toward the ready-to-wear good life. Or else it is to "get in the way of oneself." It is to wander. It is to, instead of settling down, be of two—more even—minds. I had always liked willful subjects like my eomma.

Or else, I could remember that Wittgenstein had written, "If someone says, 'How am I to know what he means—I see only his signs,' then I say, 'How is *he* to know what he means, he too has only his signs?'" My eomma's fabrications were those she could imagine, the ones the world had given her of what a good woman's good life was.

Ali put it differently: I dont think she'd let anyone steer the wheel even though the ship is busted as fuck.

Now, I looked at the captain. She hugged her knees, smiling in a slow, dreamy way at the television show, like a child. I gleaned the premise had something to do with divorcée match-making. The actors synchronized false laughter, shock.

And I thought again of Wittgenstein: "Yes, meaning something is like going toward someone."

That she had refused to say what she meant so often was a way to move away from someone, too.

And I went to my eomma's room, temporarily my room. I lay down on her mattress. I had low firepower in my body, but a nervy spigot opened, and something in me raced. It raced past night, as though that would get the whole ordeal over with.

Ali: Maybe you need to take a break. She will most likely
    keep existing.
Just come here, I'll cook for you and we'll go for walks
    around the canals

In fact, I couldn't have. Wonyi had passed on information from the authorities: due to an Omicron case on my flight to Korea, home quarantine would be reinstituted for four additional days.

Ali: You must be tired
Me: It is very sad here

Because I was, indeed, tired, by way of explanation, I sent him a picture of the lurid, half-crushed toothpaste in her bathroom.

Ali: That toothpaste looks sad
Ali: Like literally sad
Me: It is the synecdoche of her life

**Ali:** Oh honey

**Ali:** You'll like her more, once you get some time away from her.

**Me:** I don't hate her at all. I just am drowning in her.

———

That drowning sense continued the next day, when Phillip called to tell me he'd learned years ago my father had gone to prison, but if it made me feel any better he would force my mother to introduce me to my brother.

It continued when we hung up, and I heard my eomma's phone ring in the other room: Phillip was doing the rounds on his calls, undeterred by my request that he not intervene in the matter of Hyeong Min.

It continued as I heard a particular register of my eomma's voice repeat, that same register as when she'd protested at Wonyi's, "She was dead! She was dead! She was dead!"

———

And because I did not want to drown in my eomma, I locked myself in the bathroom. I read news, read text messages. For instance, one from Joe Adams following the update he'd requested:

Text me your coordinates immediately. Do not let your phone out of sight for a second. Obtain a plastic bag and when you bathe, take the phone with you. Memorize my contact information, then bleach your phone of any and all possible contact with me. Do not relate any of your travel plans further with anyone. What schedule you already discussed with them, stay with that when speaking and do not give the impression that anything has changed or you have become "uncomfortable." Act naïve and trusting but be planning a departure asap. Your mission to find your mother is complete. Without further risk, if at all possible, obtain a DNA sample of your "mother". Time for me to make a call.

Out

Z said: Your PI is obviously on amphetamines
Said: I love him? You have to keep knowing him
Make up some new family mystery to keep him interested
A serial killing aunt etc etc
Said: Get some rest. Your extraction is underway.

I could laugh at these jokes, but here's a confession: when I received that message from Joe, I was so drowning in Cho Kyu Yeon, drowning in information, drowning in misinformation, drowning in the oneiric quality of sleepless life, I had not remembered that Cho Kyu Yeon was unequivocally my biological mother—proof being, I'd hopped a plane to Korea on a tip off a DNA test. Instead, I'd glommed onto my eomma's announcement that she could not provide consent for my review of additional records held by the Eastern Social Welfare Society after all, since "someone" had falsified her resident ID number in the paperwork. I'd wondered if the entire trip could be chalked up to a case of mistaken identity.

———

So I walked the streets of Seoul. All the while, Phillip and Wonyi were calling, shooting messages. My mother had returned home during a break in the middle of her shift cleaning at the local hospital or "her shift cleaning at the local hospital," only to find her child missing. Why would I do this to her? Wonyi and Phillip asked. For all my eomma knew, I could have been dead!

She seemed to think that a lot.

But once more I wasn't dead. I was sucking down iced atmosphere, eating the whole city with my feet. Every step, I pushed entire buildings backward, and the whole time I was getting somewhere, that place being away. The silver city air was made huge by generous streets deserted in the name of nineteen degrees Fahrenheit.

I saw a sign that said: GOT JESUS? And another that said: WITH JESUS WITH LOVE WITH YOU WITH COFFEE. I saw buildings made disco ball in their cleanliness. I saw the widest mist. I purchased a fish-shaped waffle filled with cream, and when I got turned around, an old man bent forty-five degrees walked me six blocks to the bus, then hobbled away without a word. I'd never liked someone as much as that stranger who, in his stoop, ferried me to the bus station. We'd never meet again, and yet, he'd been an accessory to the theft of time on my own. I got far off the direction of my own legs, drunk on my own rampancy.

This I wanted to remember.

I don't remember buying the early return ticket to New York. I do remember that I'd decided I wanted to be around the people who'd known me longer than two weeks. Inwahn asked me to come stay with her for the remaining five days of my trip. From Washington State, Phillip's telephonic participation conveyed that my sister was angry that our eomma loved me only eight thousand dollars of love, whereas she loved Hyeong Min multiple gifted buildings of love. Inwahn had told our eomma she was cheap, which, in the logic of this family, was maybe the same as being heartless. She phrased it differently to me, Inwahn.

"I cannot let you go like this," my sister told me.

I told her I would, as she requested, go stay with her. I reneged.

I do not remember what my eomma said when I told her I had decided to leave five days early. I do remember she then went hell-bent on purchasing me a pair of sneakers and that I dreamed, waking, of sleep.

At the department store Lotte, she was roused by the orange Nike sign. Plucking models off a wall, my eomma took to the Air Zoom Pegasus 38 Shields. They were hideous but the most expensive model—cause-effect, the best. Perhaps she reasoned that more money got her appreciably more intricate sculpting on the soles (shape: chemically relaxed sine wave); therefore, the soles themselves would need to expand to accommodate said intricate sculpting; and as a result of that expansion, her daughter would be more cushioned in her tread, leading to a decline in shock and joint pressure, thus easier walking—that is, easier coming and going. She would make my coming and going easier—she could buy that. Or, anyway, buying was a fun, redemptive-adjacent thing to do. She waited for the boy in a mute, closed-circuit facsimile of joy.

But the store had sold out of my size. She froze. Her eyes doubled, blackened. She shook her head as though the news were incomprehensible. Even across language I could see the boy apologized and see my eomma was tempted to hit him over the dome. Instead, she snatched back her credit card, then turned heel, pushing elsewhere nose-first, like a hound and hounded.

And I remember the black pits of her eyes rattled as she pulled me through the streets of Seoul. I remember the posterior portion of her hair that she'd missed going red. I remember her dinky legs swishing distance in Le Coq Sportif sweatpants. It was as though every bit of meat on her body had clustered in her shoulders. We took some train rides on the largesse of Kim Da Hye. My eomma's features cinched to the center of her face with focus and fear, and when I purchased a coffee—"Bad for the health!"—after she'd already been let down at Lotte, it was all too much. She left the café.

I waited. Took in pictures of lavender taro drinks hung on the wall. Pictures of drinks constructed for the sole purpose of floating whipped cream. I zoomed in and out of maps on my phone. My eomma returned with ten pairs of the flowered slippers I had told her I planned to purchase for my friends. On a nearby street corner, I understood she'd left not for the slippers alone but to call Kyu Ok and Mee Jeong for backup.

We passed a commercial high-rise my aunts declared my eomma owned. We passed stalls of vendors selling trinkets, street food. A religious group walloped drums and moaned. My eomma crawled her arms against the failed air, as Kyu Ok slung her elbow in mine.

We visited a crammed shoe store. We sideways-walked down aisles. They carried the Air Zoom Pegasus 38 Shields, but no luck on size. My eomma near-ran out the door. She'd ceased to form words, but her bowed shoulders projecting back into the street announced another store, another. Her hair was vertical.

"Please," I said. "No more." Somehow, we'd already been doing this for hours.

Paddle through the crowds. Hop that train. In the mall, a fountain gurgled. At the second Lotte store and the third store of any denomination that day, my aunts hung back as my eomma brought the floor model to a salesman. I began, for some reason, to add up the hours I'd slept over the last two weeks, but nothing in my head worked anymore. When the salesman broke the bad news on the Pegasus 38 Shields, my eomma's mouth stretched, forsaken, stunned. It seemed to me a hard blast off the heater and she'd crumble.

"These ones are better," I said to end the quest, and Google Translate translated.

"So plain," she said, and Google Translate translated.

"These are classic."

"Aniyo."

"Ne," I said.

"You must be sad your mom is ugly," Kyu Ok said, slinging an arm around me. "I understand."

"That's not why I'm going home, if that's what you think."

"You're not ugly," I told my mother, and Google Translate translated.

"She's not ugly," I told Kyu Ok and Mee Jeong, and Google Translate translated.

Mee Jeong said through Naver Papago, "Your mom did not always look that way. She is ugly now but always no."

"Jesus H. Christ," I said.

"Jesus H. Christ," I guess Google Translate said.

I don't remember much of what we did that night, my eomma and I. I do remember watching my eomma chew food, spit it in her palm, then feed it to Yu Min. My throat closed up. I remember that I thought: one more night. You can do anything for one more night.

I remember that the next morning when she went to work, I took a walk again. I'd decided to buy Osulloc tea for friends, and

I'd decided to submit a missing person report on Kim In Kee, though later that day, once it was too late, I would no longer bank on my father's name being Kim In Kee at all. Later that day, after all, my eomma at one point referred to this man as "Jung-Hee."

WHO IS JUNG-HEE? I would write in a notebook, but all I could hear was N's impression: "Who. Is. Tracy? What. Is. Words?"

And I received Cho calls again. It was been there, done that. My eomma was afraid, not knowing where I was. But I said nothing to Wonyi or Phillip of the Gangdong Police Station, said nothing of the beautiful policewoman dressed in Balenciaga or of submitting my own spit for a DNA test that might locate Kim In Kee but could not locate my appa if he were actually Jung Hee. I did not say I'd begun to wonder whether my eomma knew this man had died of something more exotic than cancer, and fifty-fifty it was a crackpot thought. It wouldn't have been the first one of the trip.

> Wonyi: I hope there is no misunderstanding.
>
> Me: No I understand
>
> Wonyi: I think your mother is not used to expressing love.
>
> Me: Why do you think I have a problem with how my mother expresses love?
>
> Wonyi: In my opinion, what your mother wants to give you is material, and what you want to receive is spiritual.
>
> Me: Did Seokgyo tell you that? He doesn't really know me.
>
> Wonyi: No I didn't tell with him. I don't like him.

I was tired. So tired.

And I bought soju for friends. I bought them jellies. I bought miniature boxes of gold caramels and glycerin face masks branded to signal a somehow propitious association with intravenous medicine. I got back to my eomma's to discover I had a niece. She was already a young woman applying for jobs.

That evening, my niece, Hyewan, understood what my eomma did not: customs might not permit me to bring home the ginseng her father, In Hyeong, offered as a gift. But at least, she ventured, like the good sport she was, I could bring the other gift her parents had sent. I had no idea to which gift she was referring, exclusively because my eomma had hidden it in a closet and never mentioned it.

My eomma had said she did not drink. Now it was time to drink. The reason: she wanted to pack for me. I was not a good sport so I asked that she keep her hands out of my bags. Her hands doubled down in my bags. I doubled down on volume. We struggled over boxes of good Jeju tea, chocolate biscuits, books. Her hands were everywhere at once. She wanted to stuff in three plastic bags of dried seaweed "as gift to the foster parents for taking care of my daughter." I told her they were not my "foster parents." They were my parents, and they wouldn't want her seaweed or her message. Only through the saving grace of dinner did she resign herself to the kitchen.

It might have been a nice dinner. I liked spaghetti.

It might have been, but as I had satisfied my need to pack my own way, she had found satisfaction elsewhere. That satisfaction derived, it was revealed over bowls of spaghetti, from a particular development. As I'd packed, she'd instructed

Hyewan, in Korean, to call the taxi company for the sole purpose of canceling my ride to the airport. Now the taxi company was closed for the night.

I screamed. She laughed. The paroxysmal glee pulled her neck back, rocked her whole cross-legged body. Hyewan was on the brink of tears, apologizing. "I didn't know! I didn't know! I swear I didn't know!"

"It's not your fault," I said. But I hadn't said it. I had shouted. I was shouting. I was shouting about exactly what and who were not funny and whose fault it wasn't and I would not be kept here, my eomma could not actually believe she'd trick me into staying, I would not stay, I would walk from Seoul to Incheon if I had to, I would buy another ticket, I did not care how much it cost, I would pay anything, did she hear me did she hear me did she hear me, get your hands out of my life and stop laughing right now before I jump out the window.

My eomma seesawed back and forth, laughing harder. At the sight of her torso pitching, Yu Min ran to a corner to cower. Hyewan pulsed her lips like a nervous fish, no language emitting, and when my eomma began babbling through the laughter, my niece shook her head in desperate affirmation.

"She says she just wanted to use her taxi company," Hyewan said. "She says she was going to get you a different taxi."

"Did she?"

"No."

"She's full of shit."

And apparently at some point I'd stood. I'd need my purse, my coat. I didn't know where I was going, but I was.

"Where are you going?" Hyewan said.

"I'm leaving," I said, "my last time seeing her. You can tell her that."

I suppose Hyewan told her that. I suppose something hit. My eomma lunged, clutched the bottoms of my purple pants from the floor, and I despised her for being so pathetic, I wanted to love her she was so pathetic, this near-horizontal miserable clown, and I could sense the danger in my arms and the weakness, and at that very second I hated myself for any and all the above, for my failure to even stick firmly in a single feeling. It was the first day she'd changed out of her NISSY NISSY HEARTHROB sweater, and as I looked down on the slapdash titivations of her eyes, her crayon-red hair, a heavy cold poured from the crown of my head down my back to the floor. I didn't think I could move, but it was only that I'd aged a few decades.

"She will get you a different taxi!" Hyewan said. "She says she will get you a taxi and she'll even pay for it!"

"She can't breathe without lying."

"I feel bad," my eomma said.

"Feel worse." But the words were automatic. I'd put no lung behind them. I didn't think I had any anymore. I was tired. So tired.

I don't remember how I ended up staying the night. I do remember the clumpy Bolognese beef clinging to bowls on the table. I do not remember whether we returned to eating. I remember I called Yu Min to me, told him not to be such a nervous fish stick.

The next morning, a taxi came. My eomma had made good on her promise to call one. I kissed Yu Min, did the downstairs lug. I dropped my bags in the trunk and made for the belt buckle.

"Incheon International," I said, "and quickly." The car smelled of nicotine and leather. I felt my pockets for wallet, for phone, for reassurance my eomma had taken nothing essential.

"Okay," the driver said. "We go." We went. I mean he hit the gas. My eomma ran alongside the car, slapping the windows and sobbing.

"Tracy-ah! Tracy-ah! Tracy-ah!"

She slapped the windows, and for freak-long seconds her face was in the back-seat window. I could see her nostrils flare and snotting tears. She was scrawny and muscled as a chicken wing, so strong. She ran hard. Ran harder. It was harder and harder for her fingers to catch the glass. Spikes of sun shattered, and in a terror, I thought I'd tell the taxi driver to stop. I thought, in a terror, I wouldn't.

And first her mouth receded, then her flaring nose. Her eyes went. That crazy amateur-dye job. The car sped up. She couldn't go on. She'd go on. But she was human, so beatable. She'd been beat and she bent down over her knees, gasping. Then the car accelerated, until she was out of sight.

Half my internal machinery had been knocked off the shelf, and the whole car swam. I floated up to the top, caught air again. My chest opened. Breath came in big and liquid. My face was damp. Hair was, neck. Jostle me, and I'd spill.

Because I was viscous. I shifted. I was cruel when not ardent. I stayed too long until I left.

And I always wanted to know more, always wanted more, stuck to my guns except when I doubted—and I doubted often because I never knew enough, always wanted to exhaust knowledge and possibility. I sneered at consolation, then like anyone wanted comfort, though I still distrusted it enough to go on the run even at times from myself; and I had wanted her, wanted everything, yet hadn't hacked much more than two weeks in Korea. Maybe, though—

A ding.

Now you know, Ali said, without having had to be told anything of that lonely hole of a car ride. Give yourself a break.

# CHAPTER SEVENTEEN

# POSTMORTEM

Brooklyn, 2021–2023

It was well over a year after the fact that I noticed a symptom associated with what, in retrospect, was little more than a few hairs plucked off an apparition—meaning meeting my eomma the first time I can remember and the second time at all. I'd no problem with the instant she launched herself into our shuddering embrace chez Wonyi, and I wished I could stop the mind right there. But when I would think of the rest of my time in Korea, it was as though I'd been drugged. A warm tingle spread behind my eyes like an inner smog, and almost instantly, I'd fall asleep.

Suppose I had a heart, or something was pumping blood anyway. I could get my heart rate up by dint of calisthenics, and that was supposed to convince sleep not to hold me hostage. Also, there was koepi, mul, keompyeoteo, and the clanging din of unfettered proximal luxury condo construction, which had once reliably exasperated me enough to not only remain awake but rail against predatory developers when drunk or sober, but especially drunk.

I had a conscious mind. It abdicated. It was not prepared to take the crown, or even conceive the word "crown."

Though the symptom was beyond my own interpretive scope, there were diagnoses. A director friend posited that one side of my brain could not fathom that life didn't conform to drama's three-act structure. An acupuncturist suggested I needed more yang and protein. According to the internet: PMS, diseases excluded from the DSM, or cancer. At night, I wished my eomma would appear to me in sleep, if only briefly and better lit. But I didn't remember dreams other than the ones in which men brutalized me.

The exception was one in which people with translucent blue skulls communicated through lights blinking in their heads. There was a woman to warn of a man in that dream, but a different species, I didn't have a light. I didn't because, it came to me in the clowned logic of the night, I had written this nightmare into existence and never thought to compose my own light to signal to her. This woman would go down and, armed only with the dark silence of my opaque head, I could do nothing: a bystander, if not entirely inculpable.

By the time I dreamed that dream, Cho Kyu Yeon had conscripted Phillip to convince me to take a deal: she would pay a matchmaking service fee of ten thousand dollars to acquire me a husband. Example: a 172-centimeter-tall, seventy-kilogram male, born 1974, currently employed by Yale University as an associate research scientist of biomedical data science, according to the dossier, whose "ideal woman would possess a warm heart, emotional maturity, good energy, sensibility, and intelligence and take good care of her own mind and body."

I refused. Phillip urged. I refused. He said he was wrong about me being smart. He said I was his lovely niece still. He said nothing and I received a text message from a number I did not recognize, the sender identifying himself as "Mr. Wu." The campaign felt long until it didn't, which was around the time Cho Kyu Yeon accused Phillip of trying to scam her in a middleman scheme, the contours of which I never caught. Phillip decided he'd had enough of Cho Kyu Yeon, and we did not speak anymore. As middleman, he had carried urgent messages. But we had related only on the basis of *her*. Or else, we had related only on the basis of his desire to be a part of a story that, as he told me many times, was like a movie to him.

And without Phillip to translate on calls, for the second time, my eomma receded from my life, this time more slowly. On the phone, I had no idea what her babble meant, and she didn't seem to notice. The frequency of calls declined, then the frequency of KakaoTalk messages. We missed months of each other's lives. I took it as I always had, though a new abyssal element had emerged: the recognition that I'd spent the better part of two years trying to stand in proximity to her, and she was still a stranger.

Sometimes, I'd think that my eomma must now wonder why I'd had to visit myself upon her, a woman of interest hiding in plain sight. My presence had declared her jig was up. The family's. They had put me to rest. I would not rest, a menace. Then, in a hot button flash, I'd deserted as Kim In Kee had, and as my eomma had, too. I'd left despite the intimate knowledge that an entire life could be missed in an abrupt walk away. And all of it, all of it—for what?

My eomma had a conscious mind. I'd wanted to know what it did on a Thursday, and not only one in 1986, when I was born, or 1982, when she took up with my biological father, Kim In Kee. I'd wanted to know what she thought about when, supposedly, she cleaned at the hospital and plowed her live toy dog around in a pram, unfettered finally by child-rearing or a routine partner. Anything real. I'd strolled through the mall beneath her apartment as Yu Min shat on the marble floors to my eomma's untrammeled glee, knowing the whole shaky enterprise relied on the dubious graces of machine learning, a handful of semiconductors, and the judgments of a multinational corporation's artificial intelligence team regarding algorithmic logic and natural language processing—or else my own chump charades.

I'd opened the app. I'd selected conversation mode. I'd told the app to tell my eomma this app was stupid, so she'd need to speak loud, slow, and clear. Then soft, rushed, and tumbling she prated, and I had no idea what she said mostly. In my salvage: only a few records—those times whether by accident or fast fingers I was able to screenshot a line off Google Translate before I lost this woman in-her-own-words to my own bum memory.

Review: "Yes, tell me right now, my mom has a taste of hand, hand, hand, hand, hand, so if you cook it with your hands, you'll be fine."

Two: "Your father is gentle and obsessed with money, so I guess that's why his health got so bad," to which I'd said—and I needed no record to remember this—"You told me he died of cancer."

"I think your father doesn't exist anymore, so don't look for it," she said.

Finally, "I heard the news that your father died, but now that I think about it, I feel so pitiful that I will die."

The clearer message: when I asked what she thought happened after death, her idea was like that of a Chandlerian detective: a big sleep.

I feared sleep, its sudden abductions. Sleep came for me anyway.

And so I resorted to all manner of herbs, "wellness practices," and the counsel of a few outright charlatans to stave off instant knockout long enough to remember her imbecilic eyebrows. Remember how she spit out food for her cathexis dog, how her hands did not shake. I remembered even as I thought of Freud and Breuer's ill-aged but no less famed maxim: "Hysterics suffer primarily from reminiscences." Remembered Ali saying, "Freud? I don't like the coke-addled bastard, but he is right sometimes."

————

The truth was that if I cared to hold her to a single authentic identity, I couldn't. There was no one real Cho Kyu Yeon. There were the stories she told, the stories her sister did, the story provided to social workers, which my eomma claimed she did not provide. There was the story of us. Her multiverse of plots included compulsive grift and those of a survivor circumventing loveless marriage, poverty, and a society more concerned with national birth rate than her happiness. My eomma was a soft-spoken libertine, a hustling fraud, a chicken farmer, a cook maybe professionally and definitely domestically, a millionaire by means extralegal or not, a mother, a woman who disclaimed motherhood, the other woman, another woman, another.

If that answer didn't satisfy, and it didn't, I could remind myself that Cho Kyu Yeon was never a convenient woman. She did not accommodate herself to the world. She—often delusionally, movingly, and to my exasperation—chased its accommodation of her inconvenient dreams as though it were merely a matter of wanting enough to, or at least running a racket. To get out of town, get a leg up, discard lives, be discarded, and love hard loves in a postwar Korea still putting the pieces together scattered by neocolonial struggle, she didn't take no for answer. She took what she could get. Some of these seizures hurt other people, only a few such reckless feints did I know, and all were ways of stealing alternate lives in a world narrowed by proscription: choices and impulses that, even as she remained drunk on the marriage plot, scrapped together a life outrunning the received narrative in which her very being peaked churning out progeny.

When I began to search for Cho Kyu Yeon, I suspected motherhood itself prevented her from offering a coherent narrative of herself, that assuming the maternal role ruptured her identity. Perhaps she'd imagined leading by her own foot, in her own direction. Children came in light, then got to be heavy baggage quickly. But this was only the speculation of a woman who, in an abrupt glitch, found the image of a friendless geriatric intolerable enough to chase her own eomma around the world, as though she might then parent the parent of her lifelong bereavement, both as she had been parented and as she had not, though or because she had refused to parent a child.

In the months after I returned from Korea, I came to believe that in motherhood, as much as in any other con, Cho Kyu Yeon squeezed life for more life. She never really stopped impersonating the various people who could get what she was after, and that was as true with her children as anyone else. There was the mother she was to In Hyeong and Inwahn as a small-town operator, dutifully married until she dropped the family. There was the mother she was to Hyeong Min, as she tells it, broke until she—even with a "useless" husband—pushed her way to a Hanam high-rise. There was the missing mother she was to me, until she was found, an old woman chasing what I cannot deny was a getaway car.

This was the Cho Kyu Yeon not embarrassed by dog shit but embarrassed, she told me, that I didn't have "a normal life," that is, a husband. The one who did not like adventures, which I did not believe. The one who told me she did not like books, which was evident. Between the loan to Kim In Kee and the actual moneybag for me, I could see that my eomma wanted to buy love, as a lot of abject losers do. But by the time we met, she was also looking for a deal—I mean a love that would fit the story she was improvising as she went. Once, when I showed Ali her picture, he said, "Looks like she just tries something new every day." And she did live in ad lib. Credibility was no object. She got caught but never stayed down for the count, and not staying down for the count led her often to a great deal of pain.

She seemed to me a lonely woman. I wept for her.

Her instinct as a storyteller was to insist that Kim In Kee stuck around awhile, and I suppose she needed to tell that story for the same reason that I needed to tell the story of her. Because she was. Because whether or not she believed in God, in the act of wanting too much, an infractionary godliness bobbed to the drab surface of routine like a dead body. Because she had broken past sustenance, trying her dumb luck for more.

There is reasonable doubt that that was enough for her.

One day, after I'd not heard from her for a full season, she asked if I was getting married any time soon, because she worried about me. "What are you afraid will happen?" I asked.

"It's not like that," she said, according to Google Translate, "it's stable only when you have a family and live. My mother's wish is to get married quickly and live well."

———

When over a year had passed since I located Cho Kyu Yeon, I ate more protein. I took the herbs for more yang. In sudden grips of drowse, I forgot that the profit imperative was driving New York City renters to Coxsackie. And I wanted to be someone whose life was changed by yoga nidra. I wanted to be someone whose life was changed by ignoring my phone until noon. "If you dribble when you piddle, be a sweety and wipe the seaty," a tragic sign in the acupuncturist's bathroom said, as though anyone needed a re-minder I was there, to some extent, to be babied. Still, I made appointments that occasioned reading that sign. I bought FDA unregulated supplements a podcast wacko with an appointment at Stanford recommended to "optimize," though I'd settle for six-teen straight hours of sentience. The gambit was any spaghetti, any wall, and a medium told me, "You would not try to hold a bird." I was advised to ruminate on blue and purple.

I walked outside. I did not see much blue or purple. The season changed, and without me much noticing when it happened, blue and purple reappeared. There were the boxes of forget-me-nots, sky, a silk dress I considered for a party, and in my own memory, the violet pants my eomma clutched my last night in Daejeon, begging for a longer story out of us.

And I wrote what I remembered of her. I wrote even if the

whole search resembled that story Ali once told me: This person received a neighbor's package. They obsessed over getting it over to the neighbor, leaving a thousand notes (never knocking on the door or engaging them directly). After eighteen months, they very carefully opened the thing. . . . It was flowers. They touched the flowers, and the flowers just crumbled to dust.

I still, after all, would rather open a box of crumbling flowers than open nothing.

One theory on the impulse to write what I remembered:

Absence persists—I must endure it. Hence I will manipulate it . . . language is born of absence: the child has made himself a doll out of a spool, throws it away and picks it up again, miming the mother's departure and return: a paradigm is created.

—ROLAND BARTHES

Another theory: When I was a child, my father told me original bedtime stories about a girl named Elvira who, when her town is hit by a mysterious illness, goes in search of a cure. She finds a witch, who is not, after all, a witch, but a scientist in possession of medicine with which Elvira can save her family, but only because she is willing to see the stranger as more than she appears. "You mean you can make your own stories?" I asked as a child, then insisted that in place of accepting his narratives, I would imagine more of strangers my own way, in my own stories.

And in 2023, I wrote a version of my departure the way I guessed my eomma remembered it. It ended: "She had gotten her daughter. She had gotten her daughter to look." I intended the play on "gotten," both "received" and "tricked." In that version, she did not call out, "Tracy-ah! Tracy-ah! Tracy-ah!" She called, "Yu Min! Yu Min! Yu Min!" I wrote that, surmising there was only fiction when I reached the end of memory.

But maybe not.

At the end of an investigation, after all, there is just more time. I did not end the moment I located my eomma or left her. I only breathed through rather incoherent experiences; numbed out on the resolve to just keep going, break on through, stick with the schedule; then one day saw a lumpy dump of time whose loose meaning, only in retrospect, did I catch overspilled the search for Cho Kyu Yeon, as it always had. I had for many years suspected that my life paradoxically was conditional on and had little to do with this woman, but to hypothesize that something is logically true and to live out a question until one knows that something is senselessly true—they differ.

And I stopped nodding off, perhaps because I no longer expected remembering Cho Kyu Yeon to define the shape of my story.

———

What I mean: Go back to December 30, 2021. Maggie picks me up from JFK. We eat lunch outside at the place with incredible bathroom wallpaper and good amba. It isn't warm, but the Brooklyn winter air rinses away the trapped plane atmosphere. We drag fat pita in tahini. We scald ourselves gulping coffee. On discovering a shared love of the Korean word for cheeseburger, we whisper, demand, plead: "Chijeubeogeo! Chijeubeogeo! Chijeubeogeo!" so many times, we cry. I still haven't slept. I want to sleep, but I want to occupy the same time as Maggie, here outside the endless looping past of my eomma's life, a little longer, too. We stroll. We sip the now-cooling coffee. We take Maggie's gold Corolla back to my place, hit parking luck, then bring the bags up to my apartment.

"You've got to be shitting me," Maggie says, opening the door.

The apparent cause of her being shitted: bedsheets covered in dog vomit on the floor, dog bed covered in vomit by my desk. N has left them filthy nearly two weeks. The whole place stinks, but Cowboy, my old man puppy, leaps face-height.

"Who's my especial cute boy? Who's my baby gorilla love?" I say, and to Maggie, "Not shit per se. Vomit."

She mutters rhetorical questions about N. I move the suitcase to the corner, go for the dog treats.

"Come on, you fluffernutter sandwich. There's a biscuit here with your name on it."

"Okay, where's your purse? We're going to the laundromat," Maggie says. "You're not doing this alone."

"No, no. I've got it. You have a life to do, too."

This utterance comes out nasal, a consequence of the fact we are both covering our faces, trying not to retch.

"I'm doing it with you because I hate him," Maggie says. "And because this is not the way to come home."

And so I am home after all. And so she will help me make it more home, too. That she changes out dollars for quarters, rips a few butts, then helps me dump dirty water as I mop the floors—that is love as family does it, I think. She asks where the bleach is. She curses the paper towels. There isn't much glamour to it. It is just the everyday maintenance of a messy life.

For a time, I try to do only the everyday maintenance of messy life: mine, others. I sleep at length for the first time in weeks, right through the New Year's Eve parties. I roast vegetables, do dishes,

TRACY O'NEILL

brush Cowboy so that clumps of fur large as puppies tumble down the street. Wonyi needs medication sent to her son in Boston, and when I hit the post office, I see a message on my phone: What's your status?

**Me:** I'm back in the US.

Thank goodness, Joe Adams writes. Prove it.

I send a photograph of myself there, with the postal eagle and the keylock boxes. I still look tired. I still *am* tired, but I'm in Brooklyn, I'm following my own feet again, I see people who think it matters how I come home.

Where is the dog?

And that is Joe, of course. Suspicion communicates that he gives a shit. You matter enough for him to be suspicious that you are "back in the US" yet "running errands" without the dog about whom you are so crazy. People suck. Dogs don't. He's convinced enough on that front to have it on a T-shirt. But you don't suck so much that he doesn't want you safe in a true story. For whatever reason, maybe a shtick, maybe a desire to remain in the optimism of a search, this man I never met in person—presuming William James correct in his position that your experience is what you pay attention to—made me a part of his.

In my maintenance of messy life, days are long drives to Poughkeepsie, taking the Taconic, not Marty Cardona's favored Thruway. Days are teaching, which is almost exclusively asking questions. I have questions. I question. I down coffee, down talk. One day, my father asks what happened in Korea. I tell him.

"Okay," he says. "Well," he says. "Just wanted to hear how it went," then gets off the phone.

"Sounds like your birth mother's crazy," says my mother, roused and exultant when we next speak. "Tell me everything."

"It would appear," I say, shaking for want of un-come grace, "that you already heard."

I can hear her hurt, as she says, "Oh, okay." Then, "I just wanted to catch up."

Life goes on.

So, I go to Philadelphia for a writing conference, come back. The school year ends. I slip in the shower, feed Cowboy a mis-cooked scallop. I consider how unruly story forms imply how a writer believes the shape of life goes. Maggie texts me from the airport.

**Maggie:** I'm sitting next to a 60ish man who's on what's app on his laptop

**Maggie:** He's got the Dali lama on his Apple Watch

**Maggie:** And he's sexting

**Maggie:** Saying things like "holes"

**Maggie:** He named his peen

**Maggie:** Ingam

**Maggie:** He says it's on the outside of his pants and all I can say is it better not be

**Maggie:** He's instructing her to ride someone in a group

**Maggie:** He says he's going to cum in his pants now. HE HAD BETTER NOT

**Maggie:** She says she misses his fluids

**Maggie:** He's gonna connect w her once we get WiFi

**Me:** "Connect"

**Maggie:** she said I'm going to come my dearest

**Maggie:** His wife is sitting on the other side of the aisle

**Me:** Maybe it's his sister

**Maggie:** Matching wedding bands

**Maggie:** He said he's come

**Me:** He's "taking off"

**Me:** He's "strapped and ready"

**Me:** She can't wait to reconnect with his Ingam but

**Me:** JUST GIMME THE PICS I'M TAKIN OFF

**Me:** I AM SCREAMING WITH PLEASUREEEEE

"What you are laughing about?" N says.

"Oh I'm just pretending to sext with Maggie like the man beside her on the plane."

"Why would you do that?"

"Because she's flying home to be with her mother for her dead father's birthday, and this is what you do when you love someone."

"I don't know what you are talking about," N says.

"Haven't you ever sensed someone was so sad the only way they could breathe is if you got them to laugh?"

"No," he says.

At the time, we have been living together for two months. In another room, as he begins, quits, and begins another coding boot camp, I try to write about my eomma. Many days I cannot name an eyelash of significance. I write to demand for the encounter to have meant something. I write to ask what the stakes were, who I am for having searched, to ask that there be less arbitrariness to my life. I write to unwind the contradictions, to see her.

I want to see.

I want to see.

And what that looks like is, briefly, writing about N. At the time, I think of it like this: he, too, was part of the search for Cho Kyu Yeon, with all its goner prospects. I mean that the search is not always the search you think it is, that the search for her is a search for home, a search for a center beyond random conditions: devouring pandemics and faulty systems, screwed-up atmosphere and turned-around logic. I mean that the search for my eomma was always both for her and the person I might become investigating what it could be to live the life of a woman of interest, and that becoming happens not only as a self but in the everyday of which N has been a part.

And I start. I stop. I close my eyes and stir up the year before: *N says pow-pow, nice-nice in the busy, in fact cocaine, piece of leek.* From the other room, I wonder whether what I'm writing suggests that I love this person, if it is suggested that this love is present but thin, fragile. One night, my stomach is full of firing jumper cables, beside his sleeping body. I leave for a party at 10:00 p.m., and when he calls later he is frightened and angry. Another night, when he is scandalized that I stayed at a wedding until midnight, his position is that I live dangerously; I live the way someone who gets raped lives. I laugh, say, "Is midnight a rapist now? Is ten thirty? Nine o'clock has a mother, sister, and daughter, but I hear in college it interfered with some co-eds." Then he threatens to fly back to Serbia, as he does when I wish to review the timeline on his citizenship bid or discuss how he expresses anger. Before the chapter on N is finished, we break up.

I wish I could say that choice is carefully considered—better, that it illuminates my eomma's life. Untrue. The final straw is simply that on a day like any other, he begins looking at soft-core on his phone as he drives us home in my Outback. I say he can do whatever he wants on his time but not at the wheel of my car. He says he is a good driver and cannot change for me. My reply: if watching porn while driving my car is a fundamental facet of his identity, it is over. And, despite his eleventh-hour apologies, it is.

On certain days, I tell myself that through every encounter one gains insight. All I come up with is that a prime feature of breaking up with a mover is they get out quickly and that sometimes showering off shit is in fact showering to muffle low-volume iPhone pornography three or four times a day.

That is what I think for a few months, but then in late 2022, N does what I'd always guessed he would do. Once granted US citizenship, he moves back to Serbia permanently after a decade of waiting to become an American. And no matter how irrational that choice might seem to an outsider, I understand. I understand that the circuitous routes a person takes to get home need not hold water. They simply need to deliver you to a singular feeling.

And I know that the people who delivered me moments of home as I investigated Cho Kyu Yeon were in Berlin and Brooklyn. They were in Portland and Milwaukee, Los Angeles. I know that means there is so much home, and in so many places, both because we talked nonsense and because we talked real. I forget this is true. I remember again. One does not get one's story straight until it is over, which is to say, when life is. Once, an artist friend spent six years constructing a paper house large enough for an adult to stand inside. She cut the design carefully, built her paper joists, laid a roof. It was all she could think of, the folds of this home, its walls. Then she took it apart and placed it in storage. She began to paint instead.

I do not know how she put that house away. But then again, did she? Now hers are oil paintings of the interiors of homes, sometimes homes within homes. The layers of homes may never end.

Which, of course, loving Borges, I love.

And I write this, and I keep writing. I think that in the writing it would be wonderful to reach closure or even the vatic utterance. But I do not know what will follow. I do not know, regarding my eomma, whether I mean half of that phrase: bogo sip-eoyo, I miss you, I want to see you. I do not know whether, as she wonders, I will marry or have children. I do not know what I will do next week. I have wanted to solve myself. You do not solve your diffuse self any more than solving a case cracks the mystery of ongoing evil, though. To a friend, I admit I keep thinking my story is done and then, inconveniently—though I prefer it to the alternative—I keep living.

Prefer it a great deal because all things being equal, I hate endings, and I think that's why I've rarely lost a friend. My friends may be the best part of me. I find it embarrassing to win. I get my hoots strolling, dancing, and writing. I write. My style of dancing happens primarily in the arms.

At the point that I no longer nod off at the thought of my eomma, I am just someone who eats two to five times a day. Even at five times a day, I never eat breakfast unless forced. I have crises of faith about language touching the Other Mind. I find ideas emotional. I am not only talking about the idea of God. I miss cigarettes every ten minutes, and even used to while I was smoking if I wasn't paying attention to my life at the moment. I want to pay attention to my life at the moment. I resolve. I don't believe resolution happens. I pay attention to my friends because to do so is to make my experience turn on love. I see them as of

TRACY
O'NEILL

interest as any child or spouse. It is easy for me to revel in weddings, never having done one myself.

And I don't like easily, but I love easily. Eventually, I love in detail. I will have a fight with my brother, then take inventory of all the ways he's a kinder, more generous person than I. I will believe this subtracts some harm and then be irritated with myself for buying that. I will believe my own half-baked hope. I will spend too much time pondering whether it's optimistic or pessimistic that "I will" can begin a phrase that is either habit or future action. I don't have hobbies.

I will say things like "even when it confounds, the mystery of how to find the always-missing person we've not yet become is a thrilling case worth pursuing." I have never told someone to eat shit and die. I can be cold. I worry I am too strict when the concern is not personal lability. I will say I will one day have a better eye for love. I will quote bell hooks: "A woman who talks of love is still suspect. . . . No one thinks she is simply passionately intellectually interested in the subject matter. No one thinks she is rigorously engaged in a philosophical undertaking wherein she is endeavoring to understand the metaphysical meaning of love in everyday life. No, she is just seen as on the road to 'fatal attraction.'" So be it.

I am not one of those maniacs who gives carte blanche credit to "the power of storytelling" and forgets propaganda, but I obsess over the question of what story form says. My father tells me my problem is I'm funny, but I forget it. I want to like more stand-up comedy. I believe I get sick easily. I rarely go to the doctor. I have heard the one that goes: hypochondria is the only illness that I don't have. I have heard the one: I don't suffer from insanity; I enjoy every minute. I enjoy some.

I always order three tacos at a time. How fun to go hog on momentum. I return most clothes, like my mother. Someone told me I was a mess. That same person told me I was fastidious. I don't like it when people say, "Science says," even when I generally agree with their politics.

I worry about how many voices I contain. I worry I am a pony with too few tricks. Sometimes I think so much I can't remember a word. I don't remember what makes it difficult to tell some people I love them. I love music and forget to listen to it.

What is unforgettable:

Cowboy dies.

I am feeding him sliced hot dog until the last moment. I am saying, "I love you, buddy bear, love my bunny. I love my beast, my boy, baby kapusniak soup." My hands run the length of black belly before the lethal injection, during, after.

I watch his breathing stomach slow. His eyes go buttony, then his mottled purple tongue falls from his mouth. It keeps moving at first because even as he is dying, like anyone, he wants to kiss and eat, but there isn't enough life. And because he wants to say goodbye to the little guy, too, S sobs on the floor at the vet's, trying to roll the tongue back in, maybe trying to undo death: Put it back, put it away.

That I don't stop saying, "I love you, bunny" is what prompts the vet to clear her throat, say, "He's at peace."

After that, I still look for his tail when the heater comes on to comfort my animal who was so afraid of noises. I still feel happy for him, the edge of that question—"Who's a lucky duck?" on my tongue—when I drop food on the floor. These legs of mine hit mystified air in the morning, no longer needing to waddle a wide gait around Cowboy's sleeping body in the cool passage of the hallway.

In such moments, I can see that I feared the mother who was always missing would be afraid to die alone, but contrary to my predictions, my animal's is the death I feel on a Tuesday or at the heater's hiss, eating fish tacos—and I was there to the last second. S tells me I gave Cowboy a good death, that it is the way he hopes against the odds to exit life, and I want to believe there are qualitatively superior deaths, and I doubt it sometimes. It is for the living to assess, without knowledge, death. How much does it hurt to leave life, on a scale of 1 to 10? No one answers. A chosen death still is senselessly circumstantial, which is to say biological.

"He was so happy as he was dying," I tell Ali. "He was smiling at death because I tricked him. And I know he was a lunatic galoot, but he was my lunatic galoot, and I killed him."

"You loved him," Ali says.

"I did," I said. "I do."

"Light a candle for him for forty days," he says. "This is what we do in my part of the world, a ritual to light the way for the soul to leave the body."

That elemental language: This light is for you. This light is for you. Ali tells me he passed a burned-down building and someone told him, "No one died. Only a cat died." It crushed him to hear this life called "only"; promise him I will light the candle. And I observe a great many fatuous gestures on any given day but never think a life was "only." So: This light is for you. This light is for you. This light is for you. This light is for you. This light is for you. This light is for you. This light is for you. This light is for you. This light is for you. This light is for you. This light is for you. This light is for you. This light is for you. This light is for you. This light is for you. This light is for you. This light is for you. This light is for you. This light is for you. This light is for you. This light is for you. This light is for you. This light is for you. This light is for you. This light is for you. This light is for you. This light is for you. This light is for you. This light is for you. This light is for you. This light is for you. This light is for you. This light is for you. This light is for you. This light is for you. This light is for you. This light is for you. This light is for you. This light is for you.

The flame wags like a fat tail.

And I do write the past, but I also think about how to live next. I decide I will soon go to Berlin. I will one day go to Mexico. I remember I am free. I romanticize freedom, but I tend to want to leave a dinner when people quote movie lines at each other for more than two back-and-forths. I usually know when someone's done a lot of musical theater. I can never guess when I will make exceptions for someone for life. During an afternoon drive, I ask my friends Peter and Mary what the distinction between acceptance and resignation is.

One day Jelly disappears again. One day I file a missing persons report. One day I pick him up from the psych unit, mop shit off his bedroom floor, then carry jars of my friend's urine from his apartment down to the garbage. Over bad burritos, we laugh about his newest roommate, who insisted when I filed the missing person report that Jelly looked more disheveled now, more closely resembling the shoddy photocopy of his license than the image I'd provided to the police. "No one looks like that," I said. "That's just a black smudge." And at some point, we've retold the story enough times, just like the old stories, that Jelly can recite the punch line: "Even the cop agreed."

Then when it gets to be the time I previously anticipated, I get to Berlin, where Ali and I eat lahmacun. We go to see a woman sing who declares she once walked out of her bedroom so pleased with a newly written song she thought, "Bitch, I invented music." He tells me that his grandfather always instructed him never to lose the home located in the corner of Turkey with good air, sight of blue. We talk about never losing. We talk about it again another drunken night. Ali allows me to hold his Italian greyhound, TV.

"He's so small I'm afraid I'll break him," I say.

"You won't," he says.

I coo again. I ask again who has good paws. I see the most beautiful white peony, touch this life gently but touch it.

In the vast streets, walking opaque canals buttressed with chestnut leaves, home bobs up in the shared observations that at a good bar there ought to be a few people whose faces look like melting candles, that an opening act at a concert performs like the best person at a karaoke joint midweek, that at the Russian-Turkish bathhouse in the East Village some man will always end up waterboarding one of us. The waterboarded one of us is always me. Home peeks out in temporary patterns: as Ali cooks beef, pasta, quick-brined cucumber—and as it is understood that if I am present, I will be the one to make coffee, do the after-dinner dog walk. Home urges through even when, punk mourners, we go to the bar favored by queer Turkish ex-pats the night it's learned that the autocrat Erdoğan will remain president, that for Ali and nearly everyone there, the chance at a home country more home remains years away.

When asked why I am in Berlin, I say I'm seeing family.

Because I don't understand why it's incredible—that is,

unbelievable—for someone to live out theories but not values. I read horoscopes so that I can tell my friends unwarranted good news. I talk to friends all day even when I don't see their faces. This is what we give each other at distance: language. I think all of my friends love to play with language. Like any game, this is dangerous.

I know, after all, it is painful to be conned by language. I know it is painful to be conned. I know it is painful to witness language fail. My words are mistaken. It is mistaken what I mean and therefore who I am, who we could be to each other. When I wanted my eomma to trust that I'd not resent her if she showed me something true and human, I told her my interest in her was that she was not a saint.

I regretted those words, rewrote them in my mind as though history is fungible. What I ought to have said is that when I love I want to keep it going longer, even though I think love, just as it is, should register enoughness.

I have been told I am the last person still speaking to too many people. I have been, multiply, estranged. I want to like more. I hate that I think striving necessarily includes strife. I hate to say things like "a story is more than plot; it is also to say: 'I want to give you something; I want to feel, together; I want to feel together.'" But I do.

On occasion, I even believe myself. I ask questions. I talk too much. I called Cowboy everything, and I was always calling him. I named him into infinity out of love, all these nonsense words to say: "You are home." Sometimes it is not what I say but that I say. I am attracted to Lacan's sense that language cuts us off from the Real. I long for language to deliver me to it. Here is what I think about what language does: the talking cure never worked for me, but I keep writing. This is an act of faith. I find it shameful to acquire things for myself that aren't books. I have bad habits. One: I return to myself through wanting. Two: I repeat myself like a compulsion. It is hard to knock almost anything off after so long, though in retrospect change appears both random and reified. I twice met a stranger named Cho Kyu Yeon. I began. I began again. I'll begin again.

# ACKNOWLEDGMENTS

My immense gratitude goes out to the team at HarperOne: especially Rakesh Satyal, who I cannot thank enough for the visionary reminder of laughter, and Ryan "Always on His Game" Amato (believe me, I noticed). Rakesh, you heard me through the whole nine yards—and supported every insane formal shot I just had to shoot. That is the editorial gift of which every writer dreams.

Meredith Simonoff, brilliant and there every step of the way, I feel so lucky to have had a bona fide woman of interest back my case. From the get, I knew in a way that I am rarely capable of knowing that you understood this book down to the bone; I trust you so much and will always appreciate you letting me call to, in a fever pitch, ask, "But is this book a banger?"

Thank you, Yaya, Justin, the Open City crew, Treska, Jelly, Sean, and Maggie for the friendship and the stories, and for chatting stories. Thank you, Stas, for talking "intransigence of vision" past your bedtime. Thank you, Sebe, for bullying random Mini Bar patrons into holding the "Go, Tracy!" sign in the final stretch. Thank you, Joe. When I first called you, I needed someone to believe I wasn't crazy or was just crazy enough to do the damn thing. Thank you to my family and family of friends who have been a part of this investigation that keeps going, and who have kept me going, especially my brother, Ali.

# ABOUT THE AUTHOR

**Tracy O'Neill** is the author of the novels *The Hopeful* and *Quotients*. In 2015, she was named a National Book Foundation 5 Under 35 honoree, longlisted for the Center for Fiction First Novel Prize, and was a Narrative 30 Below finalist. In 2012, she was awarded the Center for Fiction's Emerging Writers Fellowship. O'Neill teaches at Vassar College, and her writing has appeared in *Granta, The New York Times, Rolling Stone, The Atlantic, The New Yorker, Bookforum*, and other publications. She holds an MFA from the City College of New York and an MA, an MPhil, and a PhD from Columbia University.